Even Spinsters Need Company

By Louise Crouch

Copyright © 2016 by Louise Crouch

ISBN: - 978-0-6484878-0-7

All rights reserved. This book or any portion thereof may not be reproduced or used in any manner whatsoever without the express written permission of the publisher except for the use of brief quotations in a book review.

This is a work of fiction. Names, characters, places and incidents either are the product of the author's imagination or are used fictitiously, and any resemblance to actual persons, living or dead, business establishments, events or locales is entirely coincidental.

For more from Louise Crouch please visit
http://loucrouch.wordpress.com

Dedication

To my family for their love and support

To my children for their patience

To my husband for saying yes

Table of Contents

Chapter 1

Horse drawn carriages splashed mud onto plain cottons hems and weather-worn faces in Hannah Evan's new home town. She couldn't remember how many long miles had passed since the coach left the Turnpike but her hind quarters had felt every gutter, root and stone. Hannah rolled her shoulders and greeted the afternoon sun, letting the golden rays warm her skin, the scent of ash-white pines seeping into her lungs. Behind her, the coach doors closed on her past and she gently balanced hooped skirts and round toed boots to the rear of the coach, the driver already releasing her cases onto the Trading Post stoop.

Although Hannah had left Philadelphia with all her worldly possessions bequeathed by her late mother and grandmother, she managed to pack the meagre store and her medicine chest into three average sized trunks. Hannah thanked Mr Stuart and took in the main thoroughfare of her new home town. Hidden in the far northern corner of Lancaster County, Franklins Shallows held an unspoken promise of prosperity, independence and safety. Hannah couldn't hide her smile.

She hefted one trunk and her boots slid out from underneath sending Hannah reeling backwards. Expecting to feel the ice sharp pain of landing on her backside, Hannah gasped when a solid mass caught her. The scent of clean leather and warm oils flooded her senses. Hannah's heels spun under her embroidered hem as she tried to right herself and found the pavers remained elusive. This time, the warmth evolved into two strong arms that surrounded her waist. A low chuckle reverberated through Hannah's back sending a flash of hot anger into her skin.

Hannah's balance returned and she spun around to confront the mocking tones, her gaze moving slowly up the black sleeves that widened into a broad set of shoulders, the left pocket of a black vest decorated by a shiny silver star. Hannah's stomach somersaulted as the Sherriff pushed her out of his embrace. Dark gentle curls contrasted the piercing blue eyes that they framed.

"Ma'am." He said sending caramel shivers down her spine and into her toes.

"Ah, Sir… Sheriff I mean." The colour rose to Hannah's cheeks and she bit back a curse. It would do no good, if the towns-people overheard their new Schoolmarm cursing in the main street.

"Hoffman, and you are?" A grin ghosted across his stubbled jaw.

Hannah spent considerably more time, fussing with her skirts than necessary to ensure the colour had drained from her skin before she returned his gaze, the heat stalking up her neck.

"Miss?"

"Yes!" Hannah snapped as she tried to gain control of her skirts. "I apologise Sheriff, you caught me off guard there and I'm grateful for your assistance."

"If that is a thank you, then you are welcome." His voice gruff and his words brisk, he stood a good foot above her, and she raised her chin to look him in the eye.

"What do you mean? *If* that is a thank you, of course it is."

"In Franklins Shallows, we usually apply the words 'Thank' and 'You'." The Sherriff said, the shadow of a grin, returning to a full blown smirk, dimples endearing his cheeks. The result instantly transformed his stern expression, blue eyes now sparkling in the afternoon light. Hannah couldn't resist smiling in return. "Before your gracious thank you, you were about to tell me your name."

"Thank you Sheriff, I'm Hannah Evans."

The Sherriff didn't take her hand, but briskly collected her trunks instead. "How do you fair, after the long journey from - ?"

"Philadelphia, I'm a little sore -" Hannah closed her mouth quickly.

"I can take you to the Doc if you need. Where exactly are you sore?" Eyes well trained in appraisal raked over her stiff movements.

Rather than rub her hindquarters, Hannah said "Never mind" and fell into step beside the tall Sherriff. A quick glance informed Hannah his dimples had cameoed. "I'm fine."

Hannah concentrated on stepping lightly and safely across the shopfronts yet her eyes wandered to her companion. His sun-kissed skin softened the dark colouring of his brows and she guessed he had a few years on her age of twenty one. The rest of his black curls lay hidden under the sharp edge of a black Stetson and Hannah marvelled at how he remained sweat free as heat flushed under her collar. Tall enough that she would have to crick her neck to look him in the eye, strong enough to carry her three trunks in a single load. His waist tapered to a gun belt where a single pistol ebbed and flowed with the cant of his narrow hips.

Hannah rushed her gaze past his thick thighs clad in black, and focused on his boots, black leather and well worn.

"So I see," The Sherriff coughed, "Welcome to Franklins Shallows. We are on Main Street, every essential good or service is on Main. The Trading Post, land's office, Widow Blacks Haberdashery, the butcher, the baker…" he said, rich honey tones worked under Hannah's skin.

"The candlestick maker?"

"No I'm afraid he's on North Street."

Hannah laughed out loud and he flashed that smile her way. They crossed Main and stepped onto the timber boardwalk to avoid more mud trucking carts and horses.

"Where are you headed Hannah, rooms at the Widows Joy or the Horses Gait Inn? Maybe the Boarding House?" He gestured to a double storey white washed building, the front fenced off with white pickets and overgrown hedges. The front door closed tight, and a narrow alley leading to a stooped side entrance. Familiar sounds of women washing dubious linen oozed from the windows.

"I'm staying with Ms Baker at the school." Until she moves out, Hannah thought. Her tenure contract had very specific terms, providing Hannah with the Teachers Lodge as residence, a small dwelling with two bedrooms, a kitchen, and a cellar. Thankfully, the Lodge had been built separate from the main school house, a good 20 yards or so Hannah had been told. The contract stated the Lodge contained a solid wooden bed and bedstead, and a small portion of donated household goods. The contract entitled Hannah to receive sufficient firewood delivered and cut small for her annually. Together with her teachers' pension, her economic position had improved greatly the moment she signed the agreement. Hannah hadn't even questioned the small print.

"I'll take you there; it's just before the bridge."

"One of those lovely red roofed bridges I hope." The thought thrilled Hannah down to her boots and she daydreamed of her footsteps echoing across the timber planks.

"Yes, but only for another week."

"How so?" Hannah said.

"Old Thom, is in a bad state and not large enough. With the Rail Lines coming and the town expanding it needs to be widened to two lanes. Rather than repair and remodel, they decided a new one would save the town's funds."

"Oh that's a shame."

"You're not the only one to think so. It was a hotly debated issue with the Committee for Salvation and Restoration. They hounded the Mayor for some time. In the end finances won through." The Sheriff strolled beside her, "The School backs on to the town's namesake Franklin Shallows. Despite the name, it's quite a river. Clean, fresh and fast, especially after the snow melts in winter." His voice sounded deep and rich in her ears. She smiled at the prospect of making her first friend. An attractive, well built, tall…. Hannah redirected her thoughts. The silence suddenly stretched between them, the Sherriff paused his narration waiting for a response.

"I have never fished Sherriff, but I do love to paint. Lucy told me all about the old bridges and the stone brick fences. She never discussed the school or the river." The excitement of starting her new life had returned and her romantic vision of making a prosperous future sparked again. As they walked, most of the townspeople, tipped their heads in greeting and the Sherriff acknowledged them by first name. Hannah caught more than one young woman sighing as the Sherriff passed.

"You paint such an endearing picture of Franklins Shallows, that I wonder, what use does such a lovely town have for a Sheriff?" Hannah queried.

"There are always lawless men in the frontier towns, most just passing through, the local drunk, the local thief, the local wh...." he paused "I keep myself busy."

"I would wager, Sherriff." Hannah added forwardly. It didn't bother her in the slightest what he was referring too. Philadelphia had taken many turns in obtaining progress. She had travelled the rich and flamboyant life style of High Society and witnessed the low, dirty and desperate measures it took to survive.

"So besides painting, Ms Evans what else entertains you?"

Hannah wanted to say "medicine" but instead replied "Needle craft." It was half-true, each stich she lay into a man's skin had been neat if not pretty. Judging by the prosperous crowds they neared the middle of town.

"Besides fishing and the "let's-not-discuss-them" ladies of the night what else keeps you busy, Sherriff."

The Sherriff steps faltered, blue eyes wide and jaw tight.

"Oh, Sherriff, I'm sorry, I only just heard those words at the same time I uttered them, I wasn't inferring that *you* .... oh I'm sorry again!" She clenched her fists together. Perhaps Franklins Shallows was civilised but not as forward as Philly. Hannah glanced around at the women-folk. They didn't work at anything other than motherhood and wifedom and a woman never spoke of such things. Hannah tucked one of her wayward brown curls behind her ear and stared at her boots. Her sister Margaret, blonde and polite would know what to say next. Hannah sighed, she would miss her sister. The Sherriff released a deep golden laugh and Hannah's shoulders relaxed. As uncertain as she felt in his company, she didn't want it to end.

"Well that's ends our polite small talk. Tell me what business do you have with Headmistress Baker?"

"I am replacing her. I am to be the new headmistress."

A ripple of tension stirred in the Sherriff, "I thought Lucy Taylor was returning to us to take up that position."

"She was, Sherriff."

"So, tell me why do we have Hannah Evans instead of Lucy Taylor?"

"In a word Sherriff; marriage," Hannah faced him to continue her explanation but his smiled had faded.

His eyes glazed over, jaw set and lips thin. "So I see."

"Yes" Hannah answered slowly and walked onwards, he fell into step beside her. Hannah caught a whisper slipping from his lips. She thought she heard, *"Marry a Frey."* However that didn't make any sense, Lucy married Thomas Ramsey.

Suddenly, the dark Sheriff took quick strides up the timber boardwalk. She breathed hard trying to push away the sudden disappointment that sunk in her chest. What did I say? She followed a few steps until the Sheriff planted her cases down and entered a small stone building.

Hannah didn't know if she should follow until her eyes found the word "Sherriff" crosshatched into silver. Sherriff Hoffman returned, his curls caressing the collar of his black coat, shoulders squared, and hat dipped low.

"I have forgotten about some reports," He clicked his tongue as if moving a piece of food from between his teeth. "My Deputy will take you the rest of the way." The sun paled as it dipped lower behind the pines that edged the town, and a cool breeze flittered around Hannah's ankles.

"Christian" He called over his shoulder, as a tall youth greeted Hannah. Christian offered a curt nod before sweeping back his dusty brown hair and covering it with his hat.

At first glance Hannah registered the attractive qualities Christian possessed, young, perhaps just twenty, straight white teeth, and another set of broad shoulders. He fell a few inches short standing next to the Sherriff, but despite his appeal, Hannah couldn't help feeling rebuffed.

"Please take Ms Evans to the School." The Sherriff entered the building, leaving Christian to collect Hannah's trunks.

"Christian is it." Anger coated her voice. I didn't matter, the dark Sheriff had disappeared.

"Yes Ma'am, Deputy Christian Hoffman." He collected her bags and swaggered off towards the end of town.

"Sheriff Hoffman and a Deputy Hoffman, are you brothers?"

"Cousins Ma'am. Pardon me for asking Ma'am, but you are aware that Ms Baker is the only teacher at the School, even if she calls herself Headmistress."

"Yes. I took the position knowing that." She inhaled slowly, "I'm sorry Christian, I apologise for my rudeness." With this attitude she wouldn't be making any more new friends today.

"I'm used to it."

"Pardon. How can you be used to it, I've only arrived today."

"Begging your pardon Ma,am…" He said in the way only youth can be so innocent and polite, "but you are not the first young lady to be offset with the Sheriff."

Hannah slowed her steps to meet his, "And why is that Christian?"

He stopped when he met her eyes. "Ma,am…"

"Please stop calling me Ma'am, I am but a year or two older…"

"Sorry, Hannah, can you recall what you were discussing before he called for me?"

"Lucy Taylor? Oh my, had he been promised to Lucy? She has married another." She had probably broken his heart there and then with the news. Had she known, she would have written Lucy to do the right and proper thing. Hannah wrung her hands together. She had hurt him with her uncanny ability to mention the wrong thing at the worst possible time. She stopped fidgeting and brushed at her skirts. No, Lucy never mentioned a male caller, not any prospect of marriage in Franklin Shallows. And the Sherriff was definitely worth mentioning.

"No, he was not promised to Ms Lucy?" Christian even lips split into an awkward smile.

"He was promised to someone though?"

"Ms Evans, Hannah it is not polite to talk of Cousin Nicholas' personal affairs."

Resigned and confused, Hannah shook her head, but retained his name. *Nicholas.* Christian turned up a long gravel drive edged by worn timber slates, the shrubs barely holding the fence-line together. A small log cabin capped with an impressive stone chimney beckoned to Hannah.

"Here you are." Christian shouted and Hannah stretched out her legs to meet him at the property gate.

"You're not Lucy."

"I know that."

"Where's Lucy?"

"She remains in Philadelphia?"

"Lucy Taylor, remaining in Philly? Why?"

"I believe its Lucy Ramsey now, Ms Baker."

Ms Elizabeth Baker stood from behind her faded kitchen table and crossed to the Lodge's small but clear glass window.

"Ramsey. Marriage," Headmistress Elizabeth Baker stood facing the window with a tight bun of greying brown hair. For a moment, Hannah thought the glass might melt under Ms Bakers stare. Who would have thought a simple word like marriage could upset two people in one day, "Lucky Lucy" She said before sitting down to the wooden kitchen table and setting the porcelain tea set. Now Hannah's tea set, "School resumes in a few weeks and the children already know you are replacing me. I guess I should say congratulations on your appointment." The sarcasms dripped thick. Hannah's own scowl must have developed because Elizabeth continued "Either you upset someone very powerful or you were the dunce in your class to be sent here to Franklins Shallows."

"On the contrary, Ms Baker, I chose to come in Lucy's place." Hannah said, the warmth sliding out of her tones.

"Call me Elizabeth if you will." Baker was in her later fifty's and quite clearly a spinster. "Come to marry a Frey have we?"

The final straw snapped and so did Hannah. The Sherriff's rebuff still irked her. "That is the second time, I've heard that in a matter of an hour, I have not come here to marry and what the devil is a Frey?" Hannah had risen from her chair as Elizabeth's grimace evolved into a sickly smile.

"Whoever heard of a young woman not wanting to marry?"

"I choose the life I want to live, Elizabeth. I want to prosper. I do not want to become a man's property and when he dies, watch all my hard work be handed away." Hannah stalked to the window. Her mothers' last years played out image by image in her head. Her father had initially apprenticed as a tailor and his talent and keen business skills lead him to a wealthy life as a fabric merchant. He had done very well for himself. Her father's income had put his youngest daughter through one of the first, of many, Hannah hoped, all female classes of medicine at the Women's College of Medicine. The wars stripped her family of all their wealth with the exception of their family name. During the day time, Hannah helped her mother iron for the more affluent families and at night Hannah earnt any extra dime she could, from the City's lowest of the low. All their income went to her sister, Margaret.

Although Hannah didn't begrudge Margaret, she certainly would have liked more food on the table, rather than more fancy clothes for her sisters' social circles. The plan had worked, regardless of their secrets. Her parents had convinced Hannah that spending all their money on Margaret, would allow her to secure a rich husband. Not an aristocrat, as such before the wars, however "New Money" had arrived in Philly and "New Money" is who Margaret married.

A wealthy banker named John Smithson the Third, had taken a shine to Margaret and using all her feminine guiles, she managed to marry him, saving their name and putting food on the table again. Before Hannah could resume her studies, her beloved father had caught pneumonia and died. She had done all she could to try and save him, he was just one of many. After their father's death, Margaret's husband had inherited the estate, their home, furniture and their debts. John counted out her mother's allowance each week like a servant. John the Banker also decided that they could never again "throw" money at Hannah's education and it was not respectful for a young woman of marrying age to be a physician anyway. It was fine if she was not ready to marry yet, but she should find a more suitable occupation such as a Schoolmarm to prepare her for motherhood. Hannah arrived at Norm School with a burning desire to obtain her qualifications and leave Philly behind. In her last year, her mother passed away. Her brother in law had seen no issue, or more to the point, no financial loss in giving Hannah her mother's personal items. For that she would not hate him, just hold an intense dislike for the man. John had promised to find Hannah a husband from his wealthy associates the moment she graduated. That was the day she signed the teaching contract in place of Lucy.

Elizabeth's smile had not waivered, "I admire your conviction, for now."

Hannah sat down and patted her cheeks, hoping to chase the colour from her face.

"A Frey my dear is one of the wealthiest families in Franklins Shallows. There are four primary families in this county and each as inbred as the last, the Frey's, the Treschell's, the Krouse's and the Hoffman's and that is the order of their importance as well. The Frey's are the oldest farming family in the county and the most powerful." Elizabeth went back to her faded writing desk with rusty hinges jamming the lid, and picked up a heavy leather bound Bible, placing it in front of Hannah. She opened the front cover to display a detailed family tree of the hierarchy, "Old Ludwig Frey emigrated here with his three sisters from Germany. You've now doubt, heard of the Pennsylvanian Dutch, although they are actually German. Well Ludwig and his sisters Mary, Rebecca and Eva were four siblings born from four different mothers. Ludwig started a farming empire here, marrying off his sisters. Mary married Hance Treschells, Rebecca married John Krouse, and Eva married Edward Hoffman. Ludwig married Hance's sister Magdalin and so started the family tradition of the first born girl from a Trechsells must marry the first born son of a Frey." Elizabeth pointed out all the names to Hannah as she spoke.

"There are so many of them."

"I know birthed some myself, the whole family could have been a genetic disaster with the exception of Eva Frey who married her lover, Edward Hoffman instead. Her act of defiance, installed the forth but most *lowly* branch of the family tree. Just imagine if she married a Krouse or another Treschells."

"Hoffman." *Nicholas Hoffman.*

"Yes, it was rumoured that her hand was also promised to a Heinz and a Lutz." Elizabeth mused over her notes.

"You wrote all of this?"

"Yes, from what I've been told and who I know. You will teach their children as well as some of the children from the other local families, although the "Freys" my collective noun for the whole four families, outnumber the other children by over a half."

She ran an arthritic finger over her drawings, "I found it most useful to keep notes, so as to - how to put it correctly, not end up in the bear pit. They are unique families, with a lot of power, in this county and the neighbouring counties. Together they own a majority of businesses here. William Frey is in line for the next Mayor, come election day. Either way, it helped me to understand where to tread sometimes. If I were you, I would stay uninvolved. As much as you can, without being impolite. Who was the first person was to mention the Frey's?"

"The Sheriff," She would not call him Nicholas.

"Oh poor Nicholas."

"Poor?" Hannah had thought of many words to call the Sherriff, but poor was not one of them.

"Yes older brother still born, younger sister died before she turned two. His mother died the same year. And his father Edward, the second Edward Hoffman mind you, passed a few years back. This left him the sole Heir in the Hoffman line. Of course he has cousins but they are younger and more removed from the family tree. He was betrothed to a girl named Beth. Except she refused him and married a Krouse. Benjamin Krouse. Not as handsome as Nicholas, but twice as wealthy."

Hannah looked up and tried to appear nonchalant. No wonder he bristled at the mention of marriage. Her anger softened yet he had offended her. He had thought no more of her than a silly young thing ready to marry the local landowner or his son. It was absurd and ridiculous.

"You may keep this, it may come in handy. I would still not involve myself with the families if you can avoid it." Just then the door to the Lodge opened inward sending with it the cold air. Hannah shivered in her dress and moved to shut the door when a bundle of timber stepped into the room.

"Put it near the fireplace, Susie." Susie did as she was told and Hannah watched as the bundle of timber revealed a slim dark skinned woman a year or two older than Hannah. Trailing behind Susie was a small dark skinned child wrapped up in a coat far too big for her. Hannah could only tell that she was a little girl by the wet skirts flapping about her bare feet.

"Susie, come in here when you are done."

Susie again did as she was told and Hannah gaped.

"Susie, this is Ms Hannah Evans my replacement, do as she says." Ms Baker said sipping her tea with a wrinkled pout.

"Hello Susie" Hannah said. The little girl peered out from behind her mother and quickly hid her face at Hannah's smile.

"Susie will stay on when I leave, don't worry their wages are secured, you won't have to worry about it coming out of you monthly salary."

Susie collected Hannah's luggage and headed into the master bedroom. Thankfully Elizabeth had packed all her belongings and would stay her last few nights in the guest bedroom. Susie tried unsuccessfully to carry all three trunks and Hannah helped her facing down a bold stare Susie offered. Hannah considered letting the girl struggle on her own, but she held on tight and took the case away.

"Show me the way," Hannah said.

"Child, hurry up with those logs." Elizabeth shouted from the main room.

"Ms Baker, Elizabeth she must have a name, it cannot be Child." Hannah spoke calmly yet a hot energy burst inside her chest. Lucy might have been right to avoid returning to this place.

"Well when the mother cannot write and the child will not speak, I will call her child." Hannah's anger boiled over and she tossed her trunk on to the double bed.

"Get away Child, Susie come and assist me" Elizabeth called again. Hannah was so dumbfounded by the irony of a mother and child living at a school and working for a teacher, yet they still could not read or write. This is Pennsylvania not Virginia!

Hannah sat on the edge of the bed and shook her head. Suddenly the child entered her room. She appeared about 7 years old, with short dark hair and bright brown eyes. There was doubt she could hear, so why was she mute.

Hannah whispered softly, "I don't care if you cannot speak. I will not call you child. I will teach you and your mother both reading and writing and until then, you can name yourself." The little girl raised her eyebrows. "You point at something, I don't care, a flower, a colour, a bird and I will call you what you want." Abruptly, Susie entered the room and closed the door.

"Will you really teach her?" The words were spoken so softly, that Hannah thought she had been mistaken.

"Yes, I will teach her and you if you would like." Susie's frown evolved flashing brilliant white teeth. Susie was beautiful with slanted almost Asiatic eyes and a straight petite nose.

"After…." Susie nodded her head towards the lounge.

"Yes, after she leaves."

"I don't hear noises in the Kitchen, Susie. I will not wait for my dinner." Ms Baker called.

Susie vacated leaving Hannah and the little girl together.

As silent as a mouse, she said, "My name is Rosa."

"Rosa, how lovely, ah yes, shhh" Hannah replied as Rosa held a finger to her lips in warning.

Elizabeth called out again, "Susie, another pot of tea girl!"

"Susie please don't trouble yourself." Hannah said, which brought a questioning smile from the dark skinned beauty. "Elizabeth, I will make the tea for you." Hannah's mood had lightened and she couldn't hide her grin when Ms Baker's eyebrows raised.

Marriage. Nicholas threw his quill down onto the desk. The ink splashed across the parchment, forming silhouettes of a slender waistline and soft brown curls. He had crossed Main on the way back to his office when the sight of a pale slender hand out the coach window snagged his interest. For reasons unknown he'd loitered at the Trading Post just long enough to observe the hands owner, a slender waist with brown curls whose high cheeks bones had drawn him onto the street. He'd watched Hannah Evan's expression evolve from weariness to that of sheer delight when she surveyed his town. Nicholas had almost lost his footing when her pert lips arched open as Hannah stretched sore muscles, sending her ample chest skyward.

Then she turned and hidden her profile. Disappointed Nicholas has taken a step forward and caught his prey, soft, vanilla, intoxicating his senses and stirring his blood.

Nicholas spent the next half an hour staring at paperwork trying to make sense of the scrawled writing of others, before Nicholas gave up and faced the sinking sun. He stared at the wavering light, the clean blue turning to stone grey and thought of her eyes and a silky brown tendril falling across her pale skin. He paced from his desk to the window and glanced at the end of Main. Hannah Evans had natural beauty that seemed to multiply when she smiled, but Nicholas knew beauty meant nothing. A sinking weight returned to Nicholas stomach when he thought about her motives. Why else would she move from the city life to Franklin Shallows, if not for the purpose of securing a prosperous husband? He had had enough of avariciousness and greed in one life time.

Nicholas cursed softly and ran his hand through his hair tugging it backwards. He paced back to his desk, Hannah Evans had managed to rouse tempting thoughts Nicholas Hoffman had long put aside.

He mused over Beth. Once she was his betrothed cousin by extension and now his cousin by-marriage. Bethany Krouse would have far more luxuries and servants than Bethany Hoffman would ever have. Or so she had believed. As Benjamin was the fourth born child in the Krouse line, he could marry whoever he liked. His older siblings had already married into the other lines of the Freys and Treschelles. It never struck his cousins, how bizarre their family really was. And now Beth was part of that family. Her children might have to marry their cousins one day.

For a time he had felt in love with her. If not love, something strong, companionship. She had a beautiful smile, a polite manner. She could cook. She had made him many a fine fare to taste and it had all been delicious. Now that smile was for Benjamin, and Benjamin sampled all her wares. He distracted himself from that train of thought immediately. *Hannah*. He had her pinned as a temporary visitor to the town with her three tiny trunks. Then again, who would want to visit Ms Baker? No, unfortunately for Nicholas, Hannah had moved to Franklins Shallows and she intended to stay.

Chapter 2

Dawn arrived quicker than Hannah had anticipated, the misty morning slid silently by as the sun rose over the tree line to the east. With no tall buildings or built in apartments, the sun splashed colour over the country side without reserve. The white pines were think and tall splattered here and there with low emerald shrubbery. Their lofty heights edged downhill to what Hannah could only guess was a water source. Franklins Shallows?

What had the Sherriff said, cool, fast flowing and more dangerous than it sounded. It might have had nothing to do with wealth that this Beth chose the second beau over the Sheriff. She pushed thoughts of the Sheriff from her head and dressed as warmly as she could. The high waisted dress she chose had been cut from dark blue wool of a fine quality. She had noticed in her small wander about Franklins Shallows, yesterday that the long tight bodices and shifting silks skirts had disappeared leaving women able to dress and walk without bustles and hoops.

At breakfast, Elizabeth dryly discussed school routines and names of the "Frey" children, their particular talent, how to praise them and when to praise them to their mothers. Susie and Rosa flittered in and around them laying the table and bringing food. Hannah's thoughts drifted off to the notion of seeing Sherriff Hoffman again and she decided she would give him a piece of her mind the next time. Begging for a change of topic, Hannah asked Elizabeth about her future plans.

"I've bought a ticket overseas, England first and then the civilised areas of Europe. The ship leaves in two weeks, I will stay in Philadelphia until it disembarks. I needed to instruct Lucy, well now you properly before I left"

Hannah was amazed at the mention of Europe. "Surely you are the thriftiest person in America to afford such a retirement. I hope to do as well on my teachers' pension." She said.

"Who are you to judge how I can afford my retirement?" Susie and Rosa exited the Lodge and after a few long moments, Hannah could hear the sound of the water pump. Elizabeth gnawed at her breakfast in silence. Hannah mumbled an apology and ventured into territory she wanted to avoid, as a half-hearted attempt to remain civil.

"Tell me more about the Frey's?"

"So you can marry one, no I think not." Ms Baker's words cut at Hannah.

"So knowledgeable on marriage even for one who was unable to achieve that status?"

"Yes, Hannah because I am a spinster and I deplore the idea that other woman will obtain what I had once so desperately wanted to hold. Yes Hannah, because you have all the talents to obtain marriage and more and instead you choose not to - " Elizabeth ended as Susie and Rosa returned indoors and stoked the fire.

Hannah excused herself from the table and scolded her judgmental behaviour. She had no right to call down Ms Baker. She hadn't lived in her shoes, just as Ms Baker hadn't lived in hers. "I sincerely apologise Ms Baker." She started cleaning the dishes when Susie stormed over and ripped the cloth out of Hannah's hand. Hannah decided to ignore Ms Baker as she launched into a deplorable discussion about how people earnt their wage. Glancing out the window, Hannah spied an old chicken run, "Do you have chickens Elizabeth?"

"No but, I did. I'm sure Mac at the Trading Post wouldn't mind selling you some. He keeps laying hens out the back." The old teacher left her chipped tea cup and saucer on the table and shut herself in the second bedroom.

After finishing drying the dishes, Hannah decided she would purchase some hens and walked into town. As each cart passed it spun the dirt into the air and coated her navy hemline in a soft brown dust. The sun peaked over the shop rooves, thatched, slated and tin, sending golden rays of light onto the bustling street below. Rejuvenated by the fresh air, Hannah strolled around Franklins Shallows determined to explore her new surroundings.

She walked in and out of each store taking in the names and personalities of those she met. Sarah at the haberdashery was polite but gossipy. Asking all manner of questions about Hannah, her marital status and offering some tid-bits of information on the town, the Sherriff hadn't divulged. The Boarding House actually had a full complement of "soiled doves" who were earning their keep well. Hadn't Nicholas asked if she'd stay there! Heat flashed into her cheeks.

The butcher greeted her with a crooked smile, his wife, Sue-Lyn heavy with child number four, sought reassurance that Hannah taught differently than Ms Baker. Hannah confirmed that she did. At the only café in Franklins Shallows Hannah found the only lawyer enjoying a late breakfast with a tall thin man from the Land Title's Office, both men poured over maps and documents mumbling about silver. They ignored her as she bought a jar of cream coloured toffees for Susie and Rosa.

As Hannah returned to the sunshine, she passed a thin blonde woman clothed in a green silk dress Hannah would expect to see on the society circuit in Philadelphia.

"Oh, you must be the new teacher I've heard about."

"I, um, yes Hannah Evans, Mrs…?"

"Mrs Feronica Frey, but please don't hold that against me."

Hannah supressed a giggle and took the petite hand, the woman offered.

"Nice to meet you, Mrs Frey."

"Feronica, please Hannah. If I can call you Hannah, that is?" Feronica squeezed Hannah's hand warmly.

"Yes, please do."

Feronica smiled a small fragile thing that seemed to pierce her fine porcelain complexion. "It's nice to see a fresh face around here some times. We had all been expecting Lucy to return, but it's a pleasure to have you in her place."

"Thank you," Hannah gushed.

Feronica's deep green dress emphasised the hazel of her eyes that held soft creases in the corner. "Have you had much chance to meet any parents since you've arrived?" Feronica took Hannah by the elbow and they strolled down Main Street.

"Not as yet. School resumes in a few weeks, so I will make my introductions between now and then."

"Of course." Feronica said, "What do you think so far of our small town?"

"It's beautiful." Hannah held her tongue about the Sherriff. "I especially love the bridge, what do you call him?"

"Old Thom, yes it's a shame we lost the votes, Mrs Jameson, our president was very upset." Feronica said before turning away to nod at the passers-by, yet she didn't stop to talk to them.

"It is a shame, all that history being torn down."

"That's an excellent point. We do have one last chance to push the Mayor on the subject. Oh, Hannah, I've had a wonderful idea." Feronica's doll like face illuminated as she tugged on Hannah's arm. "Our little committee had planned to make a last ditch attempt to sway the Mayor. We can throw you a party, a welcoming feast and invite the whole town, including the Mayor. Together we can try to convince him that Old Thom is worth saving. What do you think?"

Taken aback, Hannah thought on Ms Bakers warning, "I hardly doubt I will be able to convince anyone, I've only just arrived in town."

"And yet you feel as strongly about Old Thom as we do. You said it yourself, all that history."

"I couldn't - " Hannah thought about that beautiful red roof.

"Don't be ridiculous it will be perfect. I'll have it all sorted, the whole town can come. I'll send you an invitation to – where are you staying until Ms Baker leaves us." Mrs Frey

"At the Lodge with Ms Baker."

"Wonderful I'll send it this afternoon. I have to see the Printer about an advertisement anyway. Good help is hard to find this far out from the city."

"Thank you, I must be off now as well." Wishing she had something more important to add, Hannah finished saying "I have some chickens to buy."

"Good day to you." Both women smiled as they parted. Hannah counted that as two friends.

At Mac's Trading Post she heard mumblings about Silver again, and learnt that her initial assessment of Ms Baker had not been wrong. Most parents she met expressed their gratitude when she mentioned that the school year would start a new, each child would be assessed and schooled accordingly. She gathered her three new laying hens from their pens, holding each by their feet and made her way out into the street. Still thinking about the pending party, Hannah turned down towards home when a large rumbling mass entered her peripheral vision. The large brown lump shuffled forward towards her from a darkening alley. She heard a low groaning from under hunched shoulders and in a fright Hannah threw her hands up and loosened a chicken. The man mumbled at her and swatted the bird away from his balding head.

"I'm sorry miss," he mumbled and shuffled past her. Hannah cursed herself for her rudeness. The man, in his late forty's limped with a club foot and his jaw slackened to the side. She made an assessment he was probably without his full mental faculties. She added her own apology before he'd made it completely past her.

"Not to worry Miss," he mumbled and Hannah reprimanded herself for her nervous reaction. Now she had a chicken to catch. Hannah followed the brown feathered fugitive down the alley and around corners, clucking like a mad woman. She twisted into a dead end somewhere behind a large two story white washed building, before hearing the languished giggles of working girls. She sighted her chicken pecking happily at the ground, beside a lengthy wire clothes line, burdened by many washed sheets, none of them white.

"Lost your bird Miss?" called a small voice from above her. A skinny, freckled boy about 7 or 8 years of age started making his way down a stack of wooden crates towards her chicken, "I'll flush her your way you get ready with your skirts!"

Hannah nodded and then paused - What the Hell was she supposed to do with her skirts?

Before Hannah could properly prepare, a shutter behind the boy opened and a pale skinned, blonde poked her head out to light a cheroot. Before Hannah could cry out a warning the shutter hit the boy in the shoulder, pitching him forward to the ground. He landed with a giant thump and began howling instantly. Hannah forgot her other feathered charges and rushed to meet him.

The whore above shouted in despair, "Jackson, get the Doc, I've hurt Jimmy…" Her head snapped back in the window and within moments Hannah and Jimmy were surrounded by the ensemble of Doves from the Boarding house.

Jimmy's mother came running forward, a red silk robe covering her neck to knees, tears streaming down her face. She pulled his head away from Hannah's soothing embrace and up against her ample breasts.

"Oh Jimmy, my God boy, what were you doing?"

"I was trying to help Miss here catch her chickens."

"You?" Jimmy's mother glared at Hannah and she stopped systematically probing the boys head and arms.

"I'm sorry but it was an accident."

"Jasmine is he alright?" The blonde from the window rushed out, covering her talents with a sky blue silk robe.

"You tried hurting my boy." Jasmine flayed Hannah with her jade green eyes, where they crouched together in the dirt.

"No ma it was Pippa."

"Jassie, lay off, it was me, I bumped the window… and he fell." Pippa stammered.

Jackson, another freckled youth about eleven, sped around the corner. "I've told the Doc. He's on his way."

"Well then, I'm sorry Miss…?" Jasmine said.

"Please, it's Hannah." She spied a small girl about 6 years old peak through legs of the surrounding crowd and Hannah ventured a smile, before the heart shaped face smiled back.

"I can't feel anything broken, but -" She peered into his eyes and at the swelling bump on his forehead. "You stay awake tonight okay. Maybe a concussion and you don't want to fall asleep with a concussion."

"Are you some kind of Quack?" Jasmine managed to finish the sentence without a harsh tone.

"No, I mean, I guess." Hannah started before affirming, "No, I'm the new schoolmarm." Silence greeted her. She had an attack of the nerves and kept talking as the crowd grew restless around her. "I guess I'll be seeing you all when school resumes, but my name is Hannah Evans and I would like you all to -"

Jasmine cut her off, "Why'd you think they'd see you?"

"I'm sorry? Because school starts -"

"I ne'er been to that school Miss." Hannah sat back on her haunches, dumbfounded. Of course the Frey's and any other upstanding citizen of Franklins Shallows wouldn't want their children sitting in a classroom with these. Without a worthy response Hannah stared around at the faces accusing her of the same bigotry. If only they knew.

"Thanks Miss, but you best get on your way." A small man in his fifty's handed the three hens to Hannah, their feet neatly tied with a leather throng. As she took the bundles, she rose slowly to her feet. The little girl smiled at her again unaware of the social inequalities she would find in her future. How would the cycle ever be broken?

"How many children are here?" She whispered.

"What so you can haul them off to the orphanage in Buck!" Jasmine spat.

"Orphanage? No!"

The old man gently pushed her with aged work hands, "You best get going before someone sees you here," he added but Hannah planted her feet.

"I'm not like Ms Baker. You want them to learn, send them to the school. In the afternoons or the weekends, or I can come here." Blank faces returned her gaze. She lifted her chin. "You know where I am." Her skirts swished in the dust before she stopped again. "Thanks for the birds."

After penning the chickens, Hannah spent the rest of the day wandering about the school, opening school desks and smelling the youth of the room. Trying to alleviate her concern about the children at the boarding house, she held out hope that one afternoon she might see them here.

She scratched her name in chalk on the board and then reviewed the organisation of the desks. She took a moment to search each desk and located names belonging to each children. It became clear that the Frey's, Treschelles, Krouses and to a lesser extent the Hoffmans were favoured students, their desks sat prominently in front. Hannah even found Elizabeth's teachers diary detailing the children's current marks. She found an old essay of Jonathon Krouse and was appalled at the grammar and spelling mistakes frequented in the writing. Yet it still received top marks. She spent the next hour rearranging the desks.

Throughout the day the weather had warmed and now the late afternoon chill arrived. Hannah slowed her footsteps as she basked in the country sun until the crisp clip of snapping twigs alerted her to a hidden presence. Turning around, Hannah stared into the tall shadows of the late afternoon that snared the thick brush behind the school. She watched the flickering leaves tremble in the breeze and waited.

Nothing. Not even a songbird. Hannah forced slow breaths into her lungs and turned away, counting each step to the safety of the Lodge.

As Hannah entered, she noticed Susie had gone and Rosa sat quietly at the fireplace watching the coals, stoking them occasionally. Judging by the closed door, Elizabeth had remained in the second bedroom. Hannah peered out the kitchen window to the brush behind the school. After long minutes passed and satisfied that her imagination had run wild, Hannah turned to her first student.

"Rosa?" Hannah whispered and gestured the little girl into the main bedroom. Hannah located a scrap of parchment in her belongings and began to scrawl the alphabet.

"Do you know what these are?" The little girl nodded and whispered back in such secret excitement, "Letters?"

"Yes, this one is A-" Hannah went through each letter and made their sounds with Rosa and then wrote Rosa's name as clear as she could.

"Is that my name?"

"Yes." Hannah held no doubt that Rosa had a quick mind that was begging for knowledge, "You're a very clever girl Rosa. You will catch up in no time at all."

The little girl's attention never wavered and Hannah adored her sweet nature. Rosa had a short crop of dark tight curls on her head like her mum and had the same slanted almond eyes, yet they were not as dark as her mums, nor was her skin.

"But what about Mama?"

Hannah wanted to hug her, "I bet your Mama is just as clever as you," *Where was Susie?*

Nicholas left the café carrying a roll of pork and gravy, the heat soaking into his hands, remembering the delicious morsel he held yesterday. He focused his attention elsewhere when, upon entering his office, found his cousin waiting.

"So Cousin Nicholas, sorry *Sheriff* Hoffman, how fairs thee this fine noon?"

"Hello Cousin."

William Frey the patriarch and heir of the Frey Empire sat behind Nicholas's desks clothed in his finest. From his dark brown riding jacket and elegantly gold threaded vest right down to his burgundy riding pants and shined black boots that rested effortlessly on Nicholas's stack of papers.

William stood and gestured Nicholas to take the Sherriff's chair. Nicholas noted Williams' slender physic. He was as tall as Nicholas with a willowy grace. All the Frey's and the Treschelles had a wiry build to them, nothing like himself. His thoughts drifted back to Bethany and eventually to Hannah. In her hunt for a husband, would Hannah find the Frey's and the Treschelle's more appealing than the burly and clumsy Hoffman's? He had pushed Christian into her cross hairs on purpose. Christian, he thought, embodied the ideal husband for a young woman like Hannah. Young, handsome, blonde. "What can I do for you Cousin?" The jibed each other at every turn with the familiar and seemingly unending term of endearment.

"Oh nothing Cousin Nick,"

Nicholas resumed his seat cautiously. Usually when William said 'Nothing' he meant everything. William strolled to the other side of the desk and sat down, once again placing his boots on Nicholas's desk. He would only let William treat his occupation with such novelty. Although William was a habitual philander, wealthy, self-indulgent, and overly confident, he was Nicholas' favourite of all his cousins and only 9 years his senior. William was a loveable twit with a sense of adventure in his heart that hadn't died when his father had, that had put him in charge of the farming empire and all its adult responsibilities. Plus he never cheated at cards.

William was a rogue no doubt, with his perfectly straight nose, sandy fair hair and hazel eyes that made all the townswomen swoon with adoration. Even his moustache was perfectly manicured so it *graced* his face instead of crept across it and died, like anything Nicholas tried to grow.

"I have come to receive your reply, for the feast my wife - " William's moustache twitched whenever he mentioned Feronica, "- is throwing tomorrow night."

Nicholas leaned back slowly.

William tried to recover, "I'm sure that you would have heard, the whole family is attending. Well she has sent out invitations to the whole town"

Simply put, Feronica hated Nicholas and she took every opportunity to denigrate him. He didn't have time for her either, but it still hurt to have it so publically thrown in your face.

"Sorry, Nick, more like she only told the parents of the children" William dipped his head, "And their neighbours" He spread his thumb and forefinger along his moustache, "the Mayor"

"And the candlestick maker?" Nicholas said.

William grinned.

"I see, since I have no children, neighbours and manage my store of candles affectively, I have missed out on an invitation to a feast?"

"Now, Nick don't pout. Most importantly, I want you to come and since I am who I am, my wife -" his moustache twitched again, "- will accommodate you."

"And what is this in aid of Cousin William, another meeting for the Committee?"

"No, my wife assures me that this event it for the community to greet the new Schoolmarm before school resumes. Although Geoffrey Dammier is invited. No she says it's all about being a pillar of the community or some rot. I think she wants me to take on old Geoffrey at the next election. Fat chance! Can you imagine even more eyes on me than now? Anyway, have you seen her, I haven't, but Old Jack the barber told me she is delightful sight."

A surprise flashed of anger shook Nicholas, "Will," he growled.

"Oh, so you have seen her." William stroked his moustache. "In that case I demand you to attend."

Horrible visions crept into Nick's mind of William Frey, his cousin and his better, in all his finery seducing Hannah Evans. His wealth surpassed all the other families. He could make promises and fulfil them. Shower her with gifts and trinkets till the end of time. Only to have his dishonourable way with her and leave her ruined like so many other, God only knows how many, young women to wallow in their wickedness alone.

"Do you have any morals?"

"Some, but I'll save them for the angels in Heaven!" William said.

"Or the damned in Hell" Nick laughed with him. "I will need to –"

"Nicholas, fore stall all your excuses. I insist."

Nicholas did not want to bend under the pressure those hazel eyes cast at him so he weighed his options. The whole town would be in attendance, he could avoid Hannah with ease with so many party-goers. Nicholas had to think quick. A single woman as beautiful as a Hannah would need a chaperone, especially from William. For Hannah's benefit he told himself.

"I accept, but you will have to invite the old teacher you understand." Hannah needed a chaperone and old prickly as a cactus, socially conscious Ms Baker would suit nicely.

"Who?" William removed his boots from the desk and Nicholas laughed again; of course William wouldn't have paid any attention to a woman in her later years.

"Ms Baker, the retiring teacher of your children." William and Feronica had been blessed with two living children, 7 year old Will, and 5 year old Violet.

"You don't say, Ms Baker is her name," He jested with Nicholas. "Either way Nick I expect you there front and centre. I tolerate them, my wife, my sister and the other cousins. I do this for their money, their obedience and their land. To keep our families whole and pure, but I like you Nick, for your honesty and your ruthless poker skills. Now don't think on how you may feel when you see Benjamin clasping your filly, I will be more upset to miss out on my wife's furious face when she sees you in the midst of all her society scheming."

"I accept." He feared it had more to do with a wayward curl of chocolate hair.

He sent William on his way to pass on the invitation to Ms Baker. Any other man would not push an immoral predator towards his prey, unless he knew exactly how that predator worked. William preferred his prey, pressed and dressed in their best. He would wait until tomorrow night before deviously setting upon Hannah.

He returned to his paperwork a little lighter of heart.

"I'm not going!" Ms Baker spat into her tea,

"I don't see why not, you will be here for a week or more, you might as well come tomorrow night. It can be sort of a farewell and a welcome all at once."

"I didn't see my name on the invitation. Besides, I just want to leave…." Elizabeth's grumbling interrupted by a loud knock at the door.

"Whoever it is send them away, Susie!" Elizabeth snapped. When she heard the disembodied male voice on the other side, her hands began to shake.

"It's William Frey, dear Ms Baker."

"Oh Heavens," Elizabeth rushed to the door. Within moments, the caller at the door had Ms Elizabeth Baker gushing and sighing. After a single "I cannot impose" from Ms Baker and one,

"But I insist" from Mr Frey,

Elizabeth agreed to attend the welcome feast tomorrow night as Hannah's chaperone.

William Frey had casually disregarded meeting Hannah until tomorrow night and she only caught a glimpse of his shiny black boots behind Elizabeth at the entrance. Hannah expected that after such a personal calling by a man held so high in Elizabeth's esteem would pep up her spirits but it did the reverse. "Oh how can I?" she mumbled before bursting into tears. Ms Baker secluded herself in the bedroom only emerging at supper. After supper the old teacher sat at her writing desk. Hannah didn't ask and Elizabeth didn't offer an explanation. When Elizabeth had finished, she handed the envelope to Susie. "First thing tomorrow morning. Please."

Stunned by Ms Baker's polite tone, Susie pocketed the letter in her apron. She rushed Rosa out the door and into cool night leaving Hannah by the fire.

The next day, Nicholas turned the note over in his hands. Ms Baker's precision handwriting very politely requesting, no demanding that he escort both herself and Ms Evans to the

Frey's ranch tonight. Demanding. Yes she had captured that tone perfectly with the black ink scored deep into the parchment. He wrote his reply and handed it to the coffee toned serving girl who waited. He had seen her around town before, "Susie?" She nodded before turning on her heels and dashing away.

Hannah had spent most of the day pottering about the school, avoiding the thicket in the far northern corner. She opened the windows, relocated a sparrow's nest she found in the outhouse and found time to read the children's arithmetic's. Just as she had found with the literacy, the Frey's were treated differently. Hannah started on the cleaning the back room when Rosa appeared and they had revised the alphabet. Together they checked the chickens and were rewarded with an egg. The little girl carried her reward tenderly as they returned to the Lodge.

"Elizabeth, do you know where Susie is?" Hannah asked just as Susie rushed into the Lodge.

"Did you arrange what I asked?" The young woman nodded and handed over the envelope Hannah had seen earlier. Hannah heard the regular kitchen rumblings to signal Susie making tea she sent Rosa in to her mother and hoped for lunch. "I sent her to town to find an escort to take us to the Frey's ranch. It's not far by horse and trap, Sheriff Hoffman will collect us." Hannah made an awkward about turn and faced Elizabeth, "Very unladylike to catch flies like that my dear. For a city girl, you are not very ladylike at all?" Hannah closed her jaw.

"I just - which Sheriff Hoffman will be escorting us?" Hannah couldn't work out the cause of the feeling in her stomach now,

"I hope you are not too disappointed, when poor old Nicholas arrives and not his handsome Deputy." A small smile crept onto Elizabeth's wrinkled face.

"I see" Hannah bit her lip. Aside from her day wear, all she had was one city dress, a graduation gift from Margaret. She bypassed the kitchen and entered her room. She ran her fingers over the soft green silk of the high bodice. Hannah sighed as she breathed in the faint traces of her sister's flowery perfume.

Hannah tried it on in and gasped. If she had one grace over her sister it was her ample breasts. In Philadelphia Hannah wouldn't have given a second thought to wearing this dress, but as her pale skin practically burst forward, she'd have to find a way to preserve her modesty. After several frustrating minutes of locating and threading the needle and several more minutes of finger pricking pain, she threw the clothes on to the bed and gave up. The irony of being able to stitch perfect neat lines in a man's warm wet skin, yet simple unmoving fabric eluded her! My father was a tailor damn it! And she laughed out loud.

Susie entered the room, taking in Hannah sitting in her small-clothes with a needle in one hand and the mesh and dress on the floor. "Let me help you." She whispered, "You do not want to display the milk, without someone buying the cow."

"Ah yes – something like that - can you help?"

Susie smiled and scooped up the dress.

Hannah handed her the needle.

"You will see,".

Chapter 3

Nicholas has his foreman fix his most placid mare Smoke to the trap before setting off on his destination. A strange lightness filled Nicholas's chest as the heavy strands of sunset changed to delicate dusty purple. The grey mare plodded her way back towards the town, shoed hooves and steel wheels bouncing across the timber slats of Old Thom, moss and rot covered every second beam. Construction would start on the new stone bridge soon and Old Thom would be destroyed shortly afterwards. Nicholas tried to concentrate on the bridge and what it meant for his town but his thoughts eventually slipped back to Hannah. And Beth. His heart had been discarded and his pride bruised. Hannah would meet all his wealthy cousins tonight, would she look at him the same way Beth had?

Nicholas enjoyed working, not as rich as his cousin, but he lived comfortably. Most of his cousins had accrued gambling debts and bank loans that would substantially reduce their assets, should they be called. Which prospective cousins would Hannah try to snare tonight? Nicholas thought. Samuel Frey, was one, and about Hannah's age. Willowy, like William, Samuel had been designated by the family as next to marry. The Family just hadn't decided which of his cousins would suit him best. With his recent nuptials to Beth, Benjamin Krouse was obviously off the list. Another likely option was fat Richard Trecshells, brother to Feronica. Nicholas shivered at the thought of Richard placing a pale pudgy hand on Hannah. Richard did hold the most monetary assets out of the lot, which might make Hannah overlook his physical appearance. The Brandmyer Twins, Martin and Matthew were also of an age for Hannah. Their mother, like Nicholas's grandmother had married for love and hence her offspring were not considered official Freys. His other Hoffman cousins, Jacob, Christian, Leonard and Francis were also suitable for Hannah yet their fathers, Nicholas' uncles lived on. They held no substantial wealth in their own right. By the time Nicholas reached the gravel drive to the School he had summed up and dismissed his cousins as suitable for Hannah. He'd have to wait and see which one successfully drew her attention. Instead Nicholas mentally reiterated that he would never do it again, never care so much about a woman. Especially for some silly wedding bell chaser with dollar signs in her eyes. He had repeated those words *not again* over and over in his mind, until the door to the Lodge opened.

The words evaporated leaving little hiccups in his thoughts. Hannah had pinned half her unruly curls high on her head and the others dripping down her creamy white neck. The dark green dress cut low across the nape and sat wide on her slender shoulders. Hannah clutched a burgundy coloured shawl around her upper arms and when she reached back to close the door, Nicholas groaned. A piece of thin mesh desperately tried to hide the firm curve of her breasts. Only after Hannah readjusted her shawl and turned away did he finally hear Ms Baker.

"I said, good evening Sheriff," Brown eyes slowly regarding him.

"Evening Ms Baker, Ms Evans." His voice returned, sounding a bit colder than he would have liked. Nicholas managed to assist both ladies into the trap without gaping. As Hannah passed, he breathed deeply, absorbing the delicious, fresh soap and vanilla scents. Nicholas allowed himself one more lustful thought as she climbed upwards into the trap. Nicholas returned the front, wishing the cool dusk air would chill his thoughts.

Beth had been pretty. Slight build, fair haired and wide eyed, she had been called beautiful and yet the word beautiful seemed wasted on Hannah. The word was simply inadequate. He pushed away the surge of irritation that erupted. He had thoughts, rogue, impure, thoughts about Beth during their engagement and even more shallow kisses and soft whispers wasted in her ear. All of it faded like dust in his memory when Nicholas thought of Hannah now. He had despised William for all his treacherous philandering ways but as Nicholas caught another glimpse of Hannah, the real unending desire for a woman surged through his blood. Like a man dying of thirst would want for water, Nicholas wanted Hannah. He breathed deeply of the night air and flicked the reins to send Smoke plodding away.

"All the Frey's live across the river, Dear?" Elizabeth said but Hannah couldn't concentrate. She couldn't quell the butterflies that danced in her stomach when Nicholas helped her into the trap. His touch sent shock waves racing up her neck and his eyes turned sapphire blue with the sunset. But he had greeted her with cool detachment. How could Nicholas make such grave character mistakes in his line of work, guilty until proven innocent?

She watched the fading light bounce off the messy black waves of his hair until Old Thom appeared ahead in their path. Hannah moved forward, balancing on booted heels and tapped the Sheriff on the shoulder. As the traps wheels struck timber planks, Hannah over balanced and pitched forward. At the risk of landing face first into the Sherriff's lap, her hands shot out, grabbing at anything for purchase. She found his right thigh above the knee, taunt muscles flexing under her grip. Hannah squeaked and withdrew her hand as if scorched and tried to find leverage elsewhere, flailing like a duck about to take flight. Hannah's fingers sunk into the solid flesh of his shoulder and she pushed herself backwards. Nicholas stopped the trap.

"What are you doing?" He snapped and Hannah fought the urge to cower from his glare.

"I'm sorry. I almost landed – um I just saw the bridge and -" Hannah tried to clear the shakiness from her voice.

"Are you alright Dear?" Ms Baker queried, distant from the rear.

Only then did Hannah realise they had crossed and she had missed the whole occasion because she had been too thigh-grabbing busy.

"You wanted to walk across the bridge?"

Hannah winced, "Yes or rather I did." The heat charged up her neck and Hannah wanted to hear Nicholas silvery laugh again instead she got further icy tones.

"Lucky, no-one was hurt." Nicholas ached on the inside. How had the briefest contact made him instantly rock hard? He pushed his desire aside, hoping the tightness would pass and flicked the reins once more.

Hannah resumed her seat next to Elizabeth and folded her shaking hands into her lap. He probably thinks you are throwing yourself him now? She blinked away dampness and instead looked at the passing scenery. The rolling green meadows were brimming with wheat, corn, and barley. Windmills and scarecrows pocketed the purple hued horizon and Hannah could see other traps heading north along the road. Off in the distance the soft lowing of cattle could be heard and within a few short turns, they arrived at the stone gates marking the Frey's Ranch. As they turned up the gravel drive, careful not to cut over onto meticulous lawns and manicured hedges, the Frey's ostentatious homestead appeared. Four white columns framed the double door entrance of the pale stone monstrosity that rivalled any manor back in the best parts of Philadelphia. The second story held two regal stone balconies either side of an enormous arched window that reflected crystal light and golden finishes. Hannah counted four chimneys. The Sherriff helped Ms Baker down first and Hannah stilled her nerves as Nicholas reached for her next. Thoughts of a snappy retort crossed her mind, but the Sherriff was silent. Her hand ghosted across his forearm, fingertips trailing the back of his hand. Hannah withdrew in fear she might let her touch linger for all the wrong reasons.

Hannah glanced into the foyer of the marvellous residence and observed marble tiles lined with mahogany tables, carrying marble statues.

Hannah spoke her thoughts forgetting her present company, "Mrs Frey likes her marble."

The Sherriff stifled a chuckle.

A little worm of anxiety dissolved at the Sherriff's amusement and Hannah straightened her shoulders. Why let him affect you at all, Hannah? She thought.

He led Hannah and Ms Baker onto a paved path filled with a steady trail of party goers as it snaked through aged oak and maple trees to reveal an imposing stone barn. Built into the side of the soft undulating fields, the lower level housed the Frey thoroughbreds and breeding stock, while the top level had been transformed into a great hall. The hubbub of laughter and liquor drew Hannah and her chaperones up the side and in through the double barn doors. Lanterns hung daintily from the timber rafters, and white clothed tables lined the sides of the barn separated by stock ladders that climbed skywards.

In a flurry of greetings and handshakes Hannah entered the main hall and found herself immersed by the townspeople enjoying the finery of a grand party. Some folk danced politely to the organist, accompanied by a very talented fiddler, while others took glasses of wine from starch covered waiters. It was as if Hannah had never left Philly.

The Sheriff disappeared leaving Hannah and Ms Baker to field introductions by themselves. Elizabeth ran a sideline commentary about each person, their children's names, weakness and strengths. When Hannah met a parent who was not a blessed cousin, she gave them warm greetings and reassurances that she taught differently from Elizabeth. In each such parents eyes, a glimmer of hope blossomed. How could Elizabeth be so oblivious to the dislike of her teaching standards?

"And this is our most gracious hosts, Mr and Mrs Frey."

Feronica Frey kissed both women on the cheek, "Hannah and I met in town yesterday, Elizabeth."

Beside Hannah, Ms Baker paled, a scowl creasing her thin lips, "Oh you did?"

"Yes, we had a lovely talk about Old Thom and the importance of history." Feronica said. Her illustrious mane of golden hair cascaded down her neck and her red dress fell effortlessly over her slim figure. She reminded Hannah of a brightly coloured swan.

"I see, well Hannah and that bridge! Earlier as we crossed – "

Now it was Hannah's turn to blanch, "Have you had a chance to bend the Mayors ear?" she interrupted.

"I thought that battle was done my Dear?" A voice from behind Hannah spoke.

"Hannah, this is my husband, William Frey, Ms Evans," Feronica slid backwards slightly and the gentleman everyone seemed to fear, bow to, or envy entered Hannah's vision. Tall, fair haired and with the slightest onset of sun-wrinkles about his face. The moustache made William look distinguished and she caught herself comparing his fair colouring to Nicholas's dark appealing looks.

William Frey clasped Hannah's hand in his soft, pale fingers and raised them to his lips. A shiver ran down her back as his lips lingered on her skin and his tongue touched the back of her hand.

"Nice to make your acquaintance" Hannah stammered, retrieving her hand. Instinctively she forced her attention to Feronica, the older woman's hazel eyes sad and soft.

"I should thank you for the feast on my behalf," Hannah said, "You have a wonderful home and this barn is just enormous. I can't imagine how long it took to put all this together."

"Thank you, Hannah, but think nothing of it," Feronica beamed, "I should introduce to you our Mayor Geoffrey Dammier before dinner gets under way." The salivating scent of roasting pork drifted through the crowd, snatching their attention and making Hannah's stomach stir. Feronica physically steered Hannah away from William, however he shouted over their heads,

"Cousin Nicholas, why are you hiding back there? Feronica, Cousin Nicholas is here to greet you."

Nicholas's brow creased and Hannah watched the Sherriff school his features to calm. Had he witnessed William's slimy exchange?

Nicholas strode over and gave Feronica an empty kiss on the cheek, "Cousin,"

"Cousin," Feronica greeted him with the same, icy repugnance, "Have you greeted Cousin Benjamin and Cousin Beth?"

It took all Hannah's composure not to cluck her tongue. An elusive grin dashed across Nicholas face, "Not yet Feronica, I came first to greet you and thank you for your gracious invitation."

"And yet you made it anyway," Feronica's features turned sharply to her husband,

William twitched, "So Ms Evans tell us a bit about yourself? Where did you study?"

Hannah watched the simmering tension between their gracious hostess and the Sherriff and answered without thinking, "The Women's College of Medicine."

"College? Medicine? I thought all teachers went to some backyard Norm School." William responded.

"Yes I did that too" Hannah said, before she realised Ms Baker still stood within their company, a scowl brewing on the old teachers face.

"Well please go on Ms Evans?" Nicholas said.

"I began studying to become a physician."

"Physician?" William asked.

"Yes, it's a rather boring story of a wealthy man who thought too high of himself" Hannah was of course referring to John Smithson the Third. Then she saw the expression on Feronica's face and added "My brother-in-Law, John, I mean." Nicholas laughed into his wine. "I almost completed my studies before being shipped off to Norm School."

"I need a drink." Ms Baker exclaimed loudly as a waiter orbited close by. By the sounds of her, she was well into her cups. Hannah took a second glass.

"So what components did you complete?" Nicholas challenged.

"Well I studied physiology, therapeutics, obstetrics and chemistry. Then anatomy, theory and practice of -" Hannah was about to say surgery but William interrupted.

"Theory and Practice of Anatomy? That sounds more interesting." A smile crept under his moustache. Feronica sighed loudly and disappeared into the party. William turned on his heels and followed with a daring wink at Nicholas.

"I meant to say, Theory and Practice of surgery…" Hannah tightened her jaw. Feeling his eyes on her again she managed to stammer out "But it doesn't matter."

"I see," The tone mirrored his eyes and the wine he sipped had not softened his arrogance. He glanced around the room.

Was he searching for Beth? "So, you were not asked to attend? If not for Ms Baker's demand, of course. Is it because of Beth?" Hannah's loaded question drew a glare that would cut glass. She willed herself to hold his gaze that threatened to swallow her whole.

"Feronica." He started, "She's never liked me." Nicholas finished and resumed scanning the townspeople.

"Point her out to me and I shall see if she is worthy of all this swooning."

The cluck of his tongue, told Hannah she had been her most usual socially unacceptable self thus far. He stepped closer and let his mouth drift past Hannah's ear, "The one in the blue next to the window. My cousin Benjamin is the tall one, with the ice blue vest."

His breath touched her cheek and it took her a while before her eyes focused on what he had described. Beth was there, tall, thin, graceful, fair haired, pretty. *Pretty but not spectacular*, she thought. *And what am I?* A woman grown and self-sufficient!

Nicholas remained where he stood, his face inches away from hers. The wine on his breath tickled her nose and shivers of delight spread through her abdomen. Hannah clenched her fists and smoothed her skirts.

At this proximity, Nicholas absorbed the sweet warmth that radiated from Hannah and let it hold him, unable to step away, as Hannah groomed herself. He had to stifle a groan as her movements gently tugged at the mesh on her bodice sending ripples across her soft flesh. I am no better than Will, he chided himself.

The pianist commenced a new bout of music and many couples entered the dance floor, spinning around and swapping partners in a circle of four. Hannah could only assume it was a localised form of the Waltz. William Frey chose that time to approach, and Hannah tried to think of an excuse, but he wrapped his arms around her and dragged her onto the floor. As the piano and fiddle took flight, she grabbed hold of William's hand and shoulder, his arm resting as low as he could down her back, his little finger edging the top of her petticoats.

"I'm sure you never had any trouble finding specimens for the Practice of Anatomy." His grin twisted to the side.

Before Hannah could correct him, the partners swapped and this time she faced a stranger. Tall and thin with thin brown hair and an easy smile, the man introduced himself as James Dammier.

"Yes I am the mayor's son," He answered when Hannah made the connection. "Don't hold that against me though," He laughed a welcoming sound after William Frey. His green eyes caught sight of something or someone over Hannah's shoulder and his laughter faded. The partners swapped again. This time a tall thickly built man spun into her arms, his thin lips smiled warmly and she guessed correctly that he was Richard Treschells before he introduced himself.

He spoke with a youthful voice that belied his size. "I own the Lumber Mill and the Grist Mill and Feed exchange, just north of you." Richard went on to compliment Hannah on her dress, her hair, her smile. His high pitched tones calmed her nerves until she watched his brown eyes drift down her neckline. "You let me know if you need any more of that cut firewood."

Hannah answered him politely dipping her head as he left, for her next dance partner to enter her arms.

This time Nicholas stepped into her arms and relief overwhelmed her. Hannah grasped his shoulder, the soft fabric of his coat burning her palm. Hannah concentrated on the space between their bodies, silently wishing the distance to close. His fingers folded over hers and a flash of heat coloured her neck. His hand eased down to the small of her back, turning heat into flame. How had this man crept under her skin and how would she get rid of this feeling, that she wanted him there?

"Did you have to dance with Feronica?" She asked.

Nicholas returned a quick smile, "Yes, but it is no more awkward that William dancing with her." He nodded in the couples' direction.

Hannah stole her eyes from Nicholas dimples and saw he told the truth. The couple, held each other like well-trained partners, faces impassive.

"A physician you said."

"Almost."

"That would have taken a substantial amount of money to pay for tuition fees."

"Yes." She wouldn't discuss how she earned the money.

"Any plans on resuming your studies?" Nicholas teased.

So that's what he thinks, snag a rich husband to pay for my fees? Well you had helped Margaret catch John? "That's behind me." Hannah whispered.

"Is it," Ice blue eyes traced the outline of her hips, "You don't sound sure." The music changed and the waltz ended.

"Well I am." Hannah turned on her heels and ran into Ms Baker.

"I feel rather ill." Elizabeth said, hiccupping with severity.

"I'll take you outside." Hannah gently linked arms with Ms Baker and began leading her out of the barn to the fresh air. She clicked her tongue when Nicholas grabbed Ms Bakers other elbow. Together they steered her to the rear doors of the barn. The night air brought cool relief to Hannah's temper and dark shadows to hide her roaming eyes.

Within moments of escaping the crowded and smoky room, Ms Baker improved. A servant brought a pitcher of water and a cloth and Hannah gently dabbed at Elizabeth's cheeks, pushing back grey tendrils that clung to her forehead. Nicholas rested against a hay bale, one black boot up, thumbs in his belt.

The old teacher took great gulps of water and then straightened her hair, "Stop fussing Dear, I'm quite fine now."

"Are you now, Elizabeth?"

"Yes thank you, I'm going to go freshen up if you don't mind."

"Are you right to walk?"

"Walk, yes Sherriff, I'm fine." The usual brisk tone had returned and Elizabeth entered the rear of the barn leaving Hannah and Sheriff in the darkness.

"Sheriff." Hannah dipped her head in farewell, until smooth caramel tones delayed her retreat.

"How did you know about Beth?" He asked. The light from within, threw sharp shadows across his features, the ice blue turned to sapphire, dark brown curls into wild black serpents.

"Ms Baker. She told me."

"And what do you think of my other cousins? Did you meet Sammuel? I haven't seen Christian or Jacob yet but they will be here no doubt. All of suitable marrying age. Some with wealthy fathers - "

Hannah's empathy dissolved, "Why is this town so preoccupied about marriage and wealth!" She couldn't be lost for words here. He needed to hear it, and hear it directly from her. "Unless you didn't know already, teachers on contract are not permitted to marry." The fire in her voice unmistakable, the Sherriff took a step back. "Besides that I don't want to marry.

I'm not here for a man's money. I do not want to -" She wanted to explain her mother and her sisters husband to him, to the nights working in the scum and back-alleys of Philly all to pay for another round on Margaret's social calendar. But by the end of her thoughts, Hannah had calmed. "What about you Sheriff Hoffman, after Beth?" She ventured. She wouldn't allow him to throw all the muck her way.

Nicholas walked forward until his shiny black boots almost touched hers. When Hannah looked up the Sherriff stood over her, sapphire pits, boring into her soul.

"Ms Evans will remain Ms Evans then?"

Hannah refused to retreat, and drank in all she could before her eyes lowered to his smirking lips. A shiver travelled south from her neck to her thighs. Her breath seemed trapped in her chest and she forced out her answer, "Yes".

Hannah tore herself away, and stormed inside to the party. Her thoughts heavily veiled with Nicholas that she smelt his pine and oiled leather scent before she saw him. He stormed past leaving Hannah's to ponder his refusal to answer.

After the feast of suckling pig and wild deer, that William Frey loudly exclaimed was his own personal handiwork, the guests toasted to Ms Baker and to Hannah. Hannah sat down to eat with Ms Baker at a table towards the front of the barn. Hannah had lost sight of Nicolas, yet more of his cousins sat with her.

"Isaac Krouse and Johnathon Krouse and their wives, Margaret and Martha." Ms Baker fielded the introductions as the two hefty gentlemen pulled out chairs for their stately wives.

"Krouse Brothers Constructions, Ms Evans." The elder of the two, Johnathon offered her a curt nod.

"Our boy is definitely excited about the new school year, Ms Evans."

Hannah racked her brains as to which mother addressed her,

"Oh yes, Johnathon Krouse is doing fine, Margaret." Ms Baker answered.

Hannah recalled the error laden essay that Elizabeth had marked highly.

"He is planning on becoming a lawyer."

Hannah coughed into her pork. "Is that right?" Hannah paled. Elizabeth threw her a sharp look, "Well we can work together to see he improves."

Margaret's jowls quivered and her lined lips puckered, "Work on improving?"

"Hannah has studied at a College in Philadelphia so she knows the higher education requirements better than most. She will be of great assistance and lend her superior knowledge to see that Johnathon's applications to Universities are of the best quality."

"If that's the case, I'm sure she will do her utmost to see Johnathon succeeds, just like us." Johnathon Krouse hissed as he spoke, hazel eyes winking at Hannah.

Hannah swallowed hard, disgust blending with trepidation, "We'll all work together to see Johnathon reach his full potential." There let that sit with them. If they expected her to give Johnathon junior a free pass, she wouldn't. Margaret's pucker turned into a bold daring grin and she tucked sandy fair hair into her tight bun.

Isaac and Martha Krouse nodded in unison,

"And the same for our Isaac and Henry, Ms Evans." Martha added, grinning.

Hannah resumed her pork, the juicy flesh turning to ash in her mouth. After dinner, Hannah excused herself and wandered about the guests. Smiling at most and stopping to talk with only those parents who were not a blessed cousin. Throughout her movements, Nicholas loitered at the edge of her vision. Her eyes drifting back to the dark Sherriff who dogged her footsteps, somehow feeling safer that he was there, even if just out of reach, while she waded through the Frey snake pit.

Eventually the party goers began winding down or more appropriately winding up as the pianist retired and the fiddler began some wild barn dance ditties.

"Hannah, I feel as if we should be getting home." Ms Baker said, her heavy lined face, grey in the warm lamp light. The old teacher clutched a decorative gift bag to her chest and Hannah chanced a peep, seeing a generous brandy bottle inside.

"Yes Elizabeth right before this party turns to impolite drunkenness I think." She didn't even scold herself this time. But she was right, the group of men surrounding William Frey began chatting very loudly about Fillies and it seemed clear to Hannah if to no one else which fillies they were referring to.

"Find Nicholas will you Hannah?" Ms Baker took a stool at the side but Hannah didn't have to look far. She had never seen such a room full of pitiful faces as she did then, their heads turned to where Nicholas stood conversing with his Cousin Benjamin and his new wife. A bizarre anger stirred, inside Hannah. So Nicholas's heart had been broken by this woman, and his vile family fed off it, like a wounded animal at slaughter. All at once, Hannah discovered all the Frey's disgusted her. Their insipid features all blended together, tall sandy fair haired, and hazel eyed. Hannah imagined she could paint a portrait of Ludwig Frey just by referring to the people in the room. All except Nicholas.

Hannah straightened her dress and crossed the room in twenty determined steps, leaving her shawl behind. As she crossed, Benjamin Krouse was detailing the happy couples honeymoon travels, "We went south through France and eventually stopped for a fortnight in a charming little chateau in the Austrian Empire."

"Austria, really?" Nicholas answered.

Bethany Krouse's nasal voice assaulted Hannah's ears, "Oh yes, my Benjamin refused to deny me anything my heart desired."

Nicholas gaze met Hannah's and she almost missed a step, "Sherriff Nicholas" she uttered suddenly breathless, "Excuse me," she turned to his cousins, before turning back to the Sheriffs dark glare, "Ms Baker is ready to leave if you would be so kind as to take us home now." Nicholas eyebrows furrowed and he farewelled his relatives.

As they turned, William Frey obstructed their path, "Be sure Nicholas brings you to the horse auction on Saturday then, won't you Hannah. Pleasure to meet you." He went to kiss her hand again and she protectively clasped onto Nicholas's arm, his biceps strained. The tension seeped through the fabric into Hannah's shaking hands.

Nicholas mentally slowed down his hand as he placed it over Hannah's. His body stirred as her intoxicating vanilla scent trickled into his blood. Her simple touch brought forth a syrupy heat that stirred in his thighs. His hand over hers simply fed the heat.

"No doubt he will, thank you again but we really need to be going, Ms Baker has taken ill," Hannah said nodding to Ms Baker's greying complexion.

As they climbed into the trap, Nicholas watched Hannah settle Ms Baker in the rear, wrapping a blanket around the old headmistress. Ms Baker clutched the brandy bottle to her chest as the trap passed the stone arched gate. Hannah settled her shawl around her shoulders before sitting next to Nicholas, his thigh sizzling as her leg pressed against him. He swallowed hard but did not withdraw. He flicked the reins.

"I couldn't bear it any longer. I don't know how you do. I apologise but I couldn't contain myself any longer and my anti-social talents were about show their full glory if I stayed any longer."

Shivering flushed and angry, Nicholas's raked his eyes over her skin. A chocolate curl rested against her rosy cheek. Hannah couldn't have looked more breathtaking, with her porcelain skin and her grey-blue eyes fresh and alight with frustration. His arm burned with the memory of her hands. How covetous he had become, Nicholas had always hated dancing. Had losing Beth to Benjamin turned him into a controlling jealous man? Listening to Beth had grated on Nicholas, she seemed transparent and shallow. Hannah was hot-blooded and temptingly soft. She had told him confidently that she had no intention to marry. Not a Frey, not anyone. Did she tell him what he wanted to hear? No woman would choose to remain a spinster. Did she not want to feel the passion of a man?

Hannah's shivering continued and even though Nicholas adored the view, the gentleman inside him could not bear to let it continue. He gracefully threw his jacket about her shoulders.

"Thank you."

"I see you have mastered the art of a thank you." Nicholas said. The misty moonlight offered just enough light to see Hannah roll her eyes. "Yes, my family are awful aren't they?"

"I am sorry."

"I should be gracious for your rescue." He laughed and added, "Most of them are harmless."

"Most, oh don't forget the bridge, Old Thom!" Hannah squealed as it approached.

"You're freezing, you should wait till morning."

"I'm warm now and Ms Baker is asleep, please." The persuasive tone in Hannah's voice pleased his ears. He pulled Smoke off onto the grassy shoulder. He could see that the way through was clear and helped Hannah down to the roadside. He chuffed at himself for how snug she looked in his coat and that the next time he wore it would smell of her intoxicating vanilla perfume. Together they crept forward through the eerily silent bridge. Besides their footsteps, all they heard was the slow burble of Franklins Shallows dripping over the sleek river stones. Breathlessly she uttered, "It's perfect isn't it?" Her words frosted before her lips and Nicholas fought the urge to wrap her in his arms.

"It's about to be torn down remember?" Nicholas said, daring himself to step closer.

"Isn't it a shame?" Hannah rubbed her fingers slowly over the wood.

"Not really Hannah when you see Old Thom in the light."

Hannah grinned as Nicholas' voice enveloped her and drove away the cold. He'd moved behind her and every muscle in her body tensed when she faced him.

"I can see fine now, thank you,"

The Sherriff took a step closer, his legs either side of Hannah's. His white shirt stark in the moonlight and without care Hannah let her eyes wander over the expanse of his chest. Nicholas gaze caught hers and she raised her chin to meet the challenge.

Perhaps Hannah never wanted to marry, but Nicholas knew that was different from the basic want for a man. He placed one hand on either side of the railings, snaring Hannah between them. "You're getting very good at these Thanks You's."

A soft breeze stirred, letting the cool air clear Hannah's mind. She motioned to the left and Nicholas removed his arm allowing her freedom, "What will they do with it? Maybe I could keep some part of it when they take it down?"

The moonlight dripped through the gaps in the red slate roof and Nicholas watched her increase the distance between them. Hannah pressed her back against the timber and he stepped to meet her again.

"Why did you really come to Franklins Shallows?" Nicholas asked.

"To prosper, Sheriff."

"Why Franklins Shallows then, why not stay in Philadelphia?"

Hannah hesitated.

"Enlighten me, Ms Evans."

Hannah snuggled into his coat before answering, "As I tried to tell you before, I want my own income, my own property." Mist steamed from her now pale blue lips.

"How will you buy your own property?"

"I will find a way."

"I've never heard of a young woman not wanting to marry, not wanting a husband, a man to call her own."

"Well, I don't need - " Hannah's fiery tones petered out when Nicholas closed in on her. His gaze covered with sheen of enticement and against her better judgement she let her eyes fall to his lips.

Nicholas let his breaths slow to calm his eager hand, he cupped Hannah's cheek, feeling her sharpened breaths glide over the tender skin at his wrist, sending shock waves through his system, "You think you don't have need of a man, but women were built to satisfy the needs of men." He whispered.

Hannah's eyes, darker than shadow on stone in this light, snared his own, her words came hot with rough edges, "Well I don't want –"

"Refusing to admit something, doesn't make it true," Nicholas would bet that right now, Hannah felt the tiny needles of desire in all the parts that made her woman.

Her voice thickened with courage, "I don't want to be made some mans' chattel." She pushed his hand away and Nicholas let her go, "I will find a way to buy cheap land somewhere, grow some crops." Hannah said, her fists clenching and unclenching. "For now I will live on my teacher's pension and firewood allowance."

The moment had gone and he laughed, "I'd like to see you split that firewood by yourself." He could envision her determination in swinging an axe just to prove a point.

"I will find a way." she added and walked towards the trap.

Nicholas laughed again, "Speaking of firewood, let's get you home." Nicholas couldn't resist any longer and he reached out to rub Hannah's shoulders rapidly. To Nicholas's surprise, Hannah didn't withdraw and his heat intensified.

A low mumble erupted from Ms Baker, "Oh dear Ms Baker must be freezing." Without concern for herself or the slippery timber planks Hannah dashed across Old Thom and pressed her fingers against the old teacher's icy cheek. Ms Baker rolled over in her sleep and Hannah sighed. "Let's get going then,"

"Thank you Nicholas" Ms Baker said, after Nicolas helped her down from the trap. Her sleepy voice quavering as she demanded Susie bring her a glass. Hannah made no comment, if Ms Baker wanted to warm herself from the inside out, she could.

Hannah walked Nicholas back outside and unwrapped his coat, "Thank you again."

"There you go with those words again," He said, her residual body heat seeping from his jacket into his shoulders. Hannah raised her eyebrows in mock offence and Nicholas flicked the reins but Smoke whinnied into her bridle. Again Nicholas tapped the leather onto the dapple grey's back but Smoke refused to budge. "Smoke, girl, come on," He flicked the reins once more and this time Smoke danced away from the Lodge.

A loud thump resounded from within followed by an urgent cry "Help!"

Nicholas bounded inside pushing Hannah backward as he drew his service pistol and aimed the barrel at two huddled shapes on the floor.

"Susie, what's happened?" Hannah rushed forward to Ms Baker, her sagging face slummed against the floor, her frail arms askew by her side. Susie scrambled backwards and Hannah laid a hand against the old headmistress's throat.

Hannah's voice trembled like her fingers, "No pulse."

Nicholas holstered his weapon and knelt beside them. Hannah's trembling slowed when the Sherriff checked

Elizabeth's pulse again. He rotated Ms Baker onto her back and Hannah stared at her reddening face.

"She's gone."

Chapter 4

Nicholas' words drifted away from Hannah as cold sounds collided with long dark shadows. Ms Baker had an acid tone and a rude disposition but Hannah hadn't wished her ill. Susie reached for the brandy bottle and a spare glass. The heat might settle their nerves. Hannah focused on Elizabeth's ruddy complexion and the colour sparked her interest. She bent down towards Ms Baker and smelt an unusual sickly odour. She dared herself closer to Elizabeth's gaping mouth and amongst the sweet smell of brandy, Hannah could detect a faint bitter almond smell.

"Poison!" Hannah said snatching, the brandy bottle from the dark skinned girl. The brandy smell was strong, but it did not entirely mask the odour of the killer. "Cyanide." Hannah hissed. She almost dashed the bottle into the fireplace but instead replaced the stopper and rested it carefully on the mantle.

"What is it Hannah?" Nicholas asked standing up from Ms Baker's lifeless form.

"I think she was poisoned." Tears brewed and she wiped them away with her knuckles.

"Poisoned? You're saying Murder." The Sherriff shook his head. "That's a very serious accusation. The people in this town - "

Taken aback, Hannah continued, "Nicholas, I just - " He cut her off by raising his palm to her words, not a tremble to be seen.

"I'll wait for the Doctor to examine her, before I start jumping to conclusions." Nicholas stared down at the scene before his boots. "You're wrong." He said, before turning on his heels.

Hannah and Susie waited for what seemed an eternity with Ms Baker staring lifeless to the ceiling, mouth wide and slack, tiny purple spots forming around her lips. Hannah covered Elizabeth with a throw from the chair.

"Where is Rosa?"

"Asleep."

"But asleep where?" Until now Hannah had never bothered to question the whereabouts of Susie or Rosa during the night, they appeared at breakfast and left at night after setting the fire.

"The school."

"Where do you sleep, there is a fireplace in the main room but no-where else?"

"We sleep in the back room."

"That's ridiculous. After this… all this, you and Rosa will sleep in the spare room. "

"I do not sleep well with spirits."

"Nor do I Susie, do as I say. And Rosa could do with some shoes too.... I'll…." A chill entered the front door and swept about them.

"She did not die in the bedroom, I suppose…" Susie responded before falling silent, as did Hannah when horse hooves galloped up the gravel drive.

Doctor Fitzgibbon arrived with all the pomp and splendour he could manage in his pyjamas covered by an overcoat.

"I sent the Sherriff to wake the undertaker, Ms Evans." He answered Hannah before bending over his expanding waist line to check Hannah's diagnosis. "She's dead alright."

"Dr Fitzgibbon" Hannah began,

"Yes?" Dr Fitzgibbons greying moustache turned down into his pointed beard and one green eye twitched.

"If you examine her mouth,"

"Her mouth?" Dr Fitzgibbons drew closer to Ms Bakers face and readjusted his glasses, "Yes, what about her mouth?"

"I think its Cyanide poisoning, perhaps." She ventured carefully.

"You are referring to the purple spotting, I do see that. Why do you say Cyanide? A number of conditions could mimic poisoning, heart conditions, respiratory problems, strangulation, seizures of the mind and so on."

"There is this." She handed him the green glassed brandy bottle.

His moustache bristled as he sniffed, "Yes, I smell something. I see what you're proposing, however I had seen Ms Baker on numerous occasions for her bad heart." The doctor walked around his supine patient, running his thumbs down his moustache.

"Dr?"

"Ms Evans, I treated Jimmy earlier with Jassie, I mean Jasmine. And the Sheriff mentioned you'd had some minor medical training in in Philadelphia."

Hannah straightened her back and blinked away the last of her tears. He had called her studies Minor, "I did try to tell the Sherriff."

The Doctors moustache came alive concealing a chuckle, "Never mind Ms Evans, I'll issue a certificate in the morning after I've had a better look to see if your theory isn't wrong. Goodnight Ms Evans." Hannah watched the short man mount his spindly brown mare who sagged forward in preparation for the Doctors weight in the saddle.

The undertaker arrived, a small thin man with greying hair and black eyes. He nodded kindly to Hannah as he left with Ms Baker on his cart. Hannah went to close the door on the receding blackness when Nicholas returned riding Smoke.

"Did the Doctor examine Ms Baker?"

Did he say that with emphasis? Hannah thought closing the door behind him, "Yes, he said he'd issue you a certificate in the morning." Nicholas paced to the fireplace, eyes scanning the room.

Despite the lingering doubt that circled Nicholas dark features, his presence chased shadows from the corners. Hannah sucked in a staggered breath before the tears broke forth and Nicholas brought her into his chest. She stayed there, cheek to chest, melting into the unyielding bulk of Nicholas. Hannah inhaled pine and leather, letting the aroma slide under her skin. Each beat of his heart strummed in Hannah's ears. His arms around her shoulders, strong hands rubbing down her back, the rhythm began to slow. His fingers lingered at the top of her hips before climbing her spine, under Hannah's cheek, Nicholas heart beat quickened. Hannah stifled one last sob and Nicholas released her. He approached the green glassed assassin and took a few cautionary sniffs. He returned it to the mantel and gestured for Hannah to sit while he produced a small leather bound notebook.

"Tell me everything you spoke about, everything she did and everyone she spoke to since you first arrived…"

Hannah took a deep breath as Susie placed a fresh pot of tea and cups on the table.

"We spoke about the Frey's, the children, her retirement." Hannah said,

"Retirement? What were her plans?"

As Hannah recanted Ms Bakers plans Nicholas scratched away at his notebook. Susie returned flushed with the cold and carrying a small bundle wrapped up in tatty blankets. "Rosa" Hannah answered Nicholas raised eyebrows.

Nicholas watched as Susie deposited her precious parcel in the next room. Could Susie have played a part in this? He mused and returned to questioning Hannah, "In the last few days did Ms Baker appear agitated or apprehensive?"

"Well she was always agitated." Hannah answered before covering her mouth with her fingers, "She didn't want to go to the party tonight." Suddenly her jaw snapped and a yawn escaped, as it passed her hand dropped to her lap, "Oh Nicholas she knew someone was trying to hurt her…."

"I don't think you should be jumping to conclusions like this, I'll wait to hear what the Doctor says first." A fragment of an idea tugged at Nicholas, "That's why she demanded, I escort you two tonight."

"She knew they would be there tonight."

Nicholas stopped writing in his notebook. The list of possible suspects expanded to include the whole town, and worse, his family.

"Susie," He called into the next room, "I'll need you to make a list of all the people that visited her, or sent her letters…. Susie…?"

"I cannot write Sherriff,"

"No matter, I'll help you Susie, we can think of it as your first lesson. I meant – oh, I am sorry," Hannah hands folded in her lap.

"No it's fine Hannah, Ms Baker was not well liked, and honesty will save time. I believe her list of enemies will be quite long, but there must have been some urgency to do her harm before she left… " Nicholas said, his voice drifting away. Ms Baker had no wealth to speak of, no reason to harm her in order to benefit, it seemed purely personal, he thought, "I'll need to search through her belongings too for anything of importance."

Hannah nodded, "Of course." She rose and poured another round of tea. Through the next doorway, Hannah saw Susie lying asleep next to Rosa. "The Doctor, said you mentioned something about me."

"Yes, I told him that you initially checked her pulse and had some minor medical training."

The tea cup slipped in Hannah's fingers but she managed to catch it before is splashed a drop. There's that word minor again. She seethed.

"Don't expect too much from Doctor Fitzgibbon he is very traditional." Nicholas said, pocketing his notebook.

Hannah let the comment pass and changed the topic "I didn't even think to ask who gave her the bottle." She mused.

"I will need to speak to those at the party."

"At least you know where to find them all since most are, I mean, I wasn't insinuating that – "

"My family?"

They sipped their tea in unison, the silence split only by the crackle of firewood in flames.

"When you and Susie make that list, put an asterix next to any," Nicholas paused, "Any of her lovers." He said, his voice a husky rumble causing pin pricks to surface across her bare skin. Her gaze drew circles around his face, from the solid blue of his eyes, down his straight nose to the strong jaw and up past his cheek bones back to his eyes. There they captured hers, drawing his own assessment over Hannah. He slowly let his eyes slide down to her lips and then back again, refusing to hide his actions.

"Yes I will do that, but I doubt there will be any."

"Even spinsters need company."

The elusive invitation stretched the silence between them, until Hannah gained control of herself, "Yes I guess they might."

Hannah glanced down at her tea to conceal the rising heat in her cheeks. When she looked back Nicholas still watched her and let the ice blue drip down her skin leaving shivers in their wake. He stood up abruptly.

"You're exhausted, I will let you get to bed – I mean - sleep. I'll come back after lunch for that list."

And with that Nicholas exited the Lodge. Hannah cleared the cups before taking her leave to the bedroom. Their conversation still lingered in her thoughts, the earlier darkness evaporating against the greying dawn.

Nicholas sat in his vanilla infused coat and prepared a list of all the persons he recalled in Ms Bakers' company tonight. Christian and Leonard would have to take care of any rowdy party goers for tonight. By the time he left his writing desk, the sky had paled enough for him to walk to his bedroom without a candle. In his mind, Philanders pursued Spinsters in a merry game of catch, before sleep finally arrived. Previously he enjoyed travelling to the nearby County of York to find his tumbles, and he'd never seriously taken a lover. None of those girls compared to Hannah. Would Hannah select a wealthy husband? Could he stand by and not try to win her as his own? How long had it been since he visited York, two weeks, three?

The next day during church Nicholas stifled a yawn and recorded each person's reaction to the news of Ms Bakers passing. Hannah didn't appear and he offered apologies on her behalf blaming shock, grief and exhaustion. The majority of townspeople exclaimed their surprise, the gossips picking words from the conversations like a vulture cleans a carcase. After the initial excitement passed, the Pastor blessed the construction crew as work on the new bridge was due to commence. The Mayor announced a competition to name the new bridge and then the service ended. He returned to his office and wrote more notes. Before long, lunch had passed without sustenance and he found himself walking up the drive to the Lodge.

Nicholas took deep breaths with each stride he covered. His stomach growled when the scent of roast chicken reached his nose, his hand pausing at the door. Hannah's lilting words travelled through the oak and Nicholas realised he would have to make time to travel to York.

Susie answered his knock and then went back to Rosa scrawling big and messy letters on slate next to the fire.

"In here Sherriff," Hannah shouted from the back bedroom.

Nicholas saw Hannah before she turned to greet him, sunlight streamed across her haphazard curls while she sat on the floor, legs tucked up under a full skirt. Her brows knitted and lips thin, as she rummaged through Ms Bakers possessions.

"What are you doing?"

Hannah paused her book stacking activities and faced him, eyes wide and cheeks blushing with colour.

"You're interfering with my investigation and possibly contaminating evidence."

"I'm sorry. I was trying to put it in some sort of order for you." She said.

He laughed and Hannah crossed her arms under her bust line. Nicholas had to shift his weight from his tightening pants and trained his eyes on the stack of books,

"Being out of order, is sometimes the evidence. One moment" he said and then fetched his lunch from the stove. He sat on the empty bed and dug into the bird.

"Make yourself at home." Hannah quipped and Nicholas grinned behind a full mouth.

"How considerate of Susie….it's delicious."

"Thank both of us, Sheriff. Susie believed that a chicken should be killed to exorcise any bad spirits lingering. It seemed a waste not to eat it." Hannah watched Nicholas firm lips graze the skin, his straight white teeth sinking into the hot flesh, and Hannah wondered if he devoured everything that passed his lips in this possessive manner, savouring each drop of moisture and relishing each morsel. Hannah returned to the conversation,

"You weren't at church this morning?"

"Oh God… I forgot…"

"Yes Him, don't worry I'm sure He'll understand one lapse."

Hannah laughed and rocked back on her haunches, "How can we be so jovial at a time like this?" Thick lashes blinked away the mist that threatened her blue eyes.

Nicholas cleared his throat, "Myself, I'm tired and I'm sure you didn't have a restful sleep either."

Hannah stood up for a moment hers eyes darting around the room slipping past him, like water over oil. What had she dreamed of? Nicholas thought. Hannah's proximity placed her directly between his legs and he caught his fork before it clattered to the plate. He shook his head and stared at his chicken. "Did you find anything?"

Hannah crossed to the far side of the tiny room, "Not yet, the diary is empty, it must have been a travel journal. No letters, some books…" She picked them up and tossed them onto the bed.

"Romance titles…" He mumbled around a drumstick.

"Gentleman don't talk whilst eating, Sherriff."

Together they spent the next hour poring through Ms Baker's life with no result. Nicholas turned his attention to Susie's list, written in neat precise script by Hannah.

"Almost every mother of every child is written on here."

"Motherhood is demanding." Hannah offered.

"No doubt they were voicing complaints about her teaching methods, but that's no motive to kill her."

"Hmm," Hannah replied and ran her fingertips over her temple.

Nicholas watched her delicate fingers massage the porcelain skin underneath, jealous of their contact, wishing his hands could manipulate the hidden areas of her creaminess. The bow in her top lip, dipped to her lower lip and she rolled them both inwards, the effect of their full figured return from the inside of her mouth made Nicholas desire stir. How he wanted to claim the softness for his own.

"By the way, construction begins on the new bridge next week. I suspect you will be able to watch the progress from the edge of the school's land."

"Really?" Hannah exclaimed.

Her smile melted Nicholas resolutions, and a restless energy stirred in his muscles, "Let's take a look, shall we," he said hand extending for hers. When she slipped her tender fingers into his calloused palm, a spark of fire burst in his thighs and he drew her upward from the floor. His hands ached to close over her waist and for a moment, Hannah's breathing shallowed. He released her, admitting the room was too small at present for Hannah and his desire to avoid clashing.

As they headed towards the southernmost part of the school grounds, Nicholas watched Hannah walk defiantly through mud and weeds to get to the vantage spot overlooking the construction site. The late afternoon sun played tricks with the chocolate brown of Hannah's hair, throwing gold and copper highlights in his vision. Her sweet vanilla scent glided through the cool afternoon breeze and pulled him closer, letting the splendour of Hannah wash over him.

"There?" She questioned him,

"Yes, that's one of the surveyors down there now." A heavy set man, with a woollen cap pulled low over his eyes walked the slope carrying a sketch pad. Nicholas guessed, from this distance it could possibly be Mark Turner. The man stopped for a breather and slid the cap off his head, revealing a bald scalp. Nicholas nodded, "Turner must be finished for the day."

"How exciting, I might bring an easel out here and paint as they work."

Nicholas smiled as he pictured Hannah in one of her petticoat filled city skirts being ruined by insects and mud. "Who would want to paint a bridge being constructed?"

"Me, of course, I wonder who is going to build it."

"My cousins." He stated flatly and they both laughed. "The construction company, Krouse Brothers Constructions hire men from town, keeps the money in the community and in the Family." His shoved his hands into his gun belt. They had built an empire and protected it furiously.

Nicholas pondered who had forced Mayor Dammier to accept Krouse's tender for the construction. No doubt, John and Isaac Krouse would be receiving a hefty sum for the work. In turn, the supplies would come from Richard Treschells Lumber Mill. The money earned would no doubt be banked and invested into Franklins Shallows Bank and the other holdings of William Frey. Such an incestuous link between community and family! If the Family succumbed would the whole community suffer? As devious as it sounded it they remained his family. His father had been an honest hardworking man, and had tried to incorporate some separation from the Family Empire as best he could. He worked the Hoffman businesses, farmed the Hoffman land and gained his own wealth. His father didn't scheme alongside the Krouse and Treschells, he didn't fight to gain favour with the Frey's. Although, his money was still banked at Frey's bank, their houses still built by the Krouses with Treschells timber. Even his father's cattle had been brokered through William and his father. But I like William, Nicholas thought.

Hannah's shivering brought Nicholas back to the present, and he almost chided Hannah to dress more appropriately for the county, but instead found himself, admiring her silhouette as the wind pressed the soft fabric against her slender body.

"We better get back, you're cold again."

"I know, these city dresses. But I would like to see Franklins Shallows before I head back." Hannah continued towards the tree line, "I'll be fine on my own,"

Nicholas watched the first softening rays of the sun touch the horizon and stalked to catch up with her, "Follow me," He said, relishing a few more stolen moments in her company.

As his steps fell in time with Hannah's he pondered their stolen moment on Old Thom. He had reminded himself, not again, but Hannah had a spirited mind that contradicted her body, sending temptation to creep beneath Nicholas empty promises. She might not behave like Beth, not in the slightest, but eventually the desire she withheld herself from experiencing would surface, the need and want for a man would drive her forward into someone's arms and someone's bed. Nicholas realised then, that'd he'd being doing his utmost to make sure it would be his own.

They wandered down to the tree line and entered the shrubbery that bordered the river. Hannah continued down the slope oblivious to the thickening foliage until she reached the water's edge. The cooler air prickled his skin, and Hannah bent low to dip her hand in the running water. The fading light speckled with warm bursts of deep orange blurred Nicholas vision.

"It's so cool…." Hannah said, and a rush of noise broke from the bushes behind her. Nicholas saw the Elk buck one second before Hannah did.

"Hannah get down!" Nicholas shouted. The Elk dipped his head and snorted at the ground. Then he charged, antlers down, hooves flying in the dirt.

"Nick!" Hannah screamed and she dived forward hitting the riverbank. The Elk sent his lethal hooves clawing the air, and Nicholas held his breath. He aimed his service pistol and pulled the trigger. The bullet struck solid muscle and bone. The buck turned to Nicholas, his pistol ineffective against this giant beast. Hannah squirmed beneath as the Elk leapt into the air. The buck cleared Hannah's body and he planted his front hooves on the ground, sights set on a new target. With antlers levelled at Nicholas, he charged again. He managed to twist aside as the antlers struck his jacket. They pierced the woollen fabric and tore through to Nicholas's skin. The force threw Nicholas backwards, the air forced from his lungs. The Elk snorted as devilled hooves dashed into the underbrush.

Chapter 5

"Hannah!" Nicholas called. No sound reached his ears, except his own voice, hoarse and urgent. "Hannah! Are you alright?"

Water splashed over his right shoulder and his head whipped to the sound. A light fuzz coated Nicholas vision until he shook it free, his eyes finally focusing in the fading light. Hannah clambered over the muddy stones and reached his side, her face as pale as her skirts.

"I'm fine." She said. Nicholas sighed heavily and sucked back. Only then did he feel the red hot pain that spiked through his every movement. Intense throbbing covered his left flank and he controlled his need to touch it. Hannah was safe, and he had to move in case the Elk returned. He rolled forward and to his right side, the pain of fabric snagging torn skin caused his jaw to clench.

"But you're not," Hannah said as she pushed herself under his good shoulder.

A voice called from close by, the owner hidden in the undergrowth, "Miss Hannah, I heard the shot, are you alright? Miss Hannah? Sherriff?"

"Susie, thank goodness, we're over here. Nick is hurt," The ground quivered in Nicholas's sight before he managed to shake it off. The feeling of Hannah warm and soft under his arm gave him strength to drag himself free of the riverbank.

"I see you," Susie said and rushed to his side. Together both women shuffled Nicholas back to the Lodge. The distance hadn't seem as long, he thought as they closed in on the slated roof of Hannah's home, "Get the Doc, please Susie," he said.

Hannah clicked her tongue as they jostled his bulk through to the kitchen, "Let's have a look first."

“It’s just a scratch.” Nicholas said and pealed back the corner of his jacket, the skin separating as he did. He heard Hannah gasp as the Elk’s handiwork became clear. Three marvellous gashes graced his ribs, the skin torn and puckered at the edges. Blood streamed down into his beltline. Suddenly Hannah leaned forward, affording him the barest glimpse of creamy curves. He swallowed hard when she slid her hands into his jacket and pressed firmly.

“I’ll be fine, I’m sure,” Nicholas tried to sooth her, stifling a wince.

Hannah blinked back tears, “Oh Nick, I’m so sorry. It’s my fault if I had turned back. Hannah glanced at Susie’s pale expression and purpose cracked like a whip. “Get my medicine chest please Susie.” Hannah ordered as she filled the pot and started the stove.

“It’s not so bad. I can wait for the Doc.”

“Sure, I need towels and clean linen.” Hannah said and began sliding the black wool from his shoulders.

“Wait, wait, ow,” Nicholas winced, “We can wait for the Doctor,” He pulled his arm back from her grasp.

Hannah paused and took her requested items from Rosa who rushed into the kitchen. Hannah pushed on Nicholas chest and met solid resistance.

“Mama’s gone to get to Doc, Mr Sherriff.” The little girl answered Nicholas with a nod before dashing away. Hannah pushed again, this time Nicholas took a step back. “He’ll be here soon,” Rosa peeped and handed the Sherriff a flask of whiskey. He thanked her with a smile.

Hannah rolled her eyes and let her hand rest on Nicholas chest, the heat stirring his blood. He didn’t think he had enough of the fluid left to fuel the raging torrent she called forth from him. He backed against the kitchen table.

“I might try to stop the bleeding before then.” Hannah said. Her hands worked back the wool of Nicholas’ coat, aware of his muscles bunching and stretching under the thin white material of his shirt. “Can you take off your shirt?” Hannah asked and handed over a roughly folded washer to put on the wound.

“It’s not proper.”

"What's not proper is you bleeding to death on my kitchen floor."

"I can wait for the Doctor."

"So he can do exactly what I'm going to do Sherriff?"

He took another swig of the whiskey, "I doubt it," His slick tones rolled down Hannah's neck and ended somewhere about her middle, "This isn't right for a woman to be doing this," he added. Nicholas clumsily tried to pull his shirt clear, and stopped when the collar snagged on his bulky shoulder. Hannah wound her fingers through the fabric and a groan escaped Nicholas's lips.

"Sorry."

"No, it's – fine."

The shirt landed with a splat on the floor.

Hannah couldn't avert her eyes from the specimen she saw before her. Nicholas leaned back palms flat against the table, each muscle in his chest and abdomen, taut and hard. Her eyes ran over his brawny arms and solid chest, as if he'd been carved like one of Feronica's statues. Her gaze crossed his sun-kissed chest, sparkling with a light covering of dark hair, down to the tight stomach where rows of muscles flexed into valleys and clefts that curved inwards past his beltline.

"Let's get started." Hannah said. She took her time pouring the hot water, letting the heat drain from her face, steeling her nerves for the moment her hands would touch that body. Circling her patient, Hannah saw a ragged rip on Nicholas left flank and found herself between his thighs. Hannah motioned for Nicholas to sit on the table which he complied. A silence settled between them as her hands began to shake, Nicholas's head dipped to watch her work, sending black curls to frame hungry blue eyes.

Beth had never been on the end of one of those looks, Hannah imagined, or she would never have refused him, "Now stay still" she said. Hannah took a deep breath and began washing the wound. She was used to blood and bodies, lifeless and pale, being examined and explored at the College. Those bodies didn't breathe warm air down the back of her neck, didn't flex and shudder when she touched them and definitely did not smell as tempting as this one did. Certain that the wound was clean, Hannah retrieved a folded towel and pressed it into Nicholas. His hand encased hers and held the towel in place. "Not too much pressure but enough,"

"Gentle," He said, the whisky liquefying his already smooth tones.

Hannah slid her hand out from underneath and began threading her needle. She heard the flask swish and then began to lay a row of short stiches into his skin. It rippled and twisted under her grip and his blood slicked over her fingers. To reduce the risk of infection, she refused to wipe them before she finished.

"So this is what you want to do, sew people back together?"

"Yes, amongst other things."

"If needlework is your passion, you could have learnt embroidery, ow - "

"Sorry, I slipped." Hannah tugged on the thread and stifled a laugh. "My father was a tailor,"

"Now see, that's a more of an – "

"Honest, respectful, ladylike profession."

"It would be a less grisly."

"As is teaching,"

"Yes." He raised his arm allowing better access and Hannah cursed the trembling in her hands that wouldn't settle and coaxed the metallic scent of blood into her nose, hoping the sting would increase her focus. From this angle, she could watch the movement of strength ripple across his back, "Well except for Ms Baker that is. But why choose to be exposed to all manner of illnesses and even death?"

"I bet it's for the same reason you're not farming a field, Sherriff."

That silenced him. Once finished, Hannah grabbed the linen and wrapped it around Nicholas abdomen and over his left shoulder. He slowly exhaled, and warm whiskey caressed Hannah's jawline, sending a throbbing to the hollow of her neck,

"Perhaps but that's not all you could want for your future, surely a husband and some children."

"And the same can be said for yourself, is a Sherriff's post all you want?" Hannah stretched the bandage around Nicholas' back.

She let her fingertips trail across his skin after each pass, his thighs pressed against her skirt.

"No. Not all." He said, eyes changing from ice blue to deep violet. Dark curls threatened to snare her within his thirst. In the depths of the violet, Hannah saw her own hunger reflect. Nicholas tilted forward as Hannah raised her chin. Then he pulled away, lifting the flask and pressing it to his lips, a warning or an invitation, Hannah didn't care. Without restraint, she tipped the silver neck to her own lips and slowly swallowed the golden liquid, letting the warmth speed through her body. His hand steadied the flask, the liquor waking a flurry of resting butterflies inside her. The moisture lingered on her lips and she licked it. A growl escaped Nicholas somewhere and Hannah almost faltered. What would it be like to satiate that hungry, to quench that thirst.

"Almost finished," Hannah said.

Nicholas reached out to steady her waist, "I'm not." Unhurried, Nicholas ran his hands over Hannah's waist to the outer edges of her thighs, his strong fingers large enough that they reached the pliable flesh of her buttocks, the fabric of her dress too thin to hold back the heat. Her heart thundered against her ribs as her breasts involuntarily swelled towards her patient, his eyes lowered to her body's betrayal and he grinned.

"You are finished." She said, opening an ocean between them as she returned to the sink, washing her hands in the cool water, to douse the flames Nicholas had set alight. It didn't work.

"Is that what you want?"

Hannah refused to acknowledge his last comment, his slick honey tones tempting other parts of her body to answer his call. "You're all stitched up, so don't try to move too much and you should -"

"Like this." Nicholas said and pulled Hannah back inside his grasp. He pressed his thighs against hers and circled her waist. Hannah couldn't face the desire in his eyes and kept her gaze down. It did her no good, when she stared at his belt buckle and witnessed just how much he thirsted for her. For reasons beyond her control, Hannah's tongue touched her top lip.

Nicholas raised her chin, and shimmering violet bored through her soul. She heard a whimper and then realised it had escaped her lips. He smirked, his fingers sliding behind her neck, thumb gliding over her throat, to the frantic beating in the hollow of her neck. He made a circle with his thumb and drew it up to raise her mouth closer to his.

"Slow enough?" He asked

"I - "

That was all she managed, before Nicholas seized her mouth, his lips capturing the heat within, tongue slowly lavishing hers, the whiskey sting all but gone, leaving the pure maleness of Nicholas to invade and conquer her senses. With each foray into the sweetness depths of Hannah's mouth, Nicholas's pressure increased, the demand to have his thirst slaked driving him harder and faster. He dragged her up against his body, the hardness, dominating her soft flesh, his strength flowed into her frame turning protest into surrender and she leaned forward. When her tongue responded to tease him, he groaned and drank, hard deep and fast. Hannah drew in his heady male scent, letting it soak through her skin. Surprised by the strength and demand of Nicholas's fervour, Hannah shuddered against him, she felt the rippling transfer to his own body and Hannah's body betrayed her, bringing forth liquid heat and slickness. Her hands traced the slabs of muscle across his back that rippled and quaked under her touch. As Nicholas tongue caressed hers, it sent another wave of golden heat coursing through her body and Hannah melted in his arms. All thoughts of caution, fled as he stoked the fire within. The door to the lodge opened and Hannah jumped. Her palms came to rest over his chest and she pushed back. Nicholas held tight. "Thank you for the stitches." He sent sweet kisses sipping, nipping and savouring her lips. Tender kisses made to tease, tempt and entice.

"Ms Hannah" Susie called. Nicholas released Hannah.

The room returned to focus, "In the kitchen," Hannah replied. She took her time, smoothing down her skirts and pressing trembling hands to cheeks. Please let the colour drain, Hannah thought.

As the Doctor examined Nicholas, Hannah cleaned up. It gave her precious moments to let the taste of Nicholas dissolve from her lips and his touch to fade from her skin.

"This is exceptional work Ms Evans."

"Thank you, please call me Hannah."

"Well Hannah, you have a natural ability."

"For a teacher, you mean Doc?"

A violent shudder coursed through Hannah at his slight. Hadn't he just thanked her for her stitches, how could he be so ungrateful and offensive.

"Now Sherriff," the Doctor scolded. "That wound could have been very nasty, had Hannah not been here to assist."

Nicholas began pulling on his jacket, wincing only slightly as he did it. Hannah kept the Sherriff from her sights, his comment snagging her pride like a bramble in stockings.

"Yes, bed rest, fluids and a change of dressing frequently to avoid infection. Despite his attitude, I expect the Sherriff will make a full recovery."

He sounds recovered already, Hannah thought bitterly.

A dark skinned, well weathered man arrived with Susie in tow. He dipped his head in greeting to Nicholas and shouldered the Sherriff's weight.

"I thought Carl better take the Sherriff home in the trap." Susie said. A slight tinge of pink coloured the apples of her cheeks.

"Yes good thinking." Hannah said, the anger only slightly contained.

"Before you go Sherriff, you'd like to know, I have had a chance to re-examine Ms Baker and I find that Ms Evans had concluded correctly the first time." Fitzgibbon said, repacking his brown leather carryall.

"Pardon?" Nicholas said, halting Carl.

"Upon closer examination, I detected an almond-like odour and Ms Baker appears to have developed a deep pink rash about her mouth. I have surmised the cause of death to be cyanide poisoning. Cyanide poisoning can occur by mistake, - "

Nicholas's brows rose at Hannah but he held his tongue. For once tonight, Hannah thought. How could he go from kissing her to insulting her in a quick fit? An image of William Frey popped into Hannah's mind. Hannah resumed listening to the Doctor - "For example, a contamination of drinking water, building up in the body, *eventually* resulting in death, or a sudden large dose of the poison for instant death, or both."

"And which do you believe is the case in this instance?" Hannah ventured as Nicholas ice blue eyes trapped hers.

"I do believe that if the matter had been one of slow ingestion of the poison, Ms Baker would have shown symptoms a long time before now, a weakening of the bowels, purging, changes in skin colour and so forth. In this case, I conclude an intentional poisoning."

Hannah raised an eyebrow which sparked a glare from the Sherriff.

"Thank you Doc," Nicholas answered flatly.

"Yes you're welcome. I know it's not what you wanted to hear. I'll write the death certificate and leave it at your office."

Nicholas offered Hannah a curt nod but she turned away, the image of William Frey still burning in her brain.

Carl and Susie manoeuvred the patient out the door and Fitzgibbon turned his pudgy face to examine Hannah with tender insistent fingers, "Susie said you fell?"

"It's nothing, really."

"Of course, just precautionary." He said, moustache twitching, "However, it does give me a chance to talk to you."

"About what Doctor?"

"It is a busy time of year. Newborns, the harvesting of crops and mustering of cattle not including the construction of the new bridge will start shortly."

Hannah nodded.

"There is due to be a lot of movement in and around Franklins Shallows. Pennsylvanian Rail is stretching their lines to our little County. More people, more demands. Which is not such a bad thing, you see progress changes opinions. What was traditional now becomes obsolete, what is new and fearful becomes the norm. With construction about to commence, there are bound to be accidents. People needing my assistance…" His pudgy eyes drifted from Hannah to the floor and back again. "I cannot be everywhere at once to assist people, give help when they need it. I know that you will have your hands full come the resumption of school, however I would appreciate the opportunity to have a spare set of hands, if required."

"Oh Doctor,"

"I know you haven't completed your training or obtained the full qualifications. I know you will not be capable of undertaking the more onerous tasks required of a Doctor, however you have shown considerable skill so far. I would appreciate your assistance."

"I'm not a midwife," Hannah let the Doctor finish his examination and watched his moustache bristle. Had he ever faced prejudice in his lifetime?

"I'm not talking about just birthing babies, well not the easy ones anyway. We already have a midwife in town, she is very competent, but even she cannot be in all places at once."

"I will help where I can." Hannah clasped her hands together. A chance to work in medicine, albeit limited was a start, a magnificent start, she thought.

"I'm glad you are agreeable. On that note, I have your first task for you."

"Yes, Doctor. By all means, whatever I can do to help." She clasped her hands together to stop them from shaking.

"Good. The Sherriff's wounds will need frequent dressing changes…." Hannah stopped listening.

Chapter 6

That night, Susie made a hearty beef and potato stew for dinner. Hannah had insisted Ms Baker's spirit was gone and besides, Hannah liked eggs for breakfast. After the dishes were wiped and put away, Hannah took her leave by the fire. She had come to Franklins Shallows for a prosperous future. Instead of classroom preparations her mind was busy with the Doctors offer, heavily veiled with thoughts of Nicholas. His barbed comments pocketed the shirtless visions that repeated in Hannah's mind. Worms of guilt chased away the butterflies that swarmed in her stomach. He had taunted her on Old Thom about the wants and needs of women. By the sounds of it, Nicholas's cousin William had no trouble finding compliant woman to fill his needs, then why did Nicholas tease her? Surely a man like that could have any woman he dreamed of, the common woman of Franklins Shallows made it known that he was one to swoon over. Perhaps she presented him with a challenge. Hannah would have to be cautious around him. The Doctor had requested regular checks up on Nicholas to make sure no infection surfaced. What made Hannah even more uneasy was how quickly her body had responded to his attention. How will I manage to treat and care for him, when I can't trust myself in his company? It would end my teaching contract and where would I be then, unemployed and heading back to Philly? Or worse relying on a man to keep me?

No doubt he would prefer a true Doctor to treat and clean his wounds, especially after he read Ms Bakers death certificate.

Hannah had fired her anger at Ms Baker so quickly, so resolute only days ago and now thanks to Sherriff Nicholas Hoffman, Hannah began unravelling. She went over her teachings with Rosa and Susie before going to bed determined to put Nicholas far from her mind.

Never again, Nicholas reiterated. Sweet vanilla stained his lips and the memory of soft feminine curves burned his arms. The pain of the Bucks antlers driven into his side was nothing compared to the ache he felt when taking Hannah. Or now when Nicholas thought about how her suppleness had melted against him, lips, breasts, thighs, slowly, seductively welcoming him in. He forced his thoughts back to the investigation. Whatever Hannah Evan's said, she was all hot-blooded woman and no frigid spinster. Feeling the all too familiar throbbing returning to his lap when he found himself thinking of Hannah, Nicholas refocused his thoughts.

Poisoning? While the Doc had been busy with Hannah, Nicholas has seconded the brandy bottle. For the good part of an hour he had sat at his desk and examined it for any indication as to who it belonged to before being Ms Baker's lethal downfall. In the end it was a plain green glass brandy bottle, same mark of the Franklins glass found in everyone's house. Almost every landowner operated their own still for making spirits. He discarded the bottle as a means to find the culprit and made Carl take him home. Hannah floated through his mind and his own body's ache to relieve his suffering deep inside her, fingers blazing a trail across his skin, mouth seeking and surrendering to him, whispers of pleasure, and crying out his name in ecstasy. Nicholas squeezed a pillow to his face and tried to think of work.

The next day, Nicholas woke midmorning, surprised at how much rest he had needed. He directed Carl to his office where he reviewed the guest list against Susie's acquaintance list. They could only be referred to as Acquaintances, because clearly Ms Baker never made any friends. Next he went over his notes and the notes his cousin Christian had written. Then the inventory of Ms Baker's meagre possessions. Nothing. Witnesses, he needed witnesses. Nicholas spent the next hour drafting up a list of preapproved questions for Christian to ask witnesses.

Nicholas ribs ached and the bandages felt hot next to his skin, so he asked Carl to saddle up Smoke and the trap for home. As Nicholas stepped out to the stoop, he could hear the carousing thills of the boarding house, play harmony with strained piano notes from the hotel. His cousin and Deputy will have work to do tonight. Doctor Fitzgibbon walked up the boardwalk.

"I'm still alive Doc."

"Good, has Ms Evans been to see you?"

Nicholas narrowed his eyes at the Doctor, "No, should she?" What did the Doc know?

"Well I'm sure she will be around in her own time. You should be at home resting." Fitzgibbon handed Nicholas a very elegant parchment with long scrawled ink, "I forgot to bring this over earlier. It's the death certificate of course."

"Thanks." Nicholas dropped it on top of a stack of papers, "By the way, I never thought you'd appreciate a woman telling you right from wrong Doc."

"Not so, Sherriff, I enjoyed matching wits with someone. No doubt she excelled in her class. I've been on my own here for a long time, a challenge is always refreshing."

"Refreshing." I can think of several more words to describe her, Nicholas thought. A challenge he said?

"Yes, Hannah is an excellent candidate to take over these bandages of yours."

Nicholas blanched, "I don't think that's proper Doc."

"Nonsense. She might have a promising future ahead of her, depending on her loyalty to teaching. Being a Schoolmarm suits some women. I feel her skills would be wasted if she didn't keep at it, training and practice is most important."

"But Doc - " Nicholas started.

"Good it's all settled Sherriff. Give my regards to Ms Evans. For now go home and stay home. Those stitches can come out in a few day's time, Good afternoon." The doctor hadn't once asked to look at his bandages. The portly man stopped to talk to Carl and hurried back across Main to his office. Perhaps, I should ask him to? Nicholas gently prodded the padding before closing up for the afternoon.

After Carl had helped him inside, the Foreman kept Smoke in the trap and trotted down the drive. Nicholas looked at the internal stairs and decided his work had taxed him enough. He lay down on the sunroom chaise with the afternoon shading his eyes.

"He's in here,"

Carl didn't make any sense, I'm not looking for anyone, Nicholas thought. A light weight leaned on the edge of the chaise, and Nicholas breathed in deeply.

"That smells great Odette what is it?"

"Nick." A sweet voice brought him out of a daze, instead of his housekeeper with a tray of baked goods, Hannah sat near his boots, medicine chest in hand.

"Hannah, what are you doing here?" He sat up wiping away the afternoon weariness.

"The Doctor told me he talked to you. I'm here to change your dressing."

"Carl?"

"I saw the Doc and you talking. He told me Ms Hannah would need to get here."

"Great."

"Well where do you want this done, Sherriff? Here or in the kitchen?"

"Pardon…"

"Here's better, a shade more sanitary."

"Don't let Ms Odette hear you saying that Ms Hannah. She keeps a clean kitchen."

"My apologies, Carl, I'm sure she does. Could you please ask her for a pot of hot water for me? Thank you oh and run a bath for the Sherriff."

Carl complied and Hannah stared at Nicholas, her pert mouth closed and stern. The afternoon shade dappled her complexion into whirlpools of cream and ivory. Why did she have to look so glorious?

"Well Sherriff, shirt off."

A small devious part of Nicholas wanted to challenge her to make him but instead he sighed and pulled his shirt off. He pressed his back into the chaise and faced his injured side to Hannah. It took her several minutes to wash and prepare, all the while the irresistible scent teased him, stomach rolling in hunger, blood heating in thirst. Her delicate hands started peeling away the dressing and he watched the intense concentration on her face mixed with a dash of uncertainty.

"It looks promising, a bit of swelling." Hannah pulled a hot clean cloth across his skin washing away the lingering muck and blood. His palms itched to touch her.

A booming voice called from the kitchen, "Tell that boy his bath is ready."

"Boy?" Hannah smirked

"Thanks Odette," Nicholas sighed, hoping it was ice cold.

With Hannah's help, Nicholas shuffled to his feet. He towered over her, and watched her pupils dilate and contract with his sudden proximity, the blackness ebbing and flowing around her grey flecked blue iris's. She pushed him gently on the chest as if to turn him about face, and he closed his hands over both her wrists. Slowly he let them trail down each side of his upper body and stop at his belt-line. She sucked in a sharp breath as a shimmer of hidden delight flushed her cheeks. Nicholas would enjoy this challenge.

"I'll redress it when you're done." She said and pushed again. This time he let her move him.

When he returned to the sunroom, clean and half dressed, Hannah directed him to the chaise again. While soft ministration brought winces it was Hannah's hand resting on his hip that brought forth silent moans and tight pants. He had to think of something to say, anything to stop him from pulling Hannah down on top of him, "So your father was a tailor?" Nicholas said.

"Yes."

Hannah looked down her nose while she cleaned.

"And your mother?"

"She was a good woman, always there for us."

"I'm sorry,"

"You weren't to know. My sister Margaret took it hardest. But I'm sure I will have nieces and nephews by the end of the year." Hannah moved his arm to one side to get a better view. His bicep tensed under her grip. "I'm sorry about your family. Ms Baker mentioned your brother and sister earlier."

"My mother wanted five children, or so my father said. I remember after Eva passed, the house seemed so empty." The child in Nicholas recalled squealing giggles of a joyful toddler holding his hand and walking down stairs, then suddenly open windows, and curtains blowing silently in the breeze, "Influenza."

"It took my father too."

Nicholas watched Hannah's eyes as they dipped to her hands and heard the unspoken words. "My father built this house to be filled, and look at the fine job I've done so far."

A smile flicked across her features, "I'm sure it will be one day." Her blue eyes widened, "I mean a few pieces of furniture here and there couldn't hurt."

"A woman's touch?" Nicholas dared.

"Something like that," Hannah turned away, her cheeks tinging with pink. He'd have to plan for another sleepless night ahead. Even if it tortured himself, the pleasure of awakening Hannah's womanly desires outweighed that particular pain. Until you need it satisfied Nick, he sighed.

Carl took Hannah home in the trap steered smoke across Old Thom. It didn't matter how often she crossed the worn bridge, it still delighted her. She mused over Nicholas and how he had sidestepped an apology for his ridicule the previous day. He'd let her hands slide over his hard body, and watched her shudder. Slowly but surely, Nicholas was ridiculing her, alluring, enticing and inviting her in. What was worse was Hannah's own eagerness to let him. She kept that frustration tight to her chest while she pawed over his body, little licks of flame clawing at her fingertips. Instead of a shirtless Sherriff, Hannah reflected on his family's story, saddened by how helpless a young Nicholas would have felt. How helpless Hannah had felt when it claimed her father. That marvellous house should be filled with a wife and many noisy happy children. As Carl helped Hannah down he shadowed her to the door,

"Thank you Carl."

"No worries Ms Evans." He said but hesitated at the doorway.

"Is something wrong Carl?"

Nicholas foreman rubbed his stubbled chin with dark calloused hands.

"What is it?" Hannah squared her shoulders and planted her feet. "Tell me."

"It's just Miss Susie, Miss Hannah."

"Susie?"

"Yes Miss, she said you'd been teaching her reading."

Hannah released a slow exhale, "Do you know how to read, Carl?"

"No ma'am."

Hannah leaned in and raised an eyebrow, "Would you like to learn?"

Carl smiled a long grin of perfect white teeth.

Nicholas woke the next morning later than expected and managed to dress himself without Carl. He made it to the porch and sat down in his large wicker chairs before the throbbing started. He wanted to holler for the whiskey; instead he did a round of the stables and to the front gate before resting.

From here, Nicholas took in his family's estate. The two story river stone manor had housed four moderately spacious bedrooms as well as a master suite on the top floor. His bedrooms' window box offered a glorious view of his land right down to Franklins Shallows. The roughly hewn stones stood out against the starch mortar between the smooth greys and browns. Nicholas had changed the front two rooms into a formal dining with adjoining sun room, although sparsely furnished as Hannah had pointed out. That had been left for Beth. The northern fields nearest to the road brimmed with wheat, barley, some vegetables and maize. The Frey's had passed over this land, believing the soil to be sub-standard and for food crops they were. His father had struggled to maintain a profitable quality for market, however Nicholas had realised his northern fields handled the crops better and the southern fields, bordered by Franklins Shallows, were better suited to grain. Grain for cattle. After his fathers' death Nicholas had purchased high quality stock from William. While William had become enamoured with studding, Nicholas had ventured into beef farming. The Hoffman herd had grown to be the fattest and healthiest beef cattle in the County. Nicholas even sold his surplus grain to Richard Treschells for sale at his Grist Mill and Feed exchange and hence back into Family hands.

Nicholas had a bumper year of calves and those heifers and more were carrying again. He had no intentions of accumulating more wealth than his Cousin, but he edged closer each season. The rest of his Family had no idea how prosperous he had developed his father's land. With the cattle yards hidden from view, they may never find out. Most notably he never told Beth. What if I had?

He concentrated on the workers bending their backs and loading wagons, when horses' hooves made Nicholas turn around.

"Ho there! What the devil are you doing out of bed?" William said and halted his buggy that carried little Will and Violet.

"Uncle Nick!" They squealed,

"Was he this big?" Will stretched his arms as far as his blue vest would let him.

"What was his name?" Violet leaned on the edge of the buggy, blonde curls dancing in the wind.

"Leave Uncle Nicholas rest," William instructed before he hauled Nicholas into the buggy. After Carl helped Nicholas down, the two cousins sat on the porch while Carl put both children on Smoke's placid back and plodded easily around the front yard. It wasn't long ago that Nicholas envisioned his own children playing like his niece and nephew. Only they would have had his dark curls instead of Will's burnt red and Violets shimmer of silver. That thought sent Nicholas wondering about tiny children with sweet chocolate curls and pewter eyes.

"Faster, Faster" shouted Will and Violet their screams turned into giggles as Smoke trotted up to speed.

"Not too fast Carl." Nicholas piped in.

"So, feeling better then dearest Cousin Nicholas?"

"On the mend, yes."

"And what of the Elk?" William questioned stroking his manicured moustache, "Never mind, when you are better, we will head out to the School and finish him off." Nicholas sighed. A worm of panic burrowed in his stomach. Is that reluctance or excitement at seeing her this afternoon? "Another item I need to discuss with you, the monthly meeting of the Families is coming up again, getting in early before the big auction."

Judging by Williams deepening tone, Nicholas knew what was coming next. The Family Meeting held once a month had begun as a reunion of sorts, as the Family has spread and multiplied. Nowadays, the meeting fulfilled the purpose of helping each line of the Family and their businesses maintain a strangle hold over the community. Secrets were shared, who bid on what contract, who sold and bought what stock, who could marry who.

It sickened Nicholas. "Oh yeah,"

"Yes and you really need to start attending those. You are the head of the Hoffman line, whether you like it or not you have a voice and a vote at those meetings. I expect you front and centre at the next meeting. Present circumstances excluded of course." William used his Stetson to point at Nicholas's wounded side. After his father died, the duty had fallen to Nicholas. He had attended not one single meeting.

"Send one of my many still-living uncles to sort it out."

"Ha! No, I think not. Some of the Family are a bit put out about this questioning business you've put young Christian up to."

"And why is that?" Nicholas leaned forward gently.

"Well, they are offended to say the least. Why should they be questioned as part of a murder investigation?"

"Someone killed her, Will. Someone murdered Ms Baker while she was at a gathering filled with the whole town. Last time I looked, over half are our damn cousins." Nicholas shifted his weight from one side to the other. How dare they!

"Yes, I know but it's not a witch hunt, Ms Baker had many enemies."

"I know. Who complained the loudest?"

"The Krouse brothers. They believe you've overstepped the mark."

Nicholas's laughed, "Overstepped being Sherriff? At this stage almost everyone is a suspect." He cut short his mirth and eyed William. "I will not compromise my investigation for the Family's pride. They are not excluded simply because they are related."

"Bearing in mind you're an elected official, who may one day need to be re-elected to hold your office."

"Is that a threat, Will?" Nicholas glared at his cousin as if seeing him for the first time.

"No, Nick. You will always have my vote and with my vote, comes the others by oath and duty. I told them that as well."

"You said a lot. What else?"

William grinned under his decadent moustache, "I told them I would have a word to you and I have." He withdrew a deck of cards from his jacket. "Fancy a game?"

They played until after lunch, ending when William emptied his wallet. Maybe on the account of his injury and not Nicholas's luck, but the Sherriff let the patriarch keep his bills. Will and Violet left with a final hug and pockets filled with Odette's cookies.

"Next time run faster, Uncle Nick."

"I shall Will."

"He had to run slow for Ms Evans." Violet said.

Her father eyeballed Nicholas, tilting his head to one side, "Chivalry is a dangerous business, Vi. That buck can wait till you're healed, Cus'."

"Sure," Nicholas agreed. William's devious comments about the family and elections rankled under his bandages.

Nicholas bid farewell and waved until they cleared the gate, his side aching from the effort. Crossing the porch Nicholas noticed Carl setting Smoke into the trap, Carl wheeled out the drive and Nicholas shuffled inside to help Odette with the water.

Nicholas heard Smoke's trotting daintily up the gravel drive. Proud of his efforts Nicholas greeted his nursemaid at the door.

"Afternoon."

Hannah said, eyes slipping past him as she entered, "Afternoon, Sherriff"

What happened to *Nick*? He thought. When Hannah called his name, it sounded like a soft plea that pleased his ears and thawed his chest.

Confused, Nicholas let Hannah guide him to the kitchen. When she began un-wrapping the bandages he steeled himself to think about his cattle. Which heifer would deliver first, how much time he had before each season to fatten the stock.

Hannah inspected the wound without speaking and Nicholas helped himself to a bath. Anticipating the moment when her delicate fingers would grace his hide. He deliberately buttoned his fly but left his buckle unfastened. As Hannah dried each laceration, his cattle counting ended abruptly. Hannah still hadn't spoken when she wound the bandages around his injury. She wanted something, she was waiting for him to say or do something. He tried hard not to inhale her perfume, not to stare into those innocent yet evocative eyes.

"I apologise for the other day," I should have kept my hands to myself, he thought.

Hannah looked up at him, a smile perched on her rose frosted lips. "You are?" She said.

"Of course,"

"It's a relief to hear you say it, although, it wasn't a surprise. I expected it" She walked over towards him a joyful grin on her face.

Nicholas tongue stuck to the roof of his mouth. He reran her last words, she expected it? "You did?" A strange warmth spread across his chest, she stood within his grasp, and here she stood on the cusp of admitting her desire.

"Yes, it's not the first time - "

Nicholas pushed a loose curl behind Hannah's ear. Her dark lashes brushed his cheek when he pressed his lips to hers. His hands roamed the soft bounty of Hannah's body, down to the small of her back. His lips slanted across hers and she gasped, letting him in, until his tongue found hers. His body tight and tense yearned for Hannah's warmth to slake his thirst. Nicholas pulled her against the length of his body and a moan escaped as plump breasts surged against bare skin. His hands clutched at her skirt, pulling her forward to his hips. The fabric bunching in his knuckles, the hardness of his body turning Hannah to marble. She pushed back, palms flat against his chest.

"No," Hannah inhaled sharply, her cheeks flushed and eyes unfocused.

"No?" His grip remained steady,

"I - "

"You said you expected this?" He smirked, adding kisses to her neck, chocolate curls tickling his face. "Are you back to denying your needs as a woman?"

"Not this… I meant -"

He pulled her skirts forward, keeping her off balance and letting her suppleness discover his desire, "See what you do to me," he kissed her again, his tongue courting her own, drinking Hannah's heat, coaxing her forward, drawing forth the fire she fuelled in his blood, "See how I want you," He let his arousal graze across her hips, her thighs parting for the briefest margins and he trapped her there, the hardness seeking her liquid centre, she shuddered in his arms, "And how you want me too."

Hannah broke way. "No – stop," She used considerable force to move him backwards, "I meant, for what you said to the Doctor, what you said about me - " Strength multiplied in her voice and her pupils centred, "For doubting me."

"Doubting you?" His voice sounded harsh to his ears, "So you were right about Ms Baker that does not make you a Doctor. That does not mean that you, that all this…" he gestured to his bandages. "Is proper for a woman, for you,"

Ruby flashed violently across Hannah's pale cheeks and her shoulders squared,

"Forgive me for stopping you bleeding to death then," She stormed out of the kitchen and into the sunroom.

"That's not what I meant,"

"What did you mean then?"

Hannah's warmth stretched away and Nicholas couldn't find the words to stop it.

Hands on hips, she faced him, "Women are good enough to look at and bare your children, cook for you, even warm your bed, but not save your life?"

"Hannah," He caught her arm.

"Sherriff!" A males' voice hollered from the front door.

"Here," Nicholas shouted releasing her.

Joshua, the Krouse brothers' foreman entered. "I've been sent to get you, you've got to come to the site."

"What for? What site?"

"Oh, Sorry Miss…..Sherriff – the construction site, you have to come now…" Tall and thick Joshua stood at the door and removed his faded brown hat. His sagging cheeks puffed with exertion.

"What's happened?"

"Sherriff, this morn'n we were digging the foundations when we found bones. You've got to come."

Nicholas shook his head and focused, "Give me a minute."

“Bones?” Hannah repeated, she had stopped packing her chest and stood shoulder to shoulder with Nicholas.

“Hannah - don’t - ” Nicholas managed to say nothing of what he wanted to before dressing and adding his holster. She levelled a hard flat stare his direction and Nicholas knew this was far from over.

Chapter 7

Joshua led Nicholas to the western bank of Franklins Shallows where John and Isaac Krouse stood with several construction workers. He let Ranger graze in the grass and approached the crowd huddled around an immense man-made pit. The sunlight spilled down the sharp banks of the river illuminating the grass to emerald green, yet the centre of the pit lay in shadow. As Nicholas reached the edge, he peered into the darkness to see dirt drenched bones sprouting upwards. The familiar odour of decay greeted the midday air.

"Nick" John Krouse cleared his throat before speaking again, "Sherriff." His robust cousin wiped a white handkerchief over even whiter brow. "Peter found them, we dug around them, to make sure… you see."

Nicholas kneeled on the lip of the pit. *Them?* Yes he could see it clearly now, two skulls, two rib cages, on different planes and at different heights within the grave. One skull brilliant white the other tired brown, more decayed. Nicholas climbed into the pit and circled the area on his haunches. His cousins cleared the crowd of on-lookers, while Nicholas let a handful of dirt fall through his fingers, moist and dark. He dug around the fossils, to define a better position of the bones. Then he sketched and measured the scene, jotting notes as he went. An hour later, he sent for the undertaker.

Nicholas had exposed as much of the skeletons as he could without lifting them completely clear. He had unsurfaced the limbs, fingers with ligaments still attached. No obvious signs of animal attack and definitely no accident. The skeletons were similar in size and shape, small frames with fine forearm bones. Women? Nicholas mused. Doctor Fitzgibbon will tell me more. Nicholas sifted through the surrounding soil and found nothing. Perhaps the earth had eaten their clothes or they were buried naked. At least one skeleton had been buried on higher ground, suggesting it had been buried last. Two female victims, buried at the same spot, but possibly some years apart.

Isaac Krouse pulled Nicholas out of the pit, "Nick, I appreciate your need to investigate this but, ah…"

"Once the undertaker arrives, cousin you can have your site back." Nicholas measured his steps up the difficult slope, stopping twice to grab at the ground and pull himself up. His side ached but he'd be damned if he touched it. On level ground again, Nicholas surmised the steepness of the slope, "This area's been cleared?"

Isaac followed him up the slope, "Yes, of course, to dig the foundations."

"Where are the trees?"

Isaac directed Nicholas to a stockpile of felled timber, ready for carting to the mill. Oak, Hickory, White Pine, River Birch. Nicholas searched through the pile, directing restless workers to help, until he found it.

There was no mistaking the circular pattern of bark damage on a thick trunk of Hickory. Nicholas measured the height and width of the tree before directing an axeman to chop his evidence. When the undertaker finished packing his grisly load, Nicholas mounted Ranger and followed the cart into Town.

Something had happened at the construction site and with utter certainty Hannah linked it to Ms Baker's death. Bones. A body. Another murder. Ms Baker played a part in something and she died to keep the secret. Hannah paced backwards and forwards in the front sitting room for the next few moments, before deciding to head into Town. She approached Carl and he hesitantly saddled Smoke.

Hannah steeled herself as Carl boosted her in the saddle and her memories of childhood riding lessons flooded warnings in her body. She remembered the most comfortable and secure way to sit was astride, not side saddle which could propel a person off the animal at any given moment. Hannah trotted into Town frantically conjuring reasons to visit the Doctor. She told herself that her visit had nothing to do with the fact that Nicholas would ask the Doctor to view the bones. When Hannah arrived at

Doctor Fitzgibbons office, she scanned the surroundings for Nick and his dark horse. Gladly she had beaten him into town. Hannah entered the timber panelled parlour just as the Doctor admitted another patient.

Hannah recognised the lanky frame of Thomas Hitz, a would-be student. He shuffled awkwardly into the office patted gently on the shoulder by his mother.

"Another boil is it Thomas? Well let's take a look – "

Hannah smiled at the Doctor over the mothers shoulder. His eyes heavily ringed with dark shadows.

"Oh Hannah if you aren't too busy, maybe you could assist me – " The doctor didn't get a chance to finish as Hannah strolled into the examination room and closed the door. After the boil, Hannah assisted with a fever, a pesky cough and even set a broken arm from a lad who'd rolled his wagon.

Dr Fitzgibbon complimented Hannah's skills and they discussed her studies in medicine over a cup of tea, "How far did you get through your studies?"

"I was one component short of completion, pathology. It seemed such a waste at the time."

"That it is Hannah, you have a natural talent. I have to ask where did you get the practice? I have seen many students come out with qualifications but less experience than you."

Hannah swallowed hard before answering, "I don't want you to think less of me, Doctor."

"If I know anything about this world, my dear, it's that nothing is fair and we all have to fight for our own share. Tell me, I will withhold judgement."

Hannah took a deep breath, "I had volunteered at the Women's hospital in Philadelphia but when the tuition fees dried up, I was forced to leave. I worked at ironing with my mother. It paid our bills after my father's death. At night when I returned the ironing, I crossed paths with quite a lot of working girls,"

The Doctor's moustaches twitched and green eyes bulged.

"Please let me finish, one night near the docks, I found a working girl busted up. Sally had been attacked badly, lacerations, across her face, one eye closed, chipped tooth and bleeding gums. I couldn't walk past her. She refused to attend the hospital, afraid of the consequences. I helped her back to the bordello run by a man called Dave the Grave." Hannah recalled the memory of that first meeting, the bawdy agent, carried a limp and a cudgel and was not a man to be taken lightly. "He protected his girls like a shepherd guards his flock. When Dave the Grave found out about me, he offered me frequent on-call work to keep his ladies patched up and clean. And I did." Hannah looked at her hands and recalled those last hazardous months. I have seen that side of life, the desperate and the violent, the predators and the prey.

Dave the Grave had offered Hannah a vacant spot when his second favourite Dolly succumbed to fever. She had been stern with her words, quick with her wit and even quicker with a scalpel. She had to point out, that she could earn four times the income if she patched up his remaining four girls and kept them working, than the amount she could earn on her back. He let her be after she stitched up his forearm she had so graciously opened.

Hannah relayed this to the Doctor as well and he responded by whistling through his front teeth, "Depending on your interests, I mean with the school - " The Doctor added, "If you ever felt like recommencing your studies, I could have a word with a friend of mine, he sits on the board of the AMA, or at least he did. He still might carry some sway."

"That sounds wonderful, but I don't see how I could pay for it."

"I suppose a teacher's salary is quite small?"

And then the interruption Hannah had been waiting for arrived. The Deputy Christian knocked sharply and Doctor Fitzgibbon excused himself. He returned to gather his things, "I'm sorry Hannah I must be off."

"Oh I see, anything I can help with?" She offered faintly, fingers crossed beneath the fabric of her skirt. A thick weight slid down her throat and rested uneasily in her stomach, Nick will see what I have done but perhaps if the Doctor invited me, her thoughts trailed off. He had started this, so he would see that she was worthy! Hannah straightened her spine.

"Well, it's a bit gruesome, probably best if you avoid this type of work."

"I'm not afraid, Doctor." Hannah fell in step beside Fitzgibbon as he waddled up Main towards the undertaker.

"It's still a bit macabre all the same."

"We never stop learning Doctor." She opened the double barn doors in front, and they walked in together.

"Hannah!"

"Oh hello Sherriff, I went to visit the Doctor and I've…." Nicholas crossed the room in five steps, knitted brows and eyes fierce. Grabbing Hannah by the elbow, the Sherriff turned her to face the door. "This is no place for a woman."

Hannah sighed, no place for women in medicine? Can I fight this forever? "This is the exact place for me, Sherriff. Even if this work makes you squeamish, I am exactly where I need to be." Hannah stared into deep pools of ice and Nicholas retreated from her challenge. Damn him, how can his lips offer such sweet scalding pleasure and in the next breath utter such derisive scorn!

Hannah walked back to the undertakers cart and ignored the fresh smell of over ripe deceased humanity that hung in the air. The sweet meaty smell that coated walls, clothing and hair, reminded Hannah that Ms Baker had been the most recent occupant. She pushed distractions away and walked towards the timber cart. Dirt fell from the biscuit coloured frames as the undertaker moved the bones into correct placement. Two skeletons? The ripeness had faded, no skin and only fragments of sinew remained.

The Doctor approached the cart from the other side and began measuring and taking notes. Hannah stole the notepad and took over without objection.

"I'll wait to hear your findings, Doctor." Nicholas said, the barn doors slamming his wake.

Hannah concentrated on the Doctors words, writing them down in shorthand. At the end of the examination Hannah sent the undertaker to summon Nicholas to return. The Sherriff strode in, elegant and imposing, his eyes slipped past Hannah and she turned to her notes.

The Doctor began, "Two females, both young in age, no previous broken bones, reasonable teeth, sharp unnatural marks possibly from a blade, on the lower ribs, may have been the fatal blow or a serious of wounds. One body," The Doctor paused to point out the specific one he referred to, "is older, that is for sure. Older in age of death. Killed before the other, the rate of decay with bones changes where they are buried, clothing covering the body, nature, bugs and others that eat away the flesh, so dating and aging the period of their death is difficult. But since they were buried in the same soil at the same site, in comparison to the second skeleton, this one was killed first. The next, was possibly a year, two years later."

"How long ago?" He asked, the deepness and sharpness of his tone cut through to Hannah's blood, boiling and soothing it at the same time.

"Between maybe two to ten years ago, maybe more" Fitzgibbon answered.

"Is there anything else, Doctor, that you can tell me. Something which will tell me who they were?"

"Sorry Nicholas, the only thing that stands out as odd, which Hannah pointed out, is the pelvis." Nicholas still refused to look at her.

"Go on Doctor."

Hannah stepped forward with the men, the bones between them.

The Doctor grabbed a pencil and pointed to the inside of the pelvis on the first skeleton, "This here is a tiny ridge on both sides of the pelvic bones. I haven't seen it often or at least looked for it in specimens. The ridges are present in both skeletons. It suggests that the pelvis carried weight."

"Weight?"

"Yes."

"In the pelvis? You're telling me they were pregnant?" Nicholas said, eyes dashing to the carcasses and to the Doctor. He glanced once at Hannah.

"Yes, judging by the fact that the pelvis was affected at all suggests that they were full term pregnancies. It could be related to something else, perhaps, genetic weakness, or something, but its food for thought, pardon the insensitivity."

The Doctor washed his hands, leaving Hannah and Nicholas across the cart from each other. Sapphire pits glared at Hannah. Nicholas clenched his fists by his side and a tiny muscle on his jaw twitched. Where is the right place for a woman, in your bed? But not in your admiration, not with respect, she thought.

Tears begged to spring forth at any moment, so she turned her back and started cleaning. Hannah listened as Nicholas's boots marched to the door.

Hannah skipped dinner that night and decided to go straight to bed, start anew in the morning. When the sun did rise, it failed to chase away the melancholy of yesterday. Ms Baker's funeral was scheduled for mid-morning.

The Pastor read from the Bible as Hannah studied the grass at her feet. Herself, Doctor Fitzgibbon, Susie and Rosa stood beside the plot as the pine coffin was lowered into the ground. A majority of the Frey Family stood on either side of the grassed area, few scattered parents loitered uncomfortably in the background and none of them approached the grave.

Nicholas lingered on Hannah's peripheral vision, her eyes automatically drawn to his imposing figure, resting sentry-like under the branch of a lofty Red Cedar. As the bright sun speared through the leaves, to dapple shadows across his uniform, so too, did his presence pierce Hannah's composure. Silently he watched the congression of mourners, every few moments his ice blue eyes turned to Hannah, simultaneously chilling her skin and heating her blood. She spied Christian and Leonard behind Nicholas, the Sherriff topping his deputy by a few good inches. He said a few curt words to them and sent them on their way, positioned at either end of the gathering, taking notes.

At the end of the service, the townsfolk returned to the small church hall where Feronica Frey and the Committee for Salvation had organised refreshments. From end to end the timber floor had been covered in tables with checked cloth and all manner of baked goods displayed. The committee had well rounded cooks in their brood. From glistening cakes to sugar coated pies and salacious savouries, yet Hannah couldn't eat a bite. Considering how Ms Baker had left this world, it seemed a safe choice in present company.

Nicholas watched as Thomas Hitz's mother came to offer her condolences to Hannah, followed by a string of other student's parents. He mused over how Hannah should be the one offering her condolences to them, rather than the other way around. They knew Ms Baker longer than Hannah had, yet of all the attendees, Hannah was the most upset at the old teachers passing. Hannah offered kind words to the people who approached her, the mothers pushing their children forward. Once they said their condolences, the children skipped from the hall to play in the Church's green lawns.

The whole afternoon passed in an eerie flurry of sorrowful words and smiling faces.

The Krouses approached Hannah last,

"This shouldn't affect our last arrangements Ms Evans."

John Krouse smiled into his cup of punch as he held his foreboding wife by the arm.

"I beg your pardon?"

"Our son and his applications of course," Margaret Krouse said, raising an eyebrow. Surely they didn't mean to discuss this now?

Feronica must have been within ear shot and she immediately stood beside Hannah, "I beg your pardon?"

Hannah raised her hand to forestall Feronica's interference, "Now is not the time to be discussing this." Her cutting words silenced the pair and Hannah turned away, only to face Nicholas's vigilant gaze. He stood on the other side of the long timber panelled room, the colourful light of the stained glass windows illuminated the sun kissed skin of his face and forearms. With moves that mimicked a mountain cat, he was suddenly beside her.

"Time to go?"

"Yes, if you wouldn't mind." Hannah sighed and attempted to gain Susie's attention.

"Carl can bring her," Nicholas ordered,

"Hannah, let me know if there is anything that I can do,"

"Thank you Feronica, I appreciate all the effort you and your ladies have gone to for Ms Baker,"

"You're welcome, Hannah - "

"Farewell Feronica." Nicholas cut her off.

"Cousin," She barked, hazel eyes narrowing at Nicholas abrupt dismissal.

Outside Nicholas gestured to Smoke already hitched to the trap, “I’d rather walk if you don’t mind. That is if your stitches are up for it.”

“They’ll hold up fine, the tailor did an outstanding job,” Nicholas scoffed

His teasing comment cleared the thick haze of his Family’s despicable comments that had surrounded Hannah.

“You should see how badly I can stitch fabric. Susie had to fix my dress for the Frey’s party.”

“She did a fine job of it,” Nicholas added.

Colour rose to her cheeks as Hannah reflected on the heat in his caramel tones, coated with a thick measure of appreciation.

“Flesh is so much more corporeal, tangible and substantial to control than flimsy mesh.” They strolled down the Church drive, Nicholas matching his strides to hers and the afternoon breeze buffeted her skirt against his thighs.

“That it is,”

Hannah smoothed down the dark navy material and avoided his gaze, the colour on her neck raced down her throat and her breasts swelled against her buttons. She thanked her high necked collar for some protection. She heard Nicholas cough gently and Hannah caught the shadow of a grin cross his rigid jaw. She wanted to yell at him, to demand he apologise, but her energy had waned. She sought his comfort not his ire.

He tugged at a low hanging branch of one the Red Cedars that marked the Church gate to Main.

“How goes your investigation?” She ventured.

Nicholas began shedding the slender needles from the Red Cedar twig and tossing them onto the ground as they walked, “Well, judging by what you – what the Doctor told me yesterday – both girls had children at some point. I’ll go tomorrow and search the records of the Widow Charles. I need a clearer time frame”

“Time frame?” Hannah’s curiosity bubbled,

“No point looking for someone, until you know the dates. Unless you have a theory on that too?”

“No. Only that they were young,”

“Not old spinsters then?”

Hannah rolled her eyes, “No.”

"Do you ever want children, Hannah?"

"Eventually yes, when I'm ready and on my own terms." Hannah clicked her tongue.

"Well despite your determination that's one feat you can't accomplish on your own." Nicholas smirked causing Hannah's voice to raise.

"And what about you Sherriff? Which Cousin will help you fill that big house of yours?" It was cruel and Hannah knew it, she bit down on her lip.

"I don't want any of my cousins." He held her gaze, eyes fresh like a summer sky, features set in stone, lips thin but inviting.

Hannah drew in a slow breath tasting the male scent that permeated from his proximity, "I apologise Nicholas, I shouldn't have said that."

"No it was unfair of me to begin with." He tossed the remainder of the branch onto the road and lifted his shoulders, "Right now I should be asking you what my devious Krouse cousins had reason to offend you about."

Grateful for the new direction, Hannah relaxed and released her fingers from clenched fists and strength returned to her knees.

"Something about their son's applications to University. They want him to be a lawyer. Judging by his last marks, he's going to need to improve. A great deal. I believe they almost offered me a monetary incentive that night at the Frey's, to help him make the grade."

"Interesting."

Nicholas became lost in his thoughts as they neared Old Thom. It was something, a small something. But he needed more if he was going to be throwing accusations the Krouse's way. He needed dates. The Doctor had said between two to ten years ago, that was a large time frame. They neared the slanted timber posts of the Lodge's fence and fleeting disappointment bite into Nicholas at soon parting ways.

"I wouldn't have thought teaching could be such a hazardous career." He leaned his forearms across the top rail, Hannah lingered on the other side, her hand brushing the tops of the weeds that grew between the stumps.

"Normally I would say it's not and medicine is no more hazardous."

"Surely the safety and security of a husband is more advantageous that forging ahead independently." Nicholas gestured to the Lodge behind Hannah's shoulders with an authoritative tilt of his jaw, "A nice home to be proud of, your own children to raise, and all the wifely duties to keep you occupied."

"Is this all that a woman should want?" Hannah's brow furrowed and her mouth began to pout.

"There is always a trade off, Hannah. A man cannot expect to provide for his family and care for it as well. What would the woman do?"

"Work."

Nicholas could feel the derailment of his words, but he couldn't understand the perplexing look on Hannah's face, "A woman's work is not equal to a man's"

Hannah tugged at the blossoms from the weeds, her blue-grey eyes turning to stone. Between gritted teeth she answered him, "And what if that woman chose a man's trade, worked to the same standard or even better, would you respect her then."

Hannah didn't wait for a response, she stormed off, pebbles crunching under her boots. When Hannah slammed the Lodge door she didn't even turn back to see if Nicholas had left. The man had called Doctor Fitzgibbon traditional. Perhaps Beth had made a lucky escape from marrying the Sherriff.

Chapter 8

Susie had returned home just before Hannah had properly burned the stew and managed to rescue most of the flavour. That night Hannah read with Susie until her eyes blurred and they said their farewells. Anger seethed inside Hannah every time she thought of Nicholas's words. Anger and something else, a unspoken wish that he would value her efforts. Respect. Eventually the day's events wore her down and she drifted off to sleep.

At lunch time the next day a knock on the Lodge door roused Hannah from her misery.

"It's Jasmine." Susie sighed, "From the boarding house." She added.

Hannah opened the door wider "Hello," she said. The pale haired beauty dressed in a deep navy dress with a cream coloured shawl hiding her best assets.

"Ms Evans."

"Come in and please call me Hannah."

"What about me?" Jimmy said, his freckle smudged face popping out from behind his mother's skirts.

"You call 'er Ms Evans, boy"

"Yes listen to your mother, Jimmy." Hannah smiled at the youth.

Hannah sat them both at the kitchen table and Susie made tea.

"I've come to see you about Jimmy." Jasmine finally started, "You got me thinking the other day, about Jimmy and that."

"Yes," Hannah smiled in her tea and waited.

"It's just that him and a few of the other kids seemed to be a bit of a bother and getting in the way and all that."

"Oh I see."

The doll faced beauty shifted her shawl to cover her shoulders. Hannah admired Jasmines attempts to wear something demure. “The other girls weren’t sure about your offer. So I said, I’d come and see for me self.”

“To teach them in the afternoons? Of course I was serious.”

“But we’re not sure that ya school would have them.” Jasmines green eyes dashed about the room, focusing on anything but Hannah.

“Whenever you want to send them, I’ll be here.”

“I told ya Ma.” Jimmy beamed.

“I know, I said as much too. But we can’t be paying for a heap of books and all.” Jasmine glared at Hannah pushing her index finger into the table top.

“We’ll work with what we’ve got, if that suits you?”

“Sure.” Jasmine took her finger of the table and smiled. A little guilt landed on Hannah’s shoulders, she would have to find time between Nicholas bandages, the Doctor and the School?

Hannah saw them to the door and said goodbye. As she did, a high pitched wail erupted from the riverbank.

“What the devil was that?” Jasmine said, pulling Jimmy closer.

Shivers raced down Hannah’s spine and her hand tightened on the door frame, “I don’t know,”

They rushed around the rear of the lodge, with Susie and Rosa in tow. The scream cut through the air once more sharp and loud from the boundary of school property. Hannah walked forward slowly, hoping to see something. The sun has passed its zenith and the tree-line grew dark and ambiguous.

Jasmine tried to pull Jimmy back but he bounded forward, “Jimmy Carson you get back here now.” Jasmine whispered from a tight throat. As they women took another few steps forward, the foliage parted and an Elk stumbled into view. His taupe coloured chest stained with a single line of claret. The beast stood at least 150 yards away, and limped a few steps before releasing another squealing bugle.

“That’s the one that Nicholas shot!” Hannah hissed.

“Not good enough Ma’am,” Jimmy quipped. “He’d better take another one,”

Before Hannah could stop him, Jimmy ran off.

Nicholas slowed Ranger down to a trot when he caught sight of the Treschells Mill. His last confrontation with Hannah brewed in his mind. She turned to marble when he mentioned the proper etiquette of a lady and the thing Nicholas pursued most of all, was the downright improper, sexual heat of Hannah as a woman. He hadn't found time to travel to York, and now thinking about a blue-stone eyed beauty with chocolate curls drove him to distraction. He wouldn't travel to York, he wouldn't find any other skirt to slake his thirst. Only burying himself hilt deep into Hannah, tearing his name from her lips would bring him any satisfaction. He pushed his contradictions aside and concentrated on the task at hand. Nicholas knew a little about trees, but not enough to be sure.

Old Matthew, the foreman of the mill, hailed a greeting to Nicholas, "If you're here to see yer cousin, he's gone…" In his late seventies, Matthew didn't slow down his spry approach as Nicholas haltered Ranger.

"Actually Matt, I've come to see you." No-one knew more about timber, trees, wood or lumber than Matthew. Luckily if his cousin Richard was absent he could discuss this with Matthew in private.

"Me, oh the pleasure of it Sherriff, what do yer want to know?" Matthew drawled offering Nicholas a sly smile.

"Hickory Trees?"

"Hickory trees I can help with."

Nicholas directed Matthew inside to the running floor of the Mill. The water from Franklins Shallows provided all the power needed to saw and plane the logs to fine planks of timber. The noise of each log as it was sliced and diced became too much for Nicholas to talk over and thankfully Matthew directed him to a small alcove near Richard's office.

"We can talk here, Sherriff." Nicholas grabbed his cut sample of the hickory tree and showed it to Matthew.

"Yes, its Hickory alright, some age about it to. What's the question?"

"See these marks here," Nicholas pointed out the rope damage to the bark.

"Yeah, I see it."

"Can you age the marks for me?"

Matthew pulled a pair of spectacles from his overall pocket and balanced the frames on his nose, "From this cutting, sure, give me the measurements." Nicholas gave Matthew the measurements from his notebook. Matthew ran an arthritic finger across the inner rings.

"Some mean axe marks there Sherriff." Matthew said before he entered the mill's sawing floor and planed off the rough edges. The foreman took it to the dust covered window to count in the sunlight. "They're about 7 or 8 years old."

"How sure are you?"

"Sure as eggs is eggs, Sherriff." Matthew said shoving his spectacles into his sawdust filled pocket, "What's this about, Nick?"

"Sherriff's business Matt, good day." He waved to Matthew from the back of Ranger and headed back to town. If Nicholas kept busy like this he wouldn't have to think about Hannah. Nicholas trotted Ranger to the midwife Widow Charles's house. He knocked loudly on the door for several minutes before her son, Sam came to the door.

"She's out birthing Marianne's baby, you know Marianne from Nock's Hollow. She'll probably be all afternoon and all night. Mamma said it might be breech a week ago. Do you want her to come see you when it's done, Sherriff?"

"Yes thanks son, as soon as she can." He turned away and stood beside Ranger for a while to collect his thoughts. The sun began to set. Nock's Hollow was a decent few hours ride away. Would Marianne mind the Sherriff calling on her midwife to answer some questions? He turned back to the door, "Hey Sam, does your mamma write down records of each delivery?"

"Yeah she does, come in." Sam took Nicholas inside the house. Each window sill was covered in herbs and books. His thoughts drifted back to Hannah and her medicine. What had she treasured like this? Sam directed the Sherriff to a well worked desk near the empty fireplace. Sam lifted a heavy leather bound ledger and handed it to Nicholas.

"I've see her write them in here. I've got to fetch the chickens, do you want some grub?"

"No thanks, son you go get your chickens, I won't be long." Nicholas quickly scanned through the pages coming to a specific time frame. He took in the list. Widow Charles's house may be dusty and cluttered but her record keeping skills were commendable. She had documented each birth date, mother, father (if known), weight, and measurements. She seemed to make regular visits on each mother up till the child was two years old. Nicholas could make out the additions she had later added to each record. He scanned the names for some recognition. He found numerous women who had given birth approximately 7 years ago. Racking his brain, Nicholas could place all but three women. He wrote down their names and would have to make inquiries as to where they were. Could two be lying in the undertakers shed? Was the third safe?

The Sherriff bid farewell to Sam as the boy corralled his chickens into their pen. Nicholas walked Ranger through town just as the sun crested the horizon, deepening the sky to a splendid burnt orange. The dark shadows on Old Thom threw splintered light onto the well warn timbers. Nicholas knew which gate would approach first as he headed home. Nicholas glanced to his left at the Lodge and saw a small figure sprinting towards him. He booted Ranger into motion and caught up to the child.

"Jimmy?"

"Oh Jesus Christ!" Jimmy said before he could sensor himself. "I was just looking for you, that Elk you shot. It's back, figured, you'd like another shot, maybe finish him this time."

"Lead the way," Nicholas scooped Jasmine's boy onto Ranger's back behind him and galloped up the drive.

"So, he returned?" Nicholas said. What a surprise had greeted him at the Lodge, Susie and Rosa, inside with the whore Jasmine and Hannah, all staring at the eastern border to the school. Hannah had obviously taken his comment about her dresses seriously; today she had on a dark woollen skirt, filled with petticoats and a high necked shirt, pale blue. Her spine set rigid and he guessed it had less to do with her corset and more to do with him.

Thank the Lord he had saddled Ranger with the usual, a shot gun and Kentucky rifle, his Colt pistol snug against his hip.

"You ever shot a long rifle, son?"

"Nick, No!" Hannah began, "You can't ask Jimmy?"

Nicholas had sent Susie to round up Christian before they set out. The Elk bugled this time towards the river. “He’s moving. We might lose him again.”

“I’ll be fine Miss, I’ve shot a few rounds with Jackson and Lance.”

“What?” Jasmine paled.

“It’s okay Ma, we only hit cans, I’m actually not bad.”

“I’m sure, but we’ll wait for the other Deputy or what about Leonard?” Jasmine spoke his name with such familiarity that Nicholas paused loading his weapons. Leonard? He had just passed his twenty first birthday and Jasmine, pretty as she was could be no more than twenty two or twenty three. How old was Jimmy? Hannah patted Jimmy’s unkempt hair while the sun sunk a little lower bringing with it an afternoon chill. Another scream lamented through icy air and pushed Nicholas thoughts to the pines.

“He’s in pain,” Hannah pleaded.

“And moving away.” Nicholas walked around to the rear of the Lodge carrying his rifle.

“Please, Nick wait for someone – ” but he’d already left. Hannah thought of the previous encounter with this beast and took a deep breath, “Jimmy, how do you work this thing?”

“Hannah, you’re mad, I’ll go, Jimmy can you load it?”

“It’s already loaded ma.”

“Jasmine you’re safer in here with Jimmy and keep an eye out.” Hannah scooped up the shot gun, her hands shaking on the stock.

Both mother and boy followed Hannah out, “Miss you ever shot a peppergun before?”

“Um, no,”

“Well Lance said to me, pull it into your shoulder and lean in. Its kicks like a mule.”

“Thanks Jimmy.” Hannah stalked across the open field, eyes forward on the black coat of Nicholas yards in front.

“Hannah go back!”

“I’m here now,” Hannah whispered, mirroring Nicholas slower crouched approach as they neared the tree-line.

“I can’t be worrying about you and him at the same time.”

"If you remember, I wasn't the one who came off second best."

Nicholas scoffed. "Keep out of the trees."

The high pitched scream reached their ears somewhere from the left. Nicholas moved forward, rifle at half-mast and edged upstream. He moved so silently and quickly that moments later Hannah lost sight of him. The foliage folded into dark greens with long shadows that tangled the scenery.

"Nick." Hannah hissed. "Nick!"

She pushed aside a branch with her elbow when Hannah heard shuffling and snorting behind. The Elk stood, antlers raised, saliva dripping from its loose lips and bubbles of blood frothing from his nostrils. "Nick!" She shouted before levelling the shotgun and pulling the trigger. Jimmy was right. Hannah stumbled backwards, her heel striking a tree root, pitching her into the river.

She heard Nicholas call out her name before Franklins Shallows swallowed her whole. The frigid water carried Hannah quickly, her heavy skirts tugging her under the surface. Gulping down fist full of mountain stream didn't help either. The churning and bubbling of Franklins Shallows filled Hannah's ears as the strength dragged her towards Old Thom. She succumbed again, surfacing with brown hair obscuring her view. She flailed her arms attempting to grab purchase of something, anything. Another surge of water splashed about and Hannah closed her eyes. Panic writhed through her skin and she sucked a deep breath when she finally broke free. Visions of the Elk charging at Nick again filled her head. I have to do something!

The current carried her towards the old bridge, the river banks too wide and high for any branch or handhold. Hannah prayed someone along the bank might see her or hear her, but as the aged red roof came into view, a wave of white pushed her under. Blinking water from her eyes, boulders the size of carriages filled her path.

Frantically, Hannah kicked at her boots amongst the swirling material of her skirts that trapped her legs. She clawed at her waistline, scratching and tearing her nails along her skin. Hannah wriggled on to her back and kicked her boots and petticoats free. With stocking feet forward buffering the boulders, Hannah stretched out behind, splayed fingers raking the water and coming up empty.

One breath at a time, Hannah told herself. Grey giants sped past and the sinking sun prevented Hannah from seeing the smaller ones until she connected with them. Each time Hannah pushed back with her legs, sending her back into the current, her strength decreased. How long can I hold out? Luckily Franklins Shallows ran deep enough for Hannah to avoid the worst against her back and rear end. The temperature of the water leached the warmth and strength from Hannah's limbs, soon she would be fighting to stay awake as well as afloat.

One immense boulder grew larger and larger in her path. Her energy all but spent, an image of Nick bleeding and helpless in the forest spurred her into action. Desperately whirling and lashing out Hannah cleared the obstruction. Abruptly the banks receded, and the rocks disappeared. The river widened, slowing down Hannah's speed. Hannah bobbed and dipped along like flotsam until the surface settled flat. The current still tugged at Hannah's legs, but when she turned on her side she could reach the bank. Tree roots and logs teased at Hannah's open hand, grasping the air many times before she reached a plateau. Hannah snatched at the small pebbles that found their way here just as she had and pulled herself to safety.

Lying face down, saturated, freezing and exhausted Hannah thanked the Lord. The sun had completely dipped behind the dark oaks and woodlands leaving the scenery as drained of colour as Hannah. The hard stones pressed against her chest and a dull ache spread throughout her body. She lost track of time, one minute the sun slithered between the branches, the next it had disappeared causing a fit of shakes in Hannah's bones. A thick fog rested over her Hannah's mind and she forced her arms and legs to move.

Standing upright, Hannah guessed she had stopped far south of the Township. She dragged her sodden skirts to the riverbank as the river snaked past the plateau and out of sight.

Each footstep awoke a new injury, from sore limbs, scraped back and bruised rump, agony kneaded into Hannah's muscles. Hannah considering sitting along the tree line to wait for rescue, but the rushing noise of the rapids reminded her that no one would attempt to steer a boat across those dangers. Perhaps no one knew to look for her, Nicholas might be lying unconscious or worse in the forest, waiting for a rescue of his own.

Hannah sensed movement behind her and spun quickly to hear the soft shuffling of noses and hooves. Oh God, she thought, a wild hog to charge at me is all I need. A large dark brown mass of fur ambled into sight. The smell identified cattle and no sooner had the thought crossed Hannah's mind, that the whole herd became visible.

Someone's cattle, Hannah thought. As she crested the bank, welcoming light shone from a homestead in the distance. Hannah plucked the last threads of her dress from the thistles and stumbled forward.

"Hannah?"

The wind whipped Hannah's hair stinging her numb skin, and twisting her name in her ears.

"Hannah!"

New life burned into her limbs and she dragged herself clear of the thorny underbrush. Nicholas galloped towards her astride his black horse, tuffs of earth flying from the hooves.

"Thank God!"

Hannah looked down at her soaked and shredded clothing clinging to her shaking frame.

"I thought I'd have a bath." She scoffed. A bubble of river water gurgled its way clear and without any pause Hannah threw herself behind the closest tree and retched. By the time she'd recovered, Nicholas had reached her. Relief slammed into her soul and her strength evaporated. Nicholas swept Hannah up against his chest with ease and his warmth enveloped her, with her head lolling against his shoulder it was moments later that darkness claimed her.

Chapter 9

Tiny sprinkles of rain danced on Hannah's face, forcing her awake. "I'm so sorry Nicholas, are you alright? What happened to the Elk?" She whispered as Nicholas carried her up the front porch.

"I'm fine, I finished him."

"I was worried about you. I should have made you wait."

"It's fine, Carl we need a fire. Quick."

Nicholas placed Hannah down in the front sitting room before Hannah realised her surroundings, "This is your house, but how?"

"Franklins Shallows run's past my southern border, it's just lucky you managed to stay afloat till the water calmed."

"It wasn't easy," she scoffed looking back at her soggy and torn clothing. Her eye's focused drawing away the fuzziness that coated her brain. "Oh Nick you're hurt again. I'm sorry." Hannah's numb fingers clumsily pulled the white shirt at his side.

"You first," Nicholas whispered, lips skimming her icy cheek, causing the skin to ignite. Nicholas's fingers kneaded Hannah's shoulders strumming a chord in her core. A dull ache worked from her toes up to thighs and began to thaw her limbs.

"Carl, call the search party off, and alert Susie, Ms Evans will need more clothes." Carl finished stoking the fire, bright fast flames flickered in the hearth.

Before Carl dashed out, Hannah shouted, "And my medicine chest." Exhaustion clawed at her, yet the scent of Nicholas and his home created a familiar fondness that soothed her aches. Each item echoed family history and the clay brick fireplace had been built to shoulder height. Most of all Hannah wanted to be warm, to feel his strength seeping into her weary bones.

Nicholas staggered into the hall, returning a short time later with dark heavy blankets. He stoked the fire building the flames as high as possible. Hannah shivered in her almost transparent clothing and edged towards the fire. Franklins Shallows had taken most of her petticoats.

"What was Jasmine and Jimmy doing at the Lodge?" Nicholas asked,

"We were talking about Jimmy."

"Is he in trouble?"

"No. Jasmine is going to send him and the other children from the boarding house to the school in the afternoon."

"Do you think that's proper?"

"Yes," She stomped her foot and her clothes splashed about her ankles. If only he knew the half of it, she thought but vowed never to tell him about Philly. Nicholas shifted his weight to the other leg and Hannah noticed. "I'm so sorry, about the river."

"You're okay and that's what matters." He winced.

"But you're not," Hannah gasped.

Nicholas inhaled deeply as Hannah tugged at his shirt. Dark blue and black blossomed across his flank and splotches of blood formed in the creases. Nicholas felt his desire intensify as Hannah leant forward and the blanket dipped affording him the barest glimpses of rose coloured peaks rising from the cream. "I'll be fine, I'm sure." Nicholas tried to sooth her.

"I might need to stitch that again,"

He captured her hands within his and pushed her gently away, Hannah watched his lids sink, heavy with thoughts other than his safety, "Not right now."

"If this is about not being a Doctor – "

He chuckled softly as he ran his eyes up and down her physique; Hannah shivered.

"No quite my Dear." Nicholas enjoyed watching Hannah blush and she pulled the blanket to her neckline. "Upstairs second room on the left."

Hannah stole away from the sitting room and found the room Nicholas had described. Inside a large solid timber bed dominated the room and a stark chest of drawers slinked in the corner. It was obviously the master suite totally devoid of feminine touch. She closed the door and dried herself as best she could. The main window overlooked the curve in Franklins Shallows and darkness enveloped the homestead. A storm broke as Carl returned with her medicine chest and clothing. After a gentle knock on the door, Hannah opened it just a crack. To his credit, Nicholas stood there with his eyes cast down, and handed Hannah a bundle of her clothing.

"Susie decided to stay with Rosie in this storm. She said the Doc was birthing Sue-Lyn's baby somewhere."

"Okay,"

"The Doc said he'll call on you tomorrow."

"Fine." Hannah's swollen and frozen fingers dragged at her clothes laden with river water, her wet shirt and soggy skirts were easy before. The strings are at the back, she thought and cursed herself for choosing a corset this morning. "Um, I'm stuck."

"What do you mean stuck?" Nicholas voice oozed through the cracks in the door.

Hannah closed her eyes and gulped, "I can't undo the strings." After a long moment, she heard the door creak open.

She watched Nicholas enter, taking note of how he calculated her wet skirt and shirt on the floor. Nicholas stalked behind and Hannah pulled the blankets up to her chin. Her chest tightened and as his fingers released the first loop. At the second loop, a sigh escaped her lips. The corset loosened sinking low across her bust line, the cool fabric snagging on her tight nipples, the temperature having nothing to do with her condition. Hannah froze as Nicholas plucked another loop free. His breath tickled her neck, slow and steady. Is his heart thundering like mine, she thought. I need the clothes gone and to be warm, Hannah reminded herself. His knuckles grazed her spine sending a sweet tingling sensation to her hips, the tiny hairs on the back of her neck raised and beckoned his touch.

Nicholas sensed the change in Hannah's breathing, her shakes had subsided and her neck stretched upwards when he fumbled with the ties. Her slim figure didn't require a tight bodice and she could have drowned purely with the weight. Nicholas arousal simmered to boiling point as loop by loop he revealed the pure creaminess of her skin. Nicholas reached inside the bodice to free the next loop and his fingers caressed the silkiness that was

Hannah. She shivered under his touch and the lure of desire swelled against his clothing. She was all smooth velvet waiting for him to savour the soft femineity that she possessed. The preceding hours of heart-ripping concern vanished. Hannah's travel down the river had tangled the remaining loops and using the strength of his increasing arousal Nicholas tore at the fabric in one swift movement, dropping the wet mess to his bedroom floor. The blanket around her gaped and his eyes were blinded by the creamy silk partially hidden by her camisole that he yearned to taste.

Hannah gasped. A thick fog shrouded Hannah but this time it smelt of wet pine and leather and she leaned into the movement of nimble fingers that deftly stroked her spine. Nicholas flourished kisses down her wet hair to her icy cheek. Each stroke Nicholas laid against her back, fed the fire within. Hannah surrendered and faced him, hungry lips covered hers and liquid heat danced to the rhythm of Nicholas' tongue. She drew the all-male taste of him over her lips as his dark curls brushed her nose. A rush of heat so intense made her shiver, her desire driving her arms to his neck, her hips forward to meet his.

His mouth captured hers so totally that she yielded without hesitation. He pulled her tight against his body, the blanket a dangerously insufficient barrier between his hard flesh and her molten core. Tremors stole through Hannah's body as salacious need clawed at her insides. Her breasts swelled, the taunt peaks stinging through flimsy cloth as she pressed against the potent force of Nicholas. She wanted more, an ache started deep within her abdomen, longing for fulfilment, for pleasure, for Nicholas. It scared her.

Hannah pushed on his chest, his bulk resistant, "Nick. Please."

"Why Hannah?" He kissed the line of her jaw down to her collarbone, letting his tongue cool her fever skin, "Isn't this what you want?"

She tried to inhale the surroundings, the fire, the rain, anything to dilute his lingering fragrance. "No - "

"Your body betrays you Hannah, you look at me with a woman's eyes. You answer my kisses like I've awoken a hunger, a thirst that I have yet to satisfy. Why deny this need for pleasure." Hannah couldn't argue as his tongue drank the cool river water from her throat. She wanted more, she wanted Nick but her mind cleared. She could not.

"Nick. Please. I should go."

Nicholas tilted his head to the thumping of the storm "You're not going anywhere in this,"

Thinking fast, Hannah parroted his own words, "But it's not proper,"

"Neither is shooting an Elk or socialising with working girls." Nicholas said and then seized her lips, sipping, licking and nipping. Hannah melted into the embrace, letting the leash off her desire, and ran her hands through his hair. His arousal pressed at the soft flesh between her thighs calling forth more syrup temptation begging for release. Hannah shuddered under the pressure of his strong fingers at the edge of her breasts, edging the blanket skyward, "Besides, you said it yourself, even spinsters need company."

Clarity tolled like a bell and with two hands on Nicholas's chest, she widened the gap between them. Is that what I am to him, a conquest, a spinster, disposable. "You and your cousin are cut from the same cloth, aren't you?"

Nicholas stepped back, his heavy lidded eyes snapping open, jagged pits of sapphire.

"Carl can take you home in the morning." He said and stormed from the room.

As Nicholas stalked past her, Hannah didn't doubt her accusation. His temper had been proof enough he had been only after one thing. Hannah had never wanted to marry, never wanted to belong to a man, in any sense. Yet Nicholas had made her recant on all that she had sworn herself from. The ache inside throbbed and the complexity of her emotions brought Hannah close to tears. She had denied for so long, that a man could ever make Hannah want to be a wife, a lover, a woman possessed by a man. Hannah touched her lips recalling his passion filled kisses that had left her delirious and wanton. Nicholas's hands still ghosted across her skin, as Hannah pulled the coverlet up to her chin. Somehow Nicholas had made her want to relinquish her independence, hand over her body for his purpose and pleasure and perhaps a little bit of her heart as well. She squeezed her eyes tight.

Hannah lay awake in the early hours of the morning. It's my fault, she thought. I have flirted, breathlessly in front of his cousins at the party. I have been clear with him about not wanting to marry yet I have let myself be alone with him time and time again. What else is he to think? The blame lies squarely at my feet.

The sun began to rise and so did Hannah's apprehension of a confrontation. She clothed herself as quietly as possible, boots lost to the river, and tiptoed downstairs. Carl greeted Hannah in the kitchen and introduced her to Odette. The large brown skinned woman arched an eyebrow until Carl silenced her with a glare. To Hannah, he placed a finger to his lips. Hannah dared a peak in the sitting room and saw Nicholas sprawled out, shirtless on blankets, still sound asleep. Guilt slammed into her chest when she saw his bandage undone. He had repacked it himself and Hannah would ask the Doctor to visit.

"Carl, please take me home." she whimpered.

As Carl drove Smoke and the buggy onwards to the Lodge, Hannah paid no mind to how close Nicholas lived and how far she had travelled down Franklins Shallows. Nicholas's property sat closest to Old Thom, the homestead far back from view of travellers on the road. She drew an imaginary line between the Lodge to the North West and the Homestead in the South East. Hannah deduced that Nicholas was her closest neighbour.

Along the journey, Carl whistled and hummed but spoke very little. When the trap pulled up at the Lodge, Susie spent a short few minutes speaking with Carl before he left.

Hannah crawled into her bed but didn't get much sleep. Guilt made her send Susie over to Nicholas's to check on him once he woke and within the hour she walked to town to see Dr Fitzgibbon. She spied the dark horse Ranger tied up outside the Sherriff's office and made a mental note to apologise for sending Susie for no reason. As she waited in the Doctor's foyer, the door opened and out strolled Nicholas, splendid in his dark uniform. When he saw Hannah he nodded.

"Ms Evans."

"Sherriff," So he'd seen the doctor to sew him up.

"Oh Hannah, I would have made it eventually, but you're here now. I probably don't need to tell you how lucky it is that the Sherriff found you when he did. Exposure, fever and so on." Doctor Fitzgibbon started, and Hannah smiled meekly at Nicholas, failing to look him in the eye.

"Yes, I - " Hannah stopped, had she actually thanked him. "Ah, thank you Sherriff."

"Don't mention it." He thanked Doctor Fitzgibbon and left.

Hannah followed the Doctor into his rooms and closed the door.

Nicholas crossed main and stormed into the Sherriff's building. He slammed the door to his office, only to hear it open immediately.

"Nick, I mean Sherriff " Christian poked his head around the door. "Cousin, there are some…."

"I'm about to leave." Nicholas snapped. Where did it go so wrong? He threw his belt around his hips and tightened his holsters.

"You might want to hear this."

"I said -"

"Yeah, I know Nick, but honestly you'll have to hear these men out." Nicholas let Christian lead two well-dressed men into his office. One tall and slim, dressed in a smart grey tailored suit, edged with silver and black trimmings, his moustache twitching under his up turned nose. His brown eyes squinted at Nicholas simultaneously sizing him up and dressing him down. The other man, shorter, wearing another detailed and finely trimmed suit, this time navy and stretched awkwardly across his soft middle. The shorter man removed his hat to reveal curly fair hair receding up his square forehead.

"Sherriff," The taller man spoke first and offered his hand, "I am Mr John Smith Esquire, and this is my contemporary, Daniel Musgrave."

Nicholas seized his soft hand, and shook it. "Gentlemen", Nicholas shook Musgrave's plump outstretched hand next. Neither man had ever worked an honest day in their lives, he thought. "How can I help you?"

"We are searching for a lady whom we believe has travelled to this town." Smith's nose gave another deliberate sniff.

Suddenly, Nicholas felt a noose tightening around his neck. "Yes, and who would that be?"

Musgrave edged closer, flattening his wispy hair with a pale limp hand, "My Fiancé, Miss Hannah Evans."

Nicholas stretched back in his chair and chuckled, "Fiancé' you say?" He leaned his boots on his desk and clasped his hands over his belt buckle.

"Yes, do you know of her?" Smith took his bowler hat from his head and pulled out a chair.

"Do you know her well?" Musgrave sat down his beady eyes seemed to plead for Nicholas to continue. He took a moment to imagine Hannah's reaction at this man's small fleshy hands grasping at her flesh. A flush of jealousy shot through his skin and he took a moment to steady his thoughts.

"Ah yes."

"Do you know where we can find her?"

"I suspect you'll find her at the Doctors."

"Doctors? Is she alright?" Musgrave gasped.

"Nothing serious, if she's done she might be helping him with his patients."

Smith gave a loud hiss with his tongue and twitched his moustache over his thin lips.

"Patients? I don't understand, I thought you said she was a teacher?" Musgrave said, his beady eyes darting over the other man's stern expression.

"Yes Hannah is a teacher, sometimes she assists Doctor Fitzgibbon." Nicholas found a little heat in his voice and smiled, "If she's not at the undertakers?"

"Undertakers?" Musgrave said, wringing his hands in his lap.

"Daniel, I'm sure I've mentioned her time at the College in Philadelphia, but, that time is, *will be*, all behind her, now that you have arrived."

"Yes," Musgrave nodded.

Nicholas chided himself. Here sat two men, carrying the same narrow-mindedness she had levelled at him. Mrs Hannah Musgraves. The thought produced a bitter taste to the back of Nicholas's throat.

"Please point us in the right direction Sherriff." Musgrave stood first and Smith gracefully followed his friend.

"The brick building across the street, large white writing on the door. Maybe knock before you enter. Should you wish to freshen up gentlemen, the Horses Gait Inn can accommodate you, just ask for Joseph."

"Perhaps you should freshen up before you meet Hannah. I'll fetch her and meet you at the Tavern." John's tone sat uncomfortably around Nicholas' ears.

"No John, I'll meet her now."

So the pudding had a backbone, Nicholas thought. Smith huffed loudly into his moustache and tried once more to convince Musgrave to head to the inn, to no avail.

As they left, Nicholas pushed up from his chair, shook their hands and followed them to the porch. He rested against the door frame, eagerly awaiting the reunion about to unfold.

Nicholas didn't have to wait long. Before either man had crossed the street, the doors to the Doctors opened slightly and Hannah's figure slipped out. Her head was down, and he could see her fists clenched at her sides.

"My Dearest Hannah."

Nicholas heard Smith call out. The sheriff's mind flashed back to the elk in the brush. Hannah froze, ready to dash away. Her eyes flicked to either side of her brother-in-law as if to find a place to hide. Then she spied Musgrave. Her back stiffened and her fists pressed tighter against her thighs. Hannah's eyes found Nicholas and his heart started thundering in his chest.

Chapter 10

Doctor Fitzgibbon fussed about, apologising for not coming sooner, gesturing for Hannah to sit in his patient chair.

"I feel fine, Doctor."

"Yes I'm sure."

"How is Sue-Lyn's baby?"

"Both mother and baby are doing well. I did tell you it was a busy time of year. Have you thought any more about resuming your studies?"

Hannah ringed out her hands, "I'm uncertain at this stage," She thought of the boarding house children, of Susie and Rosa and now Carl.

"Well if you change your mind, I will write to my friend. Perhaps all you need to do is sit the final exam. Between now and then I could offer you my assistance and knowledge in preparation? Think it over."

As Hannah thought over the Doctors offer, she returned to Main Street where she spied a fancy carriage with two very tired horses.

"My Dearest Hannah" A familiar voice called.

As the two men crossed to greet her, Hannah stole those last moments to glance at the Sherriff's office. There stood Nicholas lazing against the porch of his office, arms across his chest. She could see a smirk resting on his lips.

"John, what a surprise."

"Yes of course Hannah." He brushed an empty kiss against her cheek and stepped away, grabbing her elbow and forcing her to walk towards the strange small man. Hannah surmised his age in his 30's, wispy brown hair creeping back from his shiny skin. He twirled his hat in his hands and tried a pleasant smile. His bottom lip was much larger than the top turning his smile into a child's pout. "This is Mr Daniel Musgrave, I wrote to you of his offer."

Hannah reefed her elbow out of Johns' grasp and took a step back. She caught Nicholas's movement out of the corner of her eye. "Wrote to me?"

"Yes, while you were at Norm School, dear Hannah." John had turned his back to Daniel and his eyebrows arched downwards. "I wrote to you not this past month…"

The man in question stepped towards them both and added, "When John told me of your reply, I hurried, here, to meet you."

Hannah's legs began to shake. Oh no what has he done! "Mr Musgraves I think you've been mistaken."

"Hannah, don't by foolish. Don't embarrass yourself." John chuckled with effort and snatched at Hannah's elbow before Nicholas stood between them.

Nicholas crossed the street in five measured steps before he stood between Hannah and Smith. "Is there a problem, Miss Evans?" Nicholas wanted nothing more than to ground out to Musgraves and Smith that Hannah's was his, but he checked himself and relaxed his shoulders.

"I have come with an offer, if the mail has been mislaid or sent on in error, I shall make my offer again." Perhaps the pudding was prepared for Smith's scheming. Nicholas stole a glance at Hannah, ivory cheeks flushed with red, eyes like the sky after rain and chocolate curls throwing red rubies into the sunlight. Musgraves would persist for certain.

"Yes thank you Daniel, that is a splendid idea, we can all have dinner tonight, if that suits you, Hannah."

Hannah glanced at Nicholas hoping for rescue. Musgraves had travelled this far to claim a would-be-bride. He hadn't done anything wrong. Smith on the other hand, was as sly as a fox. But, Musgrave had a right to make his offer and Hannah had a right to hear it. "Well I'll leave you to your day." Nicholas dipped his hat in farewell and returned across the street, ignoring Hannah's paling cheeks.

The hours in the day drew long as Nicholas waited to see the outcome of Hannah's fiancée and brother-in-law's proposal. Surely it was to go back to Philadelphia. When the sun sunk to its lowest, William Frey entered the Sherriff's Office grinning wildly.

"Good afternoon Cousin. Are you ready?"

"Ready for what?" He grumbled.

"The family meeting of course, we can ride together. Get your coat."

"Send one of my uncles, I told you I don't want any part of those meetings."

"Of course you don't, yet it might be a good opportunity to question your cousins with a bit more authority."

Nicholas shook his head at the fair haired well moustached patriarch, "More authority than this?" He tapped the silver star on his chest.

"Yes exactly." Not a hint of mocking lay in William's voice.

Nicholas conceded and rode out on Ranger to the Frey's ranch, ready for the inquisition that was to occur.

John the Banker and Daniel Musgrave arrived at 7pm sharp just as Hannah caught sight of Nicholas and what looked like William Frey trotting over Old Thom. Hannah held her breath as she watched him enter the red roofed relic. Moments later he galloped up the road, not a backwards glance to be seen.

Damn him. I will have to share this dinner with John and Musgrave's marriage proposal dangling like an axe above my neck. And Nick will think a wealthy husband is exactly what I need. Hannah sighed. What if Nicholas had made you an offer? Would you have refused it? She thought, before a knock at the door signalled her doom.

The dinner continued as planned, and shortly after pleasantries, Daniel broached a question that must have burned him since their first encounter.

"What exactly we're you doing at the doctors?"

"Assisting him with his patients."

"And the Sherriff mentioned something about the undertakers?"

"Examining skeletal remains." Hannah said with aplomb. John's fork splattered onto his plate.

"I thought you were done with this all."

"No John, not quite." They continued on in silence. Daniel didn't seem as pompous or as rigid as John. He had a quiet and deliberate manner about his speaking and it reminded Hannah of her father. It wasn't until Daniel gently steered the conversation towards Margaret, that John discussed something other than himself.

"I could imagine that it might be handy to have a physician in the family John." Daniel said, "With all those children you're speaking of."

John sniffed. Daniel smiled warmly at Hannah.

After dinner John took his own tour of the school grounds, while Daniel and Hannah stole a moment by the fire. Hannah seized her opportunity, "I didn't receive any letter from John while I was at Norm School or here. I'm afraid that he might be - "

Daniel waved a plump hand her direction, "I figured as much when I saw the surprise on your face. Hannah, I do want to ask you - "

She cut him off, "Daniel, I'm not going to accept any offer you make. I'm sorry."

"I'm surprised that you might turn down my offer so quickly."

Hannah curled her hands in her lap and peeked at his feature. Daniels calm expression hadn't change but he faced the fire instead of Hannah. "If it is about tuition fees for medical studies, I don't mind paying. I have substantial wealth behind me, that's why John is so interested if we should be suitable."

"You wouldn't mind a wife who was a physician? Could you cope with the shame of a having a working wife? One who works with the poor, the sick and the destitute?"

"On the contrary I believe that makes you a cut above, not below."

Hannah lowered her guard, "Daniel, I don't believe that you couldn't find a more suitable wife in Philadelphia."

"I suppose. I think John has more to do with that than me. He purposely steered me here to you. He does care about you."

"I think he cares about your money Daniel." Hannah clasped a hand to her mouth as the words escaped.

Daniel laughed, "No doubt, but who doesn't."

A deep sadness swept into Hannah. He will make some woman very happy one day.

"If it is about love Hannah, I've been told, that love can grow where you least expect it."

An image of ice blue eyes penetrated her mind, "Maybe."

"Maybe it already has."

Hannah couldn't respond. Daniel stood beside her and took her hand in his.

"I thank you for your hospitality and wish you well Miss Hannah Evans." He chastely kissed the back of her hand and released her. Daniel shuffled in his pockets and fished out a business card. Handing it to Hannah he added, "You know where you can reach me if you need to."

She pocketed his card and walked towards the door as John entered, "Dearest brother, Daniel and I have -"

"Hannah and I have come to an agreement John, we will remain fast friends for now." Daniel took John by the shoulders. "Now, back to Town, I'd like to visit this Tavern before the night is too old."

John grimaced. "Farewell for now, Hannah."

Hannah resisted clicking her tongue, "Give my regards to Margaret, I do miss her."

John stepped closer, his hand shot forward before he thought better of it and withdrew, "You can come back with me to Philadelphia tomorrow, Hannah."

Hannah shook her head, not trusting her voice to say the polite words her heart wanted to scream. Both men stole away and Hannah closed the door returning to the fire. Poor Daniel.

Hannah had gotten lost in lesson plans and reading when she heard heavy hooves clipping up her gravel drive. She opened the door to find Nicholas astride Ranger. She could smell the whiskey from the doorway. Despite his current state, Hannah marvelled at how steadily Nicholas climbed down from the saddle.

Nicholas sighed. For a long moment he regaled the image of Hannah standing at the door, the black night accentuating the soft fire glow of the Lodge like a beacon. If he let himself, he could imagine that he wasn't skull thumping drunk and she waited to greet him as he returned home. She was waiting to take him into her arms, into their marriage bed and into her heart.

You've gone and done it. Fallen in love with an impossible, vanilla scented, angel who will reject you forever. The words sounded strange inside his alcohol riddled brain. Nicholas couldn't let this homecoming vision vanish and instead of climbing back onto Ranger like he should, he walked towards Hannah. Every step he took, his vision solidified, Hannah was welcoming him home, she'd forgiven him for being a twit and she would let him take care of her.

A foot away, he stopped. What did you have to say to her? Damn it. He snatched Hannah around the waist, liftering her off her toes and into his arms. She didn't resist, the warm supple feel of her breasts swelling against his chest, her lithe frame curving to fit his inflexible power. He sunk his lips to hers, closed for the barest of moments before she opened to his urgent blistering mouth. The taste of Hannah mixed with the sweet sting of whiskey only added to fuel to his fire. He ran his hands down her back to her buttocks and surged her backwards. With her back pinned against the Lodge, Nicholas let his desire guide his hips to delve into the liquid centre of Hannah, flaying his skin and swelling to bursting point. He ground his hard flesh forward, the burn seeking wet nourishment that only Hannah could provide. Before his muddled brain convinced him he should take her there and then he released her, "Have you got a husband yet?"

For a moment Nicholas thought Hannah had come to her senses as her hand ran over his shoulder. Instead, a loud crack landed across his cheek. The whiskey dimmed the sting of the reprimand. Before Nicholas could say another word, Hannah fled inside and slammed the door.

The early morning sun ached behind Nicholas' eyes and his head thumped with each footfall Ranger made. He had washed early and the icy water had brought him to his senses. The horse auction was today and there was nowhere to hide. The Family, Hannah and even his cousin and new bride-to-be would be there. Last night the Families voted Suzanna Treschells, direct cousin to Feronica and Richard, as most suitable to be his wife. It would not do. Suzanna loved James Dammier. It was a travesty and he couldn't go through with it. Suzanna wasn't unpleasant by any means, she just wasn't Hannah, he thought. That moment of realisation occurred last night at a round table discussion of pale faced Frey's who had voted his future. Hannah was his woman despite what she might think, and thanks to a bottle of whiskey, Nicholas's attempt to make Hannah an honest offer didn't go to plan. His grandmother Eva Hoffman had made her own choices and thank God she had. To Hell with William Frey and his empire!

Nicholas trotted Ranger into town, while practising an apology and preparing arguments against Hannah's notions of independence. Surely Smith and Musgrave's appearance in town would spur her on. She had the chance to choose freely before being dragged back to Philadelphia on John's terms.

Franklins Shallows teemed with life. Every man woman and child in the neighbouring three counties had arrived to Franklins Shallows for the day's events. Entering the Sherriff's building, he noticed Christian, Leonard and their younger brother Jacob preening their uniforms. Even their moustaches looked uncharacteristically neat. "Do I need to deputise anyone today?"

"Only Jacob, did you have a chance to read over my notes?"

"Yes Christian I did, you did a good job." Nicholas didn't lie, the notes had been legible and his questioning thorough. "Ruffled and few feathers by the sounds of it."

"The Krouse brothers mainly."

"I noticed that." Nicholas dusted a few specks from his coat before putting it on. "I'll catch up with them today." Both Krouse brothers were ruthless socialites. Both of their versions appeared vague and out of sequence with the nights events.

"It's not every day that you question people over a murder in Franklins Shallows is it?"

"True." Nicholas said and thought back to the last murder. Betty Jo Stephenson shot her husband David. The drunk had beaten her every day of their married life and after the last flogging she emptied his shot gun into his chest. Rather than facing the noose, she got life in Lancaster Prison. "I'll come up and do a patrol with you when it starts, see that no-one misbehaves."

"There's no need, if you are not up to it."

His stitches had begun to itch, a good sign of healing without infection. "I'll be up to it." After a quick lunch provided by Mrs

Graff from the cafe, Christian and Nicholas rode North, out of town to the stock yards. They passed numerous people heading in the same direction and Nicholas began eying the men sizing them up for signs of trouble. He had perfected the art of judging a man on whether there would be trouble by their gait, eyes and attitude. These men he would watch, steadily dogging their every move, until they retired for the night. Unless of course they decided to put on a turn. Nicholas's shoulder blades itched.

Hannah wandered around the stock yards vaguely taking in the sights of the horses auction. People teemed the streets in the best attire, ladies with bonnets and ribbons, petticoats and parasols. The men wore top hats and shiny boots, preened and pressed like prize winning roosters. The boarding house kids had finished their reading in record time and she promised they could attend the auction as a reward. Mild curiosity drew her to attend with them. That's what she told herself anyway. Susie had laid out Hannah's light blue riding jacket and matching blue split skirts. Not that Hannah would be riding anything today, but she looked the part any way.

The heat of the day had passed and the townsfolk bore it stoically. A cool breeze filtered from the north to cool the tempers of lost bids and drunken cowboys. Her eyes searched of their own accord for a dark and solid silhouette. So many visitors had Hannah catching black coats and Stetsons at each turn. She hoped her slap had brought him to his senses. What about my senses she thought as Hannah traced her bottom lip. Whiskey fuelled passion sent shivers down behind her ears to the hollow in her neck. She cleared her thoughts and stopped by a stock yard where two stallions paced gracefully through the sawdust.

"Fancy a ride." The voice slithered down her spine as William Frey came into view, just inside the fence posts and carrying a whip. He leaned one arm casually through the steel bars and stared. In tan coloured riding pants and jacket with shiny black boots turned down at the knee, he was a handsome sight, to anyone but Hannah. She could feel his eyes removing her clothing piece by piece in his mind. She thought back to

Nicholas last night, dark blue crescents in the moon light, piercing her soul. Hannah shook her head.

"No thank you Mr Frey." She said, as William sauntered closer.

He leaned both arms crossways on the bars in front and lifted one leg to rest his boot. With the slightest twist of his hips, he pressed his groin towards her. She stepped back. "Do you like what you see, Ms Evans?" He nodded his head backwards towards the horses. Hannah looked at the animals to stop her cheeks from colouring. The roan coloured stallion danced nervously around the paddock, sniffing in numerous directions. The second Stallion a wild black coloured animal paced aggressively from end to end, snorting wildly at the passing people who came too close to the fence. "They can smell a mare in heat you see." Williams smiled slowly resting his chin on his arms. "Both are mine, I am selling them to stud. I have bred them from my own stock and select a few choice mares for breeding. The best foals are from the purest blood lines, you understand. Every now and then, I'll stud them out to the towns' people, who… need my services."

Hannah squeezed her fists together and took a deep breath. How could I have compared Nick to this man!

He leaned in closer and whispered, "If you ask me, the stallions prefer the foreign mares produced for studding." Again he smiled. She couldn't think of a witty retort quick enough. Her anger boiled over and just as she opened her mouth to lash out at him she heard that deep silky voice of Nicholas behind her. She turned and saw him riding Ranger cautiously through the crowd. He hadn't been speaking to her, just some other folk who had stopped to ask his condition. Hannah couldn't help but notice the towns' young women bidding Nicholas hello and giggling when he responded.

Hannah faced William Frey. "I am well aware of your - breeding policy William Frey, but I would choose the black stallion over any horse in any stable, any day of the week. Do you understand?" Hannah resisted the urge to wag a finger since she had used her Teachers voice to scold him.

Hannah swallowed hard when William's face fell. Now you've done it, she thought. He calmly stood up, straight backed and faced her squarely. His sickly charm evaporated and instead he wore a grin of surprise. “I see Ms Evans, I didn’t know.” His words missing the usual coat of honey, “But…. I’d warn you about animals who have been broken, broken of heart I mean, they do not trust so easily again.”

Hannah relaxed her shoulders, what did he mean? Beth? “Then it just needs time to heal.” Hannah said, suddenly confused. Nicholas and Ranger slowly plodded her direction, but he still hadn’t noticed Hannah. Because you want him, you want his affection and his respect, that’s why. Hannah’s eyes began to moisten and she blinked furiously to hold the tears back.

“So be it Ms Evans. I have some work to undo, if you’ll excuse me.”

“Good day Mr Frey.” She couldn’t face Nicholas. Her heart yearned to fulfil promises she couldn’t keep. Hannah spun around and quickened her pace, running full tilt into Feronica Frey.

“Hello, Hannah.”

“I’m so sorry,” Hannah managed to grab hold of Feronica’s elbow and stopped them both going over in the mud.

“That’s fine, Hannah, I’m glad you’re okay.” Feronica readjusted her bronze silk skirts with two calm flicks of her slender graceful hands. Hannah tugged at her skirts frantically.

“I should be more careful,…”

“You’re flight down the river is quite a story. I’m glad the Sherriff found you. I hope you’re feeling better.”

Feronica called him the Sherriff not Nicholas, Hannah noted, “I am, thank you.”

“I am sorry to hear about Ms Baker, I didn’t get a chance to talk to you at her funeral and share my condolences.”

“It had been a long day, I understand.”

“Yes, I imagine. I cannot imagine being there when - well you know.” Feronica said, her golden eyes flying wide at the hint of death.

“Yes, it was unpleasant.” Hannah glanced over her shoulders anticipating a black horse and its rider strolling down the street. Will I have to hitch up my skirts and dash through the crowd? Feronica looped her arm through Hannah’s and they walked together.

"Are you alright, dear?"

"Yes, I will be in a moment."

"Well we'll just walk a bit until you are," She turned those perfect hazel eyes in Hannah's direction and she saw compassion and something else. Is it loneliness? Hannah thought.

They took a few measured paces down one auction alley and turned left into another.

"As I was saying I am sorry about Ms Baker." Feronica's reassuring hand on her arm calmed Hannah down.

"Yes, it is an awful thing to happen." Hannah's glanced up from the mud to see where they were going.

"I'm sure the Sherriff will find the culprit soon enough. Ms Baker, oh I don't want to talk ill of the deceased, but she was not well liked in town."

"So I have observed. People gossip I suppose and soon or later, as you said, the culprit will be found."

"Gossip, yes I have heard all manner of rumours. A jilted lover, gambling debts, a revengeful servant - " Hannah's ears pricked up at the thought of the towns' gossip pointing at Susie. Hannah forced a polite non-committal smile onto her lips.

"I'm not certain about the others, but Susie could not possibly - "

"Oh I know… rumours dear. And those bones at the construction site! My goodness the whole town is talking." Several men they passed dip their hats at Feronica in acknowledgement. Other women offered passing compliments, "lovely dress", "fine day" and "good to see you". Hannah took them in one by one. The women complimented Feronica honestly, yes she wore a lovely dress, it is nice weather. But in their eyes they laughed at her. They knew. They all knew her husband's true nature and what embarrassment it caused her. Hannah peeked sideways at Feronica. Hannah realised that the Frey Empress must have no friends, female friends she could trust with her husband around. For all her wealth, and power, Feronica was isolated and alone. "I must admit it has stirred a lot of interest in town." Feronica continued.

"I have kept myself away from it as much as I can."

"Yes, I understand it must have been traumatic for you. If you need to talk to someone about it - "

"Well Ms Baker, didn't speak to me about lovers or gambling debts, she only spoke about teaching and the children."

"Of course she did." Feronica still held onto Hannah's arm and a smile beamed across her dainty face. "Did she discuss my children at all with you?"

"She discussed all the "Families" children. In depth." Guilt tripped up Hannah's words, she couldn't recall one item of interest about Feronica's children to offer any compliments. Recalling the Krouse Brothers devious conversation about their children's needs, nervously Hannah kept talking, "Feronica I intend on treating the children all equally…." Feronica had a right to know what the new school term would bring.

"I see, of course you will." They had stopped outside a large white tent charmingly pitched over a patch of flattened green grass. White wooden slates had been erected enabling the seated to have a good view of the auction proceedings. Chairs and tables had also been set up and servants of all colours and creeds began serving refreshments. Hannah eyed many of the Treschells and Krouse wives perched comfortably under the tent. A young blonde woman wandered through the crowd, smiling awkwardly when approached, her gaze scanning the crowd surrounding the tent. She spied Feronica and Hannah standing together and nodded politely,

"Poor Suzanna, my cousin." Feronica answered the unasked question.

Hannah wanted to answer "Aren't they all" but kept her comments to herself. Instead she excused herself, "It was a pleasure talking to you again Feronica,"

"It was a pleasure talking to you, if you do feel the need to talk to someone or take solace to discuss anything, -" She continued.

"Thank you for your offer." Hannah could hear the concern in her voice. Hannah tried to visualise a splendid creature like Fernoica Frey in the Lodges' kitchen sipping tea out of chipped cups and stifled a laugh. Hannah took a left turn and then a right turn trying to find Main Street without success.

"Ms Evans?" Hannah heard a masculine voice call and she searched the long face for recognition. The man's green eyes crinkled at the corners like he waited for the punchline of an untold joke. Dusty brown hair poked out from underneath a tight brown Stetson. "James, Ms Evans, James Dammier? We met at the Freys."

"The Mayor's son, I apologise Mr Dammier."

Hannah recalled her one time dance partner who now looked far more handsome in rugged shirt and breeches than he had done in his finer at the party. In his thirties and still unmarried, Ms Baker had commented that James had fallen in love with Suzanna Treschells, yet the family had discouraged the match. Hannah would bet it was Dammier that Suzanna's eyes had been searching for.

"Are you alright Ms Evans?"

"Yes, I am thank you. I apologise again."

"No need Ms Evans, it's not every day a fine young lady, tries to bowl a man over. I'm flattered, literally."

A laugh escaped Hannah lips, "I wasn't watching where I was going," she said. Hannah's shoulders relaxed and he hooked an arm through hers.

"Never mind Ms Evans, I will simply accompany you to prevent further mishaps."

"Thank you for your offer Mr Dammier, but I am headed home, if you don't mind pointing me in the direction of Main, I'll be on my way."

"My pleasure" James turned about-face and strolled casually with Hannah, chatting about cattle and horses until they reached Main. There Hannah recognised the boarding house and the Sherriff's office where Nicholas stood scanning the crowd. Hannah froze. The tiniest movement on Nicholas part, made Hannah's stomach lurch. Clad in head to toe black, with that damn silver star shining on his chest, the Sherriff crossed the street.

"Another time then Ms Evans?" James farewelled, his green eyes boring a hole in Nicholas, "I believe congratulations are in order Sherriff." James grimaced and a nerve twitched in his jaw.

"Now listen, here James – I have no -"

"Congratulations?" Hannah interrupted.

"Hannah - " Nicholas voice was heavy and thick with dread.

James talked over Nicholas, “Yes .Congratulations on your upcoming nuptials to Suzanna Treschells. May you and your *Family* be very happy,” James put his hat back on.

“Congratulations.” Hannah choked on her words. The blonde under the tent had been searching for Nicholas, not Dammier. A spike of jealousy rose so fast in Hannah that she stumbled her words, “Indeed. Good day Mr Dammier. Sherriff.” She stormed off and passed William Frey crossing the road. Hannah wanted to glare at him but she couldn’t. The tears had already started to fall.

Chapter 11

Hannah's face felt red and puffy when she finally returned to the Lodge to find a messily scrawled note in either Susie or Rosa's writing. It simply said, "At Carls". Hannah's tears cleared at the thought of Susie finding companionship and love, someone worthy who would treat her well. Rosa needed a father, and whoever he was, he was nowhere to be found. And what do you deserve Hannah? She stared at the back field, chickens pecking freely in grass, a southerly breeze buffering the tops of sprouting thistles. What had just happened?

Hannah had accused Nicholas of being just like his Cousin William, seeking only to covert woman for pleasure, until his interest dried up and he moved on. Nicholas hadn't refused her accusation, he hadn't defended his actions. Now he was engaged to Suzanna Treschells? Was this William's doing or was Nicholas always intended for Suzanna. No – James Dammier was her love.

Had Nicholas agreed to this so he could hurt Hannah, that she wasn't worthy? Every time he opened his mouth, Nicholas seemed to make known, his resentment and derision at her chosen occupation.

And yet the man had the audacity to turn up last night with a skin full of whiskey and ask her if she had a husband. Then he'd kissed her, right down to her soul, awaking those hidden places that sheltered her desire, leaving her vulnerable to whatever whim took his fancy.

An onerous throbbing erupted in her chest. She didn't want a man, a lover, or a husband and here she was pining over a man who wrought sultry yearning from her as easy as water from rain. He tormented her with her own weakness, offering no promises and demanding all.

I need to take solace; Hannah thought before snatching up Ms Bakers Bible and stalking out into the meadow. She found a wide patch of soft emerald that offered a clear view to Old Thom. The ground sloped gently towards Franklins Shallows, but Hannah didn't dare move closer.

First Hannah prayed for forgiveness for Ms Bakers sins whatever they may be and to accept her spirit into His eternal love. She assumed Ms Baker had stout religious beliefs since she owned such an exceptional Bible. Next she prayed for forgiveness for her own sins. The face of Nicholas popped up into her thoughts. Finally she opened her eyes and opened the leather bound book. She flicked past Ms Bakers artfully detailed Frey Family Tree and turned to Corinthians to read His words on temptation.

By the time she had finished, Hannah slunk down the earth, letting the afternoon sun warm her skin and blind her eyes. As the sky changed from white swept blue to deep orange, Hannah sat up. She wanted to read the Lord's prayer before she left. With the beauty of the setting sun and fields pregnant with bountiful crops her spirit eased.

As she grasped the pages, her fingers identified a thickness in the chapter. She found Matthew 6:9 together with a piece of parchment folded twice.

She opened the fold and recognised Ms Baker's handwriting immediately;

"....believe that due to my contribution to your Family and the information that I bear with such guilt every day for my assistance in these events, entitles myself to continued monetary compensation. I endeavour to forward this onwards to a suitable charity so that my soul will be absolved and my hands washed clean of the blood you have covered them with. I will forward you details of...."

The writing had been edited and some words had been scratched out and re-written. It had been a draft note of some kind. Hannah frantically searched the Bible for any other scrap of paper or note, but found none. Praying for Ms Bakers sins had proved necessary.

Hannah knew she had to show Nicholas. Without further hesitation Hannah seized the Bible and dashed back to the Lodge.

As Hannah closed in, her eyes recognised the low orange glow emitted from the Lodge was not the sunset. A thin trail of black smoke stretched to the sky.

Hannah's heart leapt into her throat and tossing the book down, she bounded to reach the Lodge. Think, Hannah! Desperately grasping at thoughts, ideas, of what she needed to do, proved impossible. Hannah ran around the front door, hands empty and jaw gaping, when she heard a noise from inside.

"Susie! Rosa!"

Hannah covered her mouth with the blue sleeve of her riding jacket and opened the door. Billows of black smoke engulfed her. The outline of a person emerged from inside, a brown leather jacket pulled down low and carrying a cudgel in their meaty hand. Spots parqueted Hannah's vision and suddenly the ground struck her back. The boot on her left foot was being tugged. But why take my boots? Hannah thought, before the sickening realisation occurred, as her back scraped the threshold to the Lodge.

Nicholas had to remind James that he hadn't agreed to the match and gave his word three times that he wouldn't marry Suzanna, before the man rolled his shirt sleeves down. James held his temper in check long enough to listen as William offered a reprieve.

"For now. I will ask the Family to reconsider," William said.

"Fine." Dammier answered, shaking hands before taking his leave.

"So you'll reconsider Dammier's request?" Nicholas said biting off each word.

"I don't want you two duking it out in the middle of Main."

Nicholas pointed his finger to the chest of William "I reluctantly agreed to the match with Beth and look what happened there. I didn't fight you, I didn't even fight for her when she chose Benjamin. But this time, I don't care what you say or who you are, I will not marry a Treschells, a Krouse or any other god damn Frey. Do you understand?"

"I do cousin, it's not because of Dammier that I'm reconsidering it." Williams' eyes sought the ground.

Nicholas hands itched to punch that graceful moustache off Will's sly grin, but his fury eased. "You have to know I would never go through with it."

"I gathered as much when you stormed off, skinful of whiskey. Where did you go afterwards?"

The vision of Hannah on the stoop of the Lodge returned, "I went home."

Nicholas patrolled the rest of the Auctions' events by himself, returned to his office when his stitches finally got the better of him. He needed to hand over to Christian, Jacob and Leonard but the rooms and cells were empty. Suddenly he heard a shout from the Horses Gait Inn. Two young men had been thrown out, yelling and cursing at the barkeep. Furious, they tossed their glasses causing the front window to smash. Nicholas didn't hesitate and grabbed both by the scruffs of their necks. Both boys spun around, Nicholas's injury limited his ability to duck. One fist collected Nicholas' chin and despite his brain jarring in his skull, Nicholas managed to twist away from the second punch aimed at his stomach. The blow glanced of his right ribs. Where are my damn deputies when I need them? Nicholas thought as Joseph the burly barkeep came to his aid. One man went down, drubbed by Joseph's hammer blow. Nicholas skirted the dirt around the other boy, who took a deep breath and launched his attack. Haymakers flew at Nicholas's head and stomach, none connecting. Nicholas shifted his weight and landed one sweet punch on the man's jaw toppling him backwards.

"It's never fair fighting a drunk is it Sherriff?" Joseph commented.

"No but sometimes it's fun,"

A few sober-ish locals helped Nicholas drag the two men to the cells commenting as they lifted, "Damn York County drunks." Nicholas smiled and bit his tongue. The same would happen in York, the locals blaming Lancaster County folks instead. As he turned the key, Christian and Leonard entered astonished.

"We sent Jacob home for the night! Do we need to call him back?"

"No I don't think so. Drunk and Disorderly and Wilful damage for smashing the Tavern windows." Leonard's mouth turned down. "Never mind, the nights not over yet." Nicholas clapped both boys on the shoulder when Joseph thundered into the room.

"Fire! At the School!" The barman shouted.

Nicholas sprang into action and launched onto Ranger, he shouted orders at Christian and Leonard to round up all the able bodied men to help as half the whole town poured out of the Inn and rushed to the top of Main.

Thick black smoke filled the horizon and Nicholas kicked Ranger in the ribs. Even from this distance, he could see the interior of the Lodge was well ablaze. Nicholas launched off Ranger and the intuitive stallion slowed his pace as his rider left the saddle. The smoke obscured his vision as the flames licked his face. A dark shape lay crumpled on the floor. His heart plummeted as he made out the feminine outline of Hannah. Nicholas dashed in and grappled with her limp body. His hands slipped from her ankle. The smoke forced his eyes closed, bringing a burn within his chest. Nicholas reached again this time coming up with Hannah. He dragged and pulled, scooping Hannah into his arms. Her head lolled heavily against his shoulder.

He withdrew from the furnace that had been Hannah's home and laid her on the soft grass. Brushing back the damp hair from Hannah's forehead, Nicholas noticed a cut originating from somewhere in her scalp. She has to be alright, he thought. I need her to be alright. I need her. Nicholas gently wiped soot from her porcelain skin.

"Hannah!" Nicholas laid an ear against her chest. The crackling of the fire and splitting of timbers made it hard to hear but between the creaking and breaking, the sound of Hannah's heart reached his ears. The townspeople rushed up the drive to the lodge, buckets in hand. Someone manned the pump and others formed a line, tossing bucket after bucket to satiate the flames. Leonard brought the Doctor, who hastened towards them, black bag in hand. Hannah stirred beneath him and Nicholas choked back smoke and tears of relief.

"Hannah, Thank god," Nicholas backed away allowing her more air.

Hannah's red-rimmed eyes opened and locked onto his. She lifted a shaking hand to his face and tenderly trailed her fingers down his cheek and across his jaw.

"You're hurt?"

Nicholas laughed out loud. He'd forgotten the fight. "Is that a thank you?"

Hannah laughed and brought forward a coughing fit that took long minutes to subside. Nicholas pulled her upright to a sitting position and she prayed her stomach contents remained where they were. "Yes thank you." She managed in a smoke coated cough. She leant forward and her whole body shook in Nicholas's arms. Hannah tried to gasp small breaths of air into her lungs. She had to ask, she couldn't bear the thought. "Susie? Rosie?" Nicholas cursed out load and turned to search the lodge. She grabbed his arm and stopped him. "Check. Carl?"

Nicholas shouted to his Deputy Leonard. Hannah prayed they were alright.

"What happened?" he asked.

"I don't know." Hannah's voice croaked as she talked and she rubbed her head. Something struck her. Hard. A person? Nicholas handed her a cup of water and she drank deep, the cool water soothing her throat.

"The Doctor is here, you'll be alright."

Hannah pieced together fuzzy memories trying to see through the fog. She remembered the field, the soft breeze tickling her nose as she read. The Bible. The note! "Nicholas in the back. Ms Baker's Bible. Please get to it. Before anyone else. Please."

Nicholas rose beside her and disappeared behind the inferno, the thick logs sizzling in the chilly night air.

"What happened here?" said Doctor Fitzgibbon. He examined her quickly and thoroughly. Her lungs would clear completely in a day or two, the bump on her head, although effective in knocking her unconscious, would subside in a few days. "First the river, now this, you're lucky to be alive, *again* Ms Evans. Don't you know water and fire make steam?" He smirked to himself and then added, "I suggest bed rest and a cold compress on that wound. It doesn't need stitches but I can assist with pain relief if you need it?"

Hannah shook her head gently.

"You know all about a concussion so you need to be watched carefully, day and night for the next few days to see that you improve." The Doctor addressed Nicholas who had returned to Hannah's side, coat bundled under one arm. "Sherriff, she needs to be watched, to see that she doesn't start vomiting, dizzy spells, headache returning."

Nicholas nodded.

Hannah watched the copper flames conquer all her possessions. Mine, Ms Bakers, Susies, Rosas. Mamma's. Gran. Her eyes stung as the tears fell onto her soot covered cheeks. The townspeople tried in vain. Hannah had seen fires take over whole apartment blocks in Philly, one room after another. Hannah scrubbed at her cheeks and glanced to the darkness above, bright embers danced across the star studded sky. Everything gone.

Nicholas deposited his coat next to Hannah and leant his aid to fighting the fire. Carefully Hannah reached out and felt the think mass of Ms Bakers Bible. Unexpectedly a warm blanket dropped over her shoulders. Startled Hannah turned to see Susie and Rosa and the tears began again. She hugged them tight, Susie threw an arm around her shoulders and Rosa sat in her lap. Together they whispered words of comfort to each other, the blanket enveloping them all. After a while, Nicholas called the townspeople to a halt, the Lodge slumped into a charred wet heap, the stone fireplace all that remained upright. The fire had kept Hannah warm, while she rested on the ground and now the frosty darkness invaded the blanket and scarred her bones. One event melted into the next in Hannah's mind. Someone shouted for free drinks at the Tavern and most of the townspeople left. The Doctor gave Hannah one more check over. Carl had brought Smoke set in the trap and Ranger whickered and scratched the ground wanting to be clear the smell of the fire.

A thick black haze swirled around Hannah, only dissipating when Nicholas reappeared. With shirt sleeves rolled up and the fabric damp across his formidable chest, Hannah wanted nothing more than to collapse into his arms. His eyes bore into her soul as if reading her mind and Hannah refused to turn away. Would

Suzanna now feel the heat of the gaze her offered Hannah? Hannah couldn't take her eyes off his brawny frame, dark damp curls pressed to his proud forehead, blue eyes like a fresh river stream, calm on the surface but turbulent currents shredding Hannah's convictions. Where did he get those bruises from, Hannah wondered. Without words Nicholas wrapped his arms behind Hannah's shoulders and pulled her against his chest. She threw her arms about his neck and let her ear rest against the firmness of his chest, his heart beat steady, calming, solid. He placed Hannah gently in the back of the trap, and Rosa and Susie snuggled in close which brought more tears. The traps wheels striking Old Thom's timbers roused Hannah to her senses. "Where are we going?"

Nicholas sat astride Ranger, "Somewhere I know you'll be safe."

Hannah could find any objections to voice so she settled into Rosa's sweet cuddles and let the swaying motion of the trap sooth her soul.

Nicholas refused to let Hannah walk and carried her into the upstairs bedroom she had occupied only a week before. She sat down on the edge of the bed and let Nicholas look her over again. Up until that moment Hannah had forgotten about the Bible and the note.

Carl brought them a bottle of whiskey and set down four glasses. Susie instinctively poured the drinks while Carl started the fire.

"I'm so sorry Susie, your things. Rosa's things - "

"It's fine Ms Hannah. I'm just glad you are okay. Where would we be if you weren't?" Susie threw Carl a dark look and handed Hannah a small glass of whiskey, and finally one to Nicholas. Hannah knocked the dark liquid back without thinking and the crude alcohol burned her tongue and set alight her insides. Susie ushered the men out of the room. "You need to get out of those clothes."

"But - "

"Everything else can wait until the morning."

Weariness swept over Hannah in a storm of emotions. Susie ran a warm wash cloth over Hannah's face and undid her hair. Then Susie rummaged around in the dressers removing a large white shirt from inside. In a flurry of pulling and tugging Susie had Hannah out of her smoke riddled clothes and into crisp white cotton. It reached down Hannah's arms past her wrists and down her thighs stopping just about her knees. Hannah crawled into the bed, the soft warm sheets smelling enticing like Nicholas. Hannah heard Susie stepped out before low whispers erupted in the hallway. The door creaked open and Nicholas walked in. Hannah sat up to watch him and delighted in the feeling of her naked legs sliding across his sheets and his shirt brushing across her breasts.

Nicholas pulled a chair from the corner of the room and stretched his legs around the upholstered back sitting down to face her. She had a fleeting memory of those thighs pressed against her own and a strange wildness began to stir deep within Hannah.

"Now tell me exactly what happened." Anger layered Nicholas voice.

Hannah straightened her back. Of course he had come to ask questions, like a good Sherriff should. Hannah tried to clear the fog the coated her mind, "I don't really remember," A hand went to her head.

"Tell me what you do remember?"

"I took Ms Bakers' Bible and went into the meadow."

"Why?"

Hannah looked out the window to the darkness beyond and didn't answer.

"When you first entered the Lodge, did you see anything unusual, hear anything. Any strange odours or - "

"No nothing."

"Go over what happened next."

When she spoke about finding the note, Nicholas riffled through the pages and pulled out the parchment. His ice blue eyes scanned over the words before returning to Hannah.

Hannah swallowed hard and let her thoughts drift, calling up vague images of returning to the door. "I went back to the Lodge and I saw the fire, at the front I heard a noise." Tingles of danger sped up her spine, goose bumps flourishing across her skin. "I thought, it might be Rosa and Susie trapped inside" Hannah heard a muffled gasp from the Hallway indicating Susie had decided to stay and eavesdrop.

Involuntarily Hannah's hand went up to her face, "I opened the door, there was a man, I think. A brown coat. He hit me and I went down." The memories resurfaced and she shivered involuntarily. "I thought he was taking my boots." Tears broke across her tired cheeks and Hannah sniffled into the blanket, "he dragged me inside. That's all I remember. I need water," Her heart pounded in her ears, the heat rising to her cheeks. Smoke, tears and whiskey choked her throat and Nicholas returned with a pitcher of water and a glass.

After Nicholas handed her water, he returned to the chair on the other side of the room. Hannah swallowed harshly, the empty space dominated the room. Hannah stared at his thick arms resting on the back of the chair and rubbed her shoulders. Beth had been faired hair, Suzanna also. Why suddenly now did she feel the need to compare herself to these two women had baffled Hannah.

"Anything else you noticed? Smell, sounds, anything unusual? And I mean even before this, the day of the auction. Any reason someone would hurt you? Any person you saw lurking around."

"No." Hannah answered before all the questions had finished running through her brain. Slowly a trickle of a thought surfaced.

"Anything unusual at all since you arrived in Franklins Shallows?"

"You mean before Ms Baker." Hannah bit back. She wanted his comfort not his questions. A flurry of tingles coursed through her skin. The school? Something about the underbrush at the school.

"Wait. After my first full day in Franklins Shallows I walked to the school to nosy around. I heard a twig snap. I thought it was an animal. There was no sound in the bushes. Not even a bird."

"Did you see anyone?" Tension rolled through his body like a thundercloud.

"No, I'm sorry, everything else happened and I forgot. I put it down to an animal."

Nicholas stormed from the room. Despite the fire, Nicholas he had taken all the heat with him, and Hannah let her tears fall onto his sheets.

Nicholas rode to the Lodge, telling Carl to keep watch till he returned. As he circled the smouldering building, he noticed that any horse tracks or boot prints would have been destroyed by the good Samaritan's of Franklins Shallows, who fought to save the building. His heart almost tore from his chest when he had seen the Lodge engulfed. The attack on Hannah had stirred a base male instinct of possession and protection. He would wreck revenge on whoever had laid a hand on Hannah.

Why even hurt Hannah? Because she caught the culprit in the act of burning down the Lodge, destroying whatever evidence Ms Baker held against them.

Nicholas contemplated the facts of his case. Ms Baker had been blackmailing a member of his Family. It had to be. The way Ms Baker had highlighted "Family" in her draft note. No one else's family was capitalised, except his. She had nominated a charity, but Nicholas doubted the words as soon as he read them. Hannah had already told him of Ms Baker's plans for a lavish European retirement. Then why kill Ms Baker before her departure? Surely that would attract unwanted attention? Perhaps it was an accident or a last spiteful attempt at revenge. The bottle had been a farewell present. Perhaps Ms Baker should have drunk it on her travels far from Franklins Shallows. The community didn't care about the teacher, no one would morn her passing if she died out of town. Ms Baker had been drunk that night, she chose to have one more night cap before bed. The more Nicholas thought about it, the more the truth hit home.

He scoured the fields in the darkness, letting the light fall across the uneven earth, finding the shallow boot prints of a man on the run. The trail lead to the rear of the school as described by Hannah and Nicholas drew his service pistol as he dismounted. How long had this man been hiding in wait, bidding his time until the right opportunity. Had the man seen Hannah storm off from outside the Sherriff's office today? The lantern brought some light and no comfort as Nicholas entered the woodland. The dark trunks of Hemlock, Oak and Hickory greeted him. He listened to the eerie night calls of the forest and cautiously continued. Scanning the darkness, he followed the trail letting the scuff marks, broken leaves and bruised moss lead him forward. After an hour of stopping and checking the trail, the scrub thinned and brought him out at the stock yards, north of the town. Any person could have returned to the festivities of the day, unnoticed. Frustration tore at Nicholas. The anger seethed through his veins as he returned to the ruins of the Lodge. Hannah had almost been stolen from him by fire. And what of James Dammier? Had Hannah moved her affections on? Did James peak her interest more than Nicholas? Had he once again been pushed aside for more appealing quarry? He let his selfish worries nag at him until he reached the Lodge.

Nicholas mounted Ranger and turned south. The blood on her hands, the skeleton's in the grave. Ms Baker had known who killed them. Maybe she stumbled across them, burying the bodies. The person would have been hidden from the road, but what about the Lodge?

Nicholas trotted Ranger over the field until the grave site came into view. Yes, in the dark with a single lantern, Ms Baker could have watched the whole grisly scene unfold. Why bury the bodies here, on the western flank of Franklins Shallows. All the Frey's lived across the river, was it as far as the offender dared to travel to bury his secret? No blood on the Frey side of town. Did he know that his secret was about to be unearthed by the building of the new bridge? Perhaps. Did the Krouse brothers have any say in where the bridge's foundations were to be constructed?

With no more leads to follow, Nicholas returned to his homestead. A single lamp still burned in the second storey window.

Chapter 12

Hannah awoke to the door sliding open. After Nicholas had left, images fluttered through her mind, and she forced her eyes to stay open, until she hadn't the strength. But the images kept coming. The lantern helped push the darkness away.

"Nick?" Hannah set upright, forgetting about the covers.

Nicholas crept into the room and loitered at the edge of the mattress, "Following Doctors orders." He said looking at his hands.

"Did you find anything?"

"Nothing much."

His lack of words told Hannah enough. Someone had tried to kill her. The same person, who had poisoned Ms Baker and slaughtered the two girls in the grave. Hannah shivered. Deep inside a ball of fear began to unravel. Seeking any distraction, Hannah focused on Nicholas's fresh bruises. She tugged on his arm forcing him to sit on the bed and gently ran her fingers over the blue and purple blemishes that marred his perfect face. Sparks of energy coursed through her fingertips, as they brushed over the day's growth covering his jaw.

"What happened to you?" His eyes shone like polished metal as he twisted his face out of her grip, "Fighting drunks". Nicholas walked back to his chair, on the far side of the room.

Nicholas couldn't stand much more of this. He'd hoped to find her slumbering safely and felt his self-control waiver now that Hannah looked so vulnerable and enticing. His eyes followed her every move, from the stretching of her slender limbs, to the way his shirt barely concealed her modesty. The anger welled inside him quenched only by the desire that threatened his control. He wanted to shred the shirt, take her there and then to the depths of passion he only dreamed they could share.

"It's nothing" he said, the silence adding to his thirst.

Hannah breathed deeply, the air around her charged with the scent of Nicholas

"Thank you,"

"I will find whoever - ."

"I know, but not now. I wanted to thank you for saving my life."

Nicholas stood behind the chair like one of Feronica's statues, the only clue Hannah saw lay in the sultry depths of his darkening eyes. A pleasing shiver ran down Hannah's spine. The fire cracked and sizzled as new timber ignited, the shadows of Hannah's night chased away by Nicholas's presence. I will travel this road with him, to Hell with where it ends.

"You're welcome," his hands tightened on the back of the chair.

"You really should let me look at those bruises?" Hannah rose slowly from the bed, letting the covers slide off her thighs. Nicholas watched her like a hawk watches a field mouse.

"Right now, you should be in bed – "

Hannah threw her gaze over her shoulder to the rumpled bed clothes "I suppose"

Nicholas knuckles went white and he thought the timber would snap.

"But I want to help you,"

"Help will not be the last thing that I want from you tonight." The firelight played havoc with her wild curls, glints of ruby and burnt copper flashing across her pearl skin, she smiled transforming Hannah into a bold untamed woman.

"What of Suzanna?" She said, trembling fingers caressed his bruises, dropping her eyes to Nicholas's lips.

"I don't want Suzanna." Nicholas hands snared her small waist and his mouth captured Hannah's. She almost broke away when his tongue feverishly sort hers. His possessive energy crashed over Hannah and she entwined her fingers in thick dark tendrils pulling Nicholas down, hungry, urgent, and intense. She let his demand lead her through the surmounting confusion of her arousal. The sweet whisky flavour of his breath mingled with the scent of fresh fire and Hannah couldn't help reflect on the

Doctor's words. Water and fire make steam, what does whiskey do to fire?

Nicholas released her.

"And what do you want Hannah?" His lips savoured her cheek, the corner of her mouth, tilting her head backwards to suckle at her throat.

"Nick,"

"Tell me Hannah. I won't warn you again and I won't stop, tell me what you want?" His lips found hers, tasting, the hot flavour of Hannah's desire, the vanilla overwhelming his senses.

Her lips opened for his immediately, inviting him in, letting him tease and entice her forward. Snared in the masculine wiles of Nicholas, so heady and delightful that Hannah barely broke away to answer him.

"Nick, I need you. I want you."

As the words crossed Hannah's lips, Nicholas captured them, drawing Hannah into his embrace. She ran her hands over his sculptured chest as he rained kisses down her neck, tilting backwards Hannah exposed the tender flesh for Nicholas to scald. Her shirt puckered and gaped as he drew circles on her thighs up to her waist, until the weight of her breasts filled his hands. Like the river flowing towards an unseen end, the lightest touch, sent of burst of energy through Hannah.

"Hannah, last night I'm sorry - " At his words, Hannah pressed against him, letting Nicholas feel the thin veil that separated them, he groaned at her bold movements, taking her mouth again. His masculinity shaped her flesh, demanding surrender, enticing slick heat between her thighs. Hannah broke away,

"So am I." Frantic fingers plucked at the buttons on his shirt, revealing the hard ridges of his body. Her hands caressed his bare chest, as sapphire crescents watched on. She smiled nervously, her desire suddenly stunted by her lack of knowledge. Hannah leaned forward, wanting the velvet pelt to brush against her naked flesh. Nicholas growled at the pleasure.

"I'm not marrying Suzanna."

The moisture evaporated from her throat, and Hannah stuttered, "Good." He answered with his mouth, his tongue teasing, tempting and pulling her closer to a waterfall of pleasure just beyond her reach. As his hands captured her swollen breasts, he ran the pad of his thumb over the centre in tight circles, snagging his white shirt and exposing the taunt nipple. The sensation sent a powerful wave of heat between Hannah's thighs, and she whimpered. Nicholas chuckled softly and sent kisses down her throat to seize her flesh in his mouth, pulling it hard against his tongue. Hannah gasped and leaned into his ministrations, clawing at his rippling back, for fear that she would succumb to the whirlpool he created. She called to him to take her there, take her where she had never been before. Everything around Hannah seemed foggy and distant except for Nicholas. A deep ache throbbed in her abdomen and as he thrust his knee between her thighs, she melted against the thick powerful muscles with a shudder that transferred to Nicholas.

Nicholas turned his mouth back to Hannah's savouring the passion she offered. Hannah sought his hot sensual tongue with her own and Nicholas carried her backwards to his bed. The mattress melded to Hannah's back, the last vestige of gentle, as Nicholas's power surged forward, his weight both reassuring and dangerous.

She arched her back when his teeth nipped at her lips, bared throat, and the soft curves of her breasts. "This is need, Hannah. My need, my desire for you. Only you."

Without reservations Hannah opened underneath him, her silky thighs gliding over the rough denim of his legs and she returned his kisses with matching fury. The air around Hannah became hard to breath. When Nicholas surged forward, she returned with equalling pressure, the slickness of her loins, melting Hannah from deep inside.

"And I you. Your need is echoed within me. I need you Nicholas. Only you can take this pain away." His male aroma flooded her senses, yet the ache in her abdomen remained.

"I don't want you to feel pain, my love, just pleasure."

Hannah removed his shirt, his rippled body shimmering in the firelight. The deep violet of his eyes held her heavy lidded gaze, his weight rested above her with the help of his elbows. She cradled into his chest and ran her fingers down his washboard stomach.

"Not pain, but sweet agony, here." Hannah ran her palm across the flat planes below her navel.

"Only I have the cure for that, honey." He whispered, kissing her jaw again, his solid muscles colliding with the hard peaked centre of her breasts. A strange urgency filled Hannah and she relished the calloused hand that slipped under her shirt, his touch only intensifying not quenching her fire. The feel of his skin on hers drove the needles of arousal into every nerve ending. Nicholas grasped one breast, and traced her nipple with his thumb, the rose pink tip already raised to its full height.

"Nick," Hannah exclaimed, when his teeth nipped and suckled at her breast.

Nicholas slipped a leg between hers and into that heat, he wanted to savour. The shuddering wonder that was Hannah erupted beneath him, her pewter eyes closing in pleasure, each gasp adding to his already hard and aching flesh. She rushed to meet him, grinding downward with her heat, the moist promise of what was to come.

Hannah sought the rigid vein of Nicholas, hoping the pressure would ease. Earlier, Hannah fought the intensity of Nicholas gasping for air in a tumultuous river of pleasure, now it seemed to Hannah that Nicholas was the air, the very essence she sought for her survival.

Nicholas peeled the shirt from her frame, and Hannah sought refuge in his pillows, each vulnerable move strumming chords in Nicholas' heart. Had any man ever glanced across the marvel he now witnessed? Never, or the man would never had let Hannah go. Slowly he drew her arms away and raked his eyes over her nakedness.

"You are beyond beautiful. Exquisite."

"I am?" Hannah scoffed, thinking about her red rimmed eyes, and smoke tangled hair.

"You are. And you taste – " He kissed and licked at the hollow in her neck, a nipple trapped between rolling thumb and forefinger. He cooled the tip with his tongue.

"Like fried chicken?" Hannah giggled nervously.

Nicholas drew all of her into his mouth and sucked, sending a whirlwind of shivers to her core.

"Like the sweetest thing I've ever tasted." His practised tongue flicked slowly against the tip. Nicholas's knee withdrew from between her thighs, replaced by his palm.

Nicholas teased the slick heat of Hannah, stroking her inner core. He wanted to be gentle, bring Hannah to him, hot and wet and begging for release. His need to be sheathed inside the sweet velvet he knew waited ascended all others and it took great strength to shelve his demands. Patience's brought the greatest rewards.

He slowed down his caress and let his lips caress her throat, the supple creaminess shivering under his lips.

"Please Nick." Hannah kissed the fine cords along his neck as she begged for release from Nicholas coaxing wave after wave, drawing it to the surface and letting it burst across her skin. With her senses filled with Nicholas, he captured her whimper with a soft kiss.

Hannah threw her arms around his neck and trailed his spine until she tripped over his beltline. Nicholas acted as if he'd read her thoughts and tugged on his belt, pulling it free from the loops. He thrust forward, letting his desire bear down to the ache that called him forward. To his pleasure Hannah gasped. A shudder spread through his body and his hands pulled her thighs up to his hips.

"The heat. Nick it's more than I can handle." She cried. Each time his mouth seized part of her, she felt in the midst of drowning and with each caress, scorched to the core. How could I live without this, with this taste of his desire? A cold emptiness stole over Hannah, causing goose bumps to pepper her skin. Hannah daringly pushed her hand forward until she felt his flesh straining against his pants. She had enough medical knowledge to know what went where, but a bolt of disbelief shocked her when she stroked the full length of his erection.

"Same for me honey."

Nicholas shucked his breaches and stalked his powerful body across her, giving Hannah a few stolen moments to appreciate the all-male sight of Nicholas. He came to rest beside her and once again teased the heat from within with his deft fingertips. Hannah approached an invisible precipice and she climbed higher with each expert stroke until Nicholas pressed against the very essence of her being. She knew there would be pain, there had to be and eagerly she wanted it to pass. Nicholas paused to capture her lips, his tongue probing inwards as he slowly sheathed himself deep inside Hannah, filling her, making her whole. Leisurely he withdrew,

"No!" Hannah cried out, the pain had passed and she pulled his bulk against her body.

His chuckles tickled her neck and he thrust forward sending a jolt of energy into Hannah's core, ripples of golden wonder spread through her veins. Stronger and faster Nicholas returned, driving Hannah higher to that unseen precipice, this time the delicious threshold felt tangible and within her grasp.

"Oh Nick, take me there."

"I will and back again, Hannah. This is where you belong."

Nicholas's thirst pushed him deeper and faster into the silky tightness of Hannah. Never before had Nicholas sunk so completely into a woman. Hannah's thighs around his hips, her fingers raking his skin, hot kisses clouding his mind until he didn't know where he ended and she started.

As Nicholas descended into Hannah, he made her climb skyward, her body shaking beneath his. Hannah gasped for air and only his name came out. The strength and hardness of Nicholas invaded, dominated and pleasured the soft woman she had become. He had broken her, remaking her to fit him, to be his woman, until the waves peaked. A white heat burst forth, fragmenting her soul, the shards settling around Hannah and her man. Hannah claimed Nicholas, calling his name into her heart as he spilled his hot seed inside.

The tension slaked off Nicholas in great rolls of shuddering muscles, eyes like a winter blizzard made Hannah tremble again and he seized her mouth. She savoured the salty kiss of their laboured breathing. He rolled onto his back and pulled her against his chest and Hannah threw an arm possessively across his bulk, nuzzling into his shoulder. Nicholas's heart thundered in her ears and she couldn't separate his frantic beats from those of her own.

I have to say something, Hannah thought, tell him how I feel. Tears spilled onto her cheeks. He stroked her soft curls as

Hannah listened to his heavy breathing slowing down. Hannah fell asleep, satisfied, content and completely utterly in love.

Nicholas stirred as the moon faded from the sky and Hannah dozed beside him. He climbed out of bed and trapped his head between his hands. Nicholas knew from the moment he laid hands on Hannah, he would take her. A twang of guilt stung his insides. This is what he wanted, what he had chased and yet the bitter pain of his selfishness stung sharp in his soul. Nicholas glanced over his shoulder at the slumbering beauty behind. The words "never again" took flight and disappeared from his mind. You will try to keep her, and she will not be held. Suddenly the air seemed thick with the injustice of loving a woman who didn't want to be loved. Nicholas rose from the bed and paced about the room as if his actions could undo that word from his mind. It didn't work and he couldn't leave. It was his bed, she slumbered in. He stoked the fire instead.

"Nick," Hannah murmured.

Would he ever tire of hearing her call his name in groggy satisfied tones "Here," he tried to clear the rough edge to his voice. Nicholas sat on the edge of the bed, letting the moon highlight her delicate features. "Are you alright?"

Hannah propped her head under one arm, "Wonderful." Suddenly she sat up, the blanket unceremoniously falling to her waist. The moon transformed her creamy complexion to heavenly white. As Hannah ran her fingers down his back, each tip struck a dainty furrow in this skin. "The fight?"

Nicholas surprised by how Hannah's simple movements had left him hard and wanting. "Not the fight," he kissed her fingers one by one, "You, my Sweet."

Colour blossomed in her cheeks and down her throat, "Oh, Nick I'm so sorry,"

Hannah's coy reaction had him on edge, wide eyes, the colour of slate in the moonlight, full lips parted and breasts bare. Like sunlight cuts through a misty morning, Hannah had dissolved his earlier admonishments and Nicholas clasped her into him, supple breasts soft against his chest, the nipples already hard. "On the contrary, I hope there are more."

Hannah sought out his hot tongue for her nourishment and pleasure. Her fingertips found another set of marks near Nicholas's hips, "I am sorry for those too."

"You can treat them in the morning." He mumbled trailing his kisses down her, neck and finally to the soft roundness he searched for. She cried out his name without shame as the waves crashed down, dragging her into the sensual whirlpool of Nicholas's carnal delights. He grasped her thighs and wrapped them around his hips, Hannah ventured forward seeking the fulfilment only his hardness could provide.

"Right now, you have need of a remedy more than me." He chuckled, fingers kneading the flesh at the top of her thighs.

Hannah gave a throaty laugh that sent shivers down Nicholas spine "You are both the source and the cure of the condition that tortures me."

Nicholas found the incline of her hips and lowered her silkiness over him, letting Hannah pace the entrapment. Nicholas raked his hands through her hair and down her back, brandishing kisses and nips across her breasts that taunted him. When Nicholas arched backwards lifting Hannah up, she cried out his name.

"Then you know how I feel." He said, his lips brushed against Hannah's tasting, sipping and savouring. She gasped as she began to climb again, but it was lost in Nicholas's hot kisses. Shivers broke out across her body when he rocked beneath her hips. Words formed and vanished, sound disappeared, breathing staggered. She heard herself panting. She wanted to scream, but a deep throaty groan escaped her lips instead. She sunk her fingers into his shoulders as Nicholas bit down on hers.

As Hannah quivered around him, Nicholas couldn't restrain himself any longer, silver threads of pleasure burst forth. Sweating, salty and satisfied he clasped Hannah against his chest and pulled her down to the covers.

"And I would have it no other way." He mumbled as sleep claimed them both.

Chapter 13

Nicholas spurred Ranger faster and faster up the gravel drive. What have I done? On a night where Hannah had lost everything, you took even more. Nicholas thought about his failure and his own selfish need to possess her. In his haste, he had left them both unprotected. He had looked upon Hannah's beautiful face that morning, sprawled over his chest, her hand resting peacefully on his arm. The sunlight reflected off the burnish tips of her lashes, and Nicholas left before he could see the regret and disgust in her eyes. He had saddled Ranger and worked himself and the horse into a sweat for over an hour. Memories of last night could not absolve his shame.

He pushed Ranger to jump the irrigation ditch and suddenly a stitch popped. He slowed the black horse down to a comfortable trot and turned onto Old Thom, heading straight for town. He only remembered today was Sunday when he noticed the public congregation outside the white brick church.

The heads of his cousins and extended family turned to size him up, as he intended on riding passed. Nicholas relented and hitched Ranger, searching for Doctor Fitzgibbon.

William Frey stood in his way. Hannah is right, I am not better than Will.

"Nick, glad you could make it today. How is that Ms Evans today?"

"Fine, I'm looking for the Doctor, have you seen him?"

"Something wrong, Nicholas," Feronica piped in. "Is Hannah okay? I heard she lost everything last night" Nicholas missed a step.

"Ah yes, she's fine,"

Nicholas looked at William who suddenly developed a large grin under his perfect moustache.

"Well tell her not to worry I have set about the crowd this morning for some donated goods. She will have almost everything back in no time." Feronica's face shined with pride. Nicholas cringed.

"Almost everything." William added.

Feronica tilted her head at her husband. "In any case, I'm sure our family can arrange some charitable financial donations from the business community to rebuild the Lodge. Maybe convince our Krouse cousins to build it at a discount." She prodded.

William actually grinned at his wife and Nicholas turned away. Blood dripped down his side. Over exertion, Nicholas thought and regretted it as visions of Hannah's body rippling underneath him popped into his mind. Through the crowd he spotted the Krouse brothers,

"You will be seeing me today, after Church, in my office. Understood?" Nicholas barked.

"Sure, Nick. If we have to."

Nicholas raised his eyebrows at John and Isaac Krouse and both brothers furtively nodded their balding heads. Nicholas left without saying another word. Finally he spotted the Doctor, and after a few curt words, Fitzgibbon agreed to cut out on the sermon and see to his injury.

"What on earth have you be doing Sherriff?"

Nicholas sat on the examination bench in the Doctors back room. "Ahh riding."

"I see, well, I hope your horse is in better condition than you."

Nicholas coughed into his fist.

The Doctor wiped away the blood and applied a bandage, "It's not so bad, no need for more stitches. I'll give them a few more days to heal."

Nicholas pulled on his shirt, whilst watching the Church congregation file out into the street. One of them was a murderer, a triple murderer.

"Well, how is she?"

"Who?"

"Ms Evans, Hannah? Do I need to make a house call this morning or is she feeling better?" When Nicholas didn't answer, the Doctor started to list of symptoms.

"Experiencing any pain?"

Definitely.

"Dizziness?"

Possibly at some point.

"Sleepiness?"

Yes.

"Any vomiting"

Maybe in the weeks to come.

Nicholas kept his thoughts to himself and answered, "No, I think she is mostly fine. She is in the main house, if you want to see her. Susie and Carl are there if you need help."

"And where will you be?"

"I'll be around." The walls at the surgery started pressing in and Nicholas escaped onto Main Street. He knew he was deliberately avoiding addressing the issue. Turning yellow wasn't in his nature and it sat uncomfortable in his stomach. He concentrated on his investigation to drive Hannah from his mind. Hannah needed time. She would listen to reason after he had time to consider her options, if his seed hadn't already started to blossom. He returned to town and waited for John and Isaac Krouse to appear. When they did, John reluctantly agreed to be questioned first and provided the same vague version of events.

Today Nicholas didn't have the patience, "Cut lying to me John."

"I swear Nick, I'm not lying."

Nicholas stood from his chair and circled behind the elder Krouse. "You're withholding information and I won't hesitate to lock you in the cells overnight until your memory is refreshed."

"You can't do that!"

"Want to wager on that?" Nicholas resumed his seat. "Out with it."

"I can't " John Krouse spluttered, his double chin wobbling.

"Yes you can, you've already started."

"But the Family - "

"I don't give a damn about the Family!" Nicholas slammed his fist onto the table. John's head tipped forward and he rubbed his hands quickly across his knees.

"Will you tell William?"

"I am only interested in the truth. The Family businesses are none of my concern."

John sighed, slender shoulders cowering over a port belly. "Isaac and I were talking to Dammier."

"The Mayor? What does he have to do with any other this?" Nicholas mind spun like a tumbleweed, the Mayor?

"No, no, James. James Dammier."

"James? What about?" Intrigued Nicholas relaxed his shoulders.

"A business opportunity, that's all." Krouse said leaning back his chubby arms resting across his chest.

"Go on."

John clicked his tongue, "You know James was refused Suzanna's hand, on the basis of *purity* and wealth?" Nicholas knew only too well. Hannah shimmered in his mind. Would Suzanna feel relieved when he rejected their union? "Well you know we Krouse's aren't at the top of the pecking order. Not above the Frey's or the Treschells. Dammier thought it was safe to come to us, this is before her hand was offered to you of course."

"What the hell are you talking about?"

John leaned forward and whispered, "Silver."

"Silver?"

"Yes, Silver." John Krouse looked around like a weasel about to chase a rabbit. "James has discovered silver on his land. The first sample is good, not good, great and that's just scratching the surface. He proposes to open a silver mine. He needs construction equipment and men to help him get it running. We were working out the details of a mutually beneficial deal. Enough profits to rival the Frey's and Treschells and for Dammier a chance to win Suzanna's hand. Well until you - "

"And that's all?"

"Well, a little more respect, a little more power and a lot more money."

How could Nicholas judge him when he had his cattle for the same reasons? "That doesn't explain your whereabouts for Saturday afternoon." Nicholas said.

"Oh yes it does. James asked us to do some surveying on his land, on Auction day when everyone else was occupied. Isacc and I went alone. Were out there till sunset, I'd swear it on a stack of bibles, Nick."

"Anyone who can verify this?"

"Ask James, but please do it quietly. None of us want Frey interference in this." Nicholas nodded. William would find some way to earn coin from their enterprise to line his pocket.

It took Nicholas over an hour to locate James Dammier, bare backed, shovel in hand pulling samples from his land. Dammier reluctant to talk at first, eventually confirming the Krouse brother's version. Nicholas turned to leave when Dammier grabbed Rangers reins.

"And what are you going to do with this information now Sherriff? How will this affect you're decision on Suzanna's marriage?"

A bell tolled in Nicholas's head. "Silver or no silver Dammier, I'm voting for you, not me. I will not force a woman to marry -" Nicholas paused. A brief thought of Hannah heavy with his child appeared. "Suzanna should be able to make her own choice."

The bell kept ringing as Nicholas steered Ranger to the road. Instead of heading for home, Nicholas rode into town.

Hannah paced around Nicholas's sparse bedroom for the last time. This morning, Hannah had woken to bright sunshine and warm white linen, filled with the scent of her lover. Susie had found time to clean and dry Hannah's one set of clothes so Hannah had something to wear other than Nicholas's white shirts. Hannah could have worn them all day, like a second skin. But that had been this morning.

Carl told Hannah that Nicholas had ridden out on Ranger, early this morning and hadn't been seen since. Hannah glanced around the room again, noticed the empty tall boy, the almost bare cupboard. The crafted timber pieces were solid and well oiled, but vacant. Nicholas had left and without him, the room could be mistaken for any room in a hotel or saloon or worse, a boarding house.

Regret slapped Hannah sharply in the face. He had called you "My Dear" and "My Sweet" but not "My Love", she thought. Hannah resumed her pacing passed the curtain-less window, a tall thin stain of charcoal blotted the landscape to the North. Where could she go now that she had been cast aside? Hannah sat down on the coverlet, wiping her eyes. How foolish am I? Having her teacher's contract cancelled might be the least of her problems as a hand instinctively went to her abdomen. Return to Philadelphia, to John or Daniel Musgrave. No! Could I live with Nicholas's disdain, he already thinks I am a wedding bell chaser with wealth in my sights. He will grow to resent you, she thought.

She drove the rejection from her mind. She loved him but he didn't love her.

She glanced down at her ankle and touched the fingerprint bruise from the attacker glowing purple, raised and sore. It had to be a man, for that strength to bruise her skin. Maybe Nicholas continued his investigation, his rejection a figment of her imagination. Hannah absent-mindedly ran a finger along her bottom lip before exiting Nicholas's bedroom, determined to ask him what if anything he felt for her, the very next time she saw him.

That proved difficult by the time night fell, Hannah hadn't seen or heard from Nicholas. She'd spent the day wandering about his land taking in his two storey river stone manor house. She followed a stone path boarded by tiny white stones down to the back garden. Here a bench had been set under a large oak, offering a delightful spot to sit and watch the fields. Franklins Shallows wrapped its frothy length around the western edge, both decorating and sustaining Nicholas's property. Rosa joined Hannah under the oak, watching the butterflies drift past them to the flower and herb garden at the rear kitchen door. Odette hummed softly as Hannah watched workers in the distance fields cut and pack some produce or another.

The air was cool across her skin but the sun warmed her insides. Would it be so bad to stay here a little longer? If he doesn't love you? Hannah retired to his bed, the bitter edge of anxiety driving away the fresh strong scent of the man she loved.

The following day, with Nicholas still notable absent, Doctor Fitzgibbon came to visit.

"I'm off to visit the boarding house tomorrow, so I'll see you in a few days." Fitzgibbon prodded Hannah's scalp with his soft pudgy fingers paying no mind to his words. "I do a visit once a month."

"Doctor?" Hannah blushed.

"Some of those girls don't care to see me, but it benefits them more than me,"

Hannah froze.

"Yes everyone gets a check-up even the children," he continued.

Hannah admonished her impure thoughts. "I wouldn't mind coming along and assisting if you'll let me."

"Really, what would the Sherriff say?"

Hannah paused for a moment not wanting to think about the attack. Surely she'd be safe with the Doctor. Nicholas would see that. "I don't see why not. I have been teaching Jimmy and company to read in the afternoons, and you already know my experiences from Philly."

"I suppose you're right. I will share the fee in any case. I can't have you doing all this work without recompense. I might as well tell you and I don't want you to be cross with me."

"I won't be cross. No judgment here Doctor."

"I wrote to my friend at the AMA, for my own curiosity mainly, but he responded. It's not so much of a lost cause as first thought."

"Really?"

"Although the board changed the requirements in '52, you still qualify."

The Doctor handed Hannah a letter, the seal already broken, after scanning through the salutations and well wishes, Hannah read and re-read the last three paragraphs.

"I have to return to Philadelphia."

"For now, but I can more than fulfil the last requirements. That is, if you want to return to Franklins Shallows. This nasty business with Ms Baker and so on, I'd be surprised if you'd stick around." His moustache twitched like a laughing caterpillar.

Hannah swallowed hard. Even if someone hadn't tried to kill her, could she return to this town and face Nicholas disdain, a discarded plaything. If she wanted to become a Doctor, she'd have to take Fitzgibbons offer. Would she ever find another Doctor eager to apprentice a woman in medicine?

"I don't think I can afford the ticket." Hannah laughed.

"Let me worry about that for now."

Hannah smiled. How could she ever repay this man? By returning to take up his offer, easing the twilight years of his career and offering him the opportunity to mentor.

"Doctor, did you and your wife ever have children?"

Fitzgibbon dipped his head, "We did. Two daughters, both still born. Gerty passed ten, no fifteen years back. I've been keeping myself busy ever since."

Hannah thanked the Doctor and said her farewells from Nicholas's porch. Ideas flooded Hannah's mind like a swarm of locusts. She had to speak to Nicholas.

Nicholas spent the day in town, trying to fill in the blanks of his investigation. He still had the Widow Charles list of three missing girls and he needed to find them. Thoughts of Hannah had bombarded Nicholas throughout the morning, how to address the situation he had put them in. How to talk some sense into the woman who didn't want a husband but who would be needing one very soon.

He still had a triple murderer to catch and so far Christian, Leonard and even Jacob had managed to question the whole town. The key to link all three victims and Hannah together seemed to be as elusive and irritating as an itch between his shoulder blades. He should have this case closed, have the man caught and strung up, have Hannah safe and in his arms. At lunch he decided to walk down Main to clear his head.

As he passed the court house, Nicholas found the court registrar locking the front gates. The metaphorical itch exploded across Nicholas back as an idea suddenly bit him.

"Registrar Stephens," Nicholas called out.

"Sherriff, always pleasure. Those two from the other night got a pretty hefty fine. Foolish York County folk."

"So I hear. Stephens, have you got a moment?"

The middle aged man placed his brown bowler hat on top his balding crown, "Now Sherriff?"

"Now if you have the time."

Jack Stephens shuffled the keys in his pocket, and twitched his nose. "If I have to, but my wife Lillian has promised a special pork pie for my lunch, will this take long?"

"It might."

Stephens reopened the court and gestured Nicholas to follow inside. "What's this about then?"

"The bones at the construction site,"

"How am I supposed to help with bones?" The registrar rubbed the side of his nose with a crooked finger and stopped in his office. The shelves behind his hunched frame, dripped with paperwork and dust, causing Nicholas to supress a cough.

"Well I need to identify them and I have a list of names. I want to know if you can tell me where they are now?"

The elder man sighed, "Okay, go ahead."

"First one is a Sarah Bolder."

"Bolder?"

"Yes and Mary Thistleton?" The Registrar scratched his nose again.

"Thistleton? None of those names are remarkable. Bolder. Perhaps. I may be wrong but I believe the Bolder's moved to Buck Town. You would have to check with the mail service. Bolder yes, Thomas Bolder. Thomas. I'm sorry Sherriff. You'll have to come with me." The Registrar stood from behind the large oak desk. He pulled the keys from his pocket and left the room, "Sherriff, this way."

"Where?" Nicholas hand ghosted his holster. The Registrar suddenly reminding Nicholas of a black rat snake, coiling inside a nest of leaves.

"I keep all my books in the Cellars. I'm nothing without my notes Sherriff."

Nicholas smirked and relaxed his hand, "Yes of course Registrar Stephens, so am I."

The registrar lead Nicholas to the rear of the sandstone structure, down a set of narrow timber stairs to a stark stonewalled cellar, the walls lined with bookcases. With his record books in front of him, the Registrar Stephens instantly turned to the correct page, and located the girls' names.

"Yes, Bolder, she married Thomas. Thomas had been in a rush to obtain the marriage licence as I recall. She delivered the baby on their farm and I remember the red headed little babe in her arms when she registered his birth. Boy. They moved to Buck Town, I'm certain of it, Sherriff. If I were a betting man, that is. Next name?"

"Mary Thistleton."

"Thistleton, yes that was a scandal. Moved to Elk County. Before they left, her family tried to tell me that Mary's soon-to-be-husband had died in the wars. Well, I can tell you that isn't reflected here." Stephens tapped his bent finger into the page.

"Really? Elk County."

"And the third is Harriet Swan."

"Swan." Stephens turned the pages in a flurry of parchment. "Another scandal, refused to divulge the babes father. Her widowed mother had family in Northumberland County, so I believe."

"Buck Town. Elk and Northumberland." Finally some solid leads.

"You will have to confirm it with the postal service, Sherriff."

"Thank you Stephens, go and enjoy your pork pie." Nicholas farewelled the Registrar and set off to the Post. He'd have to wire inquiries to the Sherriff's in those counties, asking for assistance. As the afternoon arrived, a set of steel eyes permeated his thoughts. He counted down the hours to darkness.

Chapter 14

As Odette, prepared juicy beef and potatoes, she retrieved a striped table cloth from one of the many kitchen drawers and handed it to Hannah. Without objection, Hannah set the table and called Susie and Rosa from the sitting room. Carl joined them as Odette served each one in turn. Perplexed at the extra plate, the large woman paused,

"I hope you don't mind, Odette but I thought we could all eat together." Hannah said, sighing into her stew.

"Thanks Ms Hannah but I will take my leave. My Jeremy will be coming in from the field and expect me to be there when he does."

"Next time then," Hannah said smiling as the dark skinned woman left.

Hannah spent the night reading to Carl, Susie and Rosa by the fire, each noise outside pausing her teachings. Her students said nothing and in the end, Hannah fell asleep surrounded by the smell of Nicholas, without ever setting eyes on the man.

Hannah woke early, Ranger and Nicholas absent from the homestead but not her thoughts. She dressed and waited for Carl to set Smoke into the trap before she met Doctor Fitzgibbon at his office. She had spied a light coloured mare hitched outside the Sherriff's office, Christian's mount but no Ranger. Where is he?

When Hannah arrived at the boarding house, several of the working girls had to be woken from their slumber. Some dripped down the stairs in satin dressing gowns, some wore plain woollen dresses, Jasmine wore a happy medium. Bright yellow satin dress with red flowers stitched along the collar and hem.

"We all heard about the fire and so we put this together kind of as a thank you for reading to the kids and on account of you lost all your shi-"

"Thank you Jasmine." Hannah interrupted as Jimmy handed her a small timber chest and then perched himself on the edge of a Chinese jacquard chaise.

"You're welcome."

Hannah opened the small box to find a madman's assortments of jewellery, perfume, and makeup. Tears welled behind Hannah's eyes. How long would it have taken to accumulate these trinkets and the kindness it took to give it away?

"You like it."

"I love it, thank you, all, but - ." Hannah pulled out a long string of blue gemstones with matching earrings.

"They never suited me," Blonde Pippa spoke up, "But they'll go nicely with your eyes."

Hannah considered refusing their gift, on the pure value of the items they gave her. Surely they had worked hard to earn these things. However, if she refused, they would take it as a slight against their kindness. "They are lovely. Thank you Pippa."

Hannah opened a scrap of folded parchment that rested in the chest.

"That's from me and Lance, Miss" Jimmy said.

Hannah unfolded the parchment and read aloud, "One free shooting lesson."

The Doves giggled and Jasmine clipped Jimmy over the ear.

"Thank you. I might take you up on that offer. Well the good Doctor is getting impatient."

Fitzgibbon had pulled out his medicine chest and set up some instruments on the entryway table. "Indeed. Ladies if you would care to join me."

"I'll just wash up," Hannah said and Jimmy pointed her to the rear where the laundry entered the alley behind. As Hannah washed her arms to the elbows a sound from behind made her turn. A broad shouldered man shuffled up the alley way to a stack of crates.

"Miss."

Hannah searched her memory for the slack jaw and club foot.

"How's them birds Ma'am?" He mumbled.

"Good." Hannah had graciously thanked Susie, Carl and Rosa for catching them yesterday and bringing them to Nicholas's barn. They were her only possessions.

Something about the man snagged in Hannah's memory, something important just out of reach. He sat on a stack of empty crates and lit a cheroot.

"Good day." Hannah said and returned inside the brothel. As she helped the doctor conducted his examinations, Hannah asked Jasmine about the man in the alleyway.

"That's Lance, you're new shooting coach!" She laughed.

"I don't mean to be rude but - ?"

"He used to work for the Krouse's before the accident. He caught a beam with his head instead of his hands. Ain't been the same since. We keep him on for security and he does work for Joseph at the Inn some times."

"I see." Hannah shook her head to clear her thoughts.

After lunch time Hannah and the Doctor had finished giving all occupants a clean bill of health. As Hannah stepped out onto Main, she spied a dark horse hitched at the front of the Sherriff's building. Worse, in the shadows of the porch a black vested figure stood, arms crossed over his broad chest. Was he searching for her attacker? Tiny tingles of fear threatened her composure and her ankle throbbed. A layer of fog cleared in Hannah's mind and she thought back to the fire, to the brown coat and to Lance at the Boarding House. Pieces of a puzzle fell into place, except her attacker hadn't walked with a limp. She'd been wrong not to mention the smallest details before, and yet she wanted nothing more than to avoid the man who had rejected her.

As her conviction began to wane, Nicholas turned and entered his office. A fiery heat surged through Hannah's veins and blossomed on her neck.

"Sherriff," He spun around so fast at the sound of her voice that Hannah jumped back in surprise. "I need to talk to you."

"I am just heading out." Nicholas said, he pocketed a telegram and grabbed his Stetson, pulling it down over his brow.

"I can go to Northumberland Nick?" Christian chimed in from the corner.

"No Christian - ." Nicholas said through gritted teeth.

"Don't worry Sherriff this won't take much of your time." Hannah strolled into his office leaving Nicholas no choice but to follow. As Nicholas entered, he closed the door, causing Hannah's belly to turn somersaults.

"I remembered something more about that night," colour blazoned across her features before she had time to add, "The night of the fire," Her shade of crimson matched the glowing warmth crawling up Nicholas's collar.

"Go on." He said, the chill in his voice, cutting through Hannah like an artic wind.

"I told you that the man who attacked me was wearing a large brown coat, and now, I remembered where I had seen one earlier. The day I bought my chickens I ran into Lance, the man - "

"Lance Horton, the Simpleton?"

"Yes him." Hannah looked at the stone floor, the wood panelled walls, covered in wanted posters. "But I don't' remember the man limping, like he does. But I thought you should now." Her voice trailed off in a weak whimper.

"I will follow it up, where did you last see him." He opened the door behind her.

"Just now, at the boarding house," Hannah's voice cracked. She swallowed hard against her constricted throat.

"What were you doing at the brothel?" His words liked loaded shot, gave Hannah reason to pause.

"What?"

"You heard me, what were you doing cavorting in the boarding house. I know you have been teaching their kids the basics, but to be seen in the middle of the street exiting the brothel. It was a shock when I saw Jasmine at the Lodge, but honestly do you think about how this looks."

Hannah eyes flew wide, "I was helping Doctor Fitzgibbon."

"This is exactly what I was talking about, this ends now. I forbid it." Nicholas looped his thumbs into his belt and broadened his chest.

A hysterical giggle burst out, "You forbid it? Who are you to forbid anything I do?"

"That brings me to my next point. We need to talk about your predicament." Nicholas's eyes glared at her, all sharp ice and empty blue.

"My possible predicament, you mean?" Hannah bit back. She should tell him there was no predicament, prevent his awful words from gaining flight, but uncertainty held her tongue. She folded her arms under her breasts instead.

"I'm serious."

"So am I. I've told you that I never intended - that I never would – to any man." Her words all jumbled with incomplete thoughts, "What happened was a mistake, granted." There that should ease his conscious! She thought. Once she got started it was hard to stop, "But don't you dare try and be honourable and wholesome now when your actions thus far have been deliberate and deceitful."

"Deceitful and deliberate? As I remember it was you that crawled in or more correctly, crawled out of my bed." He'd stalked forward, his lips thin and jaw tight.

"How dare you!"

"I saved your life, honey!" Nicholas reached up and trapped her chin in his hands, the pad of his thumb teasing down her bottom lip.

Hannah jerked her head back, the air suddenly hot in her lungs, "And when I was at my weakest," Hannah heard the lies form on her tongue. All the pain and rejection tumbled out into words she couldn't take back. "Well this spinster" Hannah pointed at to her chest, "Can do without your kind of company Sherriff!"

"Hannah -" She opened the door and dashed out to where Christian sat wide eyed and opened mouthed.

He grabbed at her elbow, stopping her dead. "You go home, straight home."

"You have no right."

Nicholas closed the distance, his face an inch from hers, chipped ice stabbing into her tearful eyes.

"In this I do, Hannah. You've forgotten that I'm the Sherriff and that night" His eyes softened only slightly, "Someone tried to kill you. If don't go home, where I can keep you safe, I'll have you in the lock up."

Hannah pulled back her elbow but he held fast. Her bottom lip wobbled and she squared her shoulders.

"You wouldn't dare?"

"Try me."

Nicholas watched her throat bob up and down as she swallowed hard, pert lips moulding into a delightful pout he wanted to seize. He released her elbow and she stepped back.

"Fine," She smothered her skirts and then with more control that Nicholas thought Hannah could muster, she dipped her head and farewelled Christian.

Without hesitation Hannah marched across Main Street to where Carl waited and climbed into the trap.

Nicholas sat poleaxed as to how this had gotten out of hand so suddenly. Last time he had been skull thumping drunk when he tried to talk sense into her and just now, he had tried to be clear, concise and stern. She wouldn't marry for wealth and yet she wouldn't marry whilst possibly carrying his child. Deliberate and deceitful she'd called him and she wasn't far wrong. "All I wanted to do was protect her." He murmured whilst pacing around his office. Protect her and cherish her. To love her and have Hannah love him in return. Nicholas faced his smirking Deputy, "Yes, something to say?"

"I can ride Northumberland way if you like, it'll be an adventure."

"No that won't be necessary," Nicholas touched the telegram in his top pocket. The postal service of Sunbury, Northumberland could not confirm Harriet Swan had moved or still lived in their county. Her family were recorded there, but no Harriett. The telegram went on to say the old Sherriff had been recently shot, and the replacement Sherriff had been curt, telling Nicholas if he wanted something done, he could ride out and do it himself. He had made plans to do just that until Hannah marched in. "Beside you might have to ride to Spring Creek." The telegram from Elk County had been just as vague, Mary Thistleton might be in Spring Creek, Elk County.

Christian broke the silence, "Good luck, Nick."

"Thanks Cousin." Nicholas answered flatly. Carl had smoke already plodding away to Old Thom. Nicholas spent the rest of the afternoon talking with Lance and all those at the Boarding House before he could effectively remove the man as a suspect. As the final hours of the day wound down, Nicholas realised he had a lot of repair to do. He tugged Rangers reins free from the hitching post and put his boot in the stirrup, glancing at the Doctors office. Somehow, he had to show Hannah how he felt and what she meant to him. Hannah had lost everything in the fire, her family's treasures and her own. What did Hannah treasure? Nicholas strolled over to the Doctors office after his best idea dawned.

"Sherriff, what can I do for you this afternoon?" Fitzgibbon said, leading Nicholas into his office. The smell of rubbing alcohol and a myriad of other chemicals and herbs assaulted Nicholas' nostrils. This is what Hannah wanted for herself?

"I'd like to set you straight about letting Hannah in that boarding house, but I've decided to keep it to myself."

The Doctor chuckled into his chins, "Keep it yourself, hey? So I see, well it never bothered her in Philly, why should it bother her now."

"I beg your pardon, Doc."

Fitzgibbon shuffled in his shirtsleeves. "Oh, gone and done it now, haven't I Sherriff. I assumed she told you."

"Why would you assume Hannah would tell me anything, Doc?"

"Oh come now Sherriff, only the way you say her name like it's the final breath in your body. And the way that girls eyes light up at the mention of you. She fights harder for your respect and support than any ones else's, despite what she says. Why else would she tell me about Philly and not you? Surely you would understand the underbelly of life better than anyone."

When the Doctor finally spilled the beans, Nicholas sighed heavily. Hannah had worked for a Philadelphia Brothel fixing working girls to earn her keep. Her sisters keep more to the point. An overwhelming urge to beat her brother-in-law senseless made his hands shake. No wonder Hannah fought so hard to strike anew and keep her independence. Everywhere Hannah had turned she saw the trappings men had made on women. But not all men were alike, nor all women. Most relished the role of wife and mother. Nicholas would bet at least one whore somewhere liked her job. The only other option was schoolmarm and Hannah had grabbed that with both hands.

"Have you come to ask me to refuse my offer of assistance then?"

"What offer?"

"Gee's you aren't having to work hard for my answers today Sherriff. She's planning on returning to Philadelphia, to resume her studies of course."

"You encouraged this?"

"Yes. Sherriff. Hannah has a great talent and it would be such a waste. I figured it is her choice in the end. If not to pester me about the offer or provide me with your not-so-silent-opinions on working girls, what did you come here for then Sherriff?"

Another bell tolled in Nicholas's brain. "I had meant to ask you for some supplies. For Hannah, she lost her medicine chest in the fire and I thought to replace it. Seems pointless now." Nicholas paced inside the Doctor's tiny room.

"I take it your betrothal to Suzanna is off the cards for now?"

The bell continued to toll, distracting Nicholas from forming clear thoughts. What had the Doctor said? "Pardon?"

"Nothing Nick, I think the supplies make an excellent peace offering." Fitzgibbon started ransacking his own office, bandages, scalpels and balms.

The tears Hannah had earlier scrubbed from her face returned when she spotted the charcoal remnants of the Lodge. You only have yourself to blame, Hannah thought as the trap passed the gate. Lust is not the same as love, she murmured through parched lips.

A tiny voice inside Hannah wondered what life would be like, having Nicholas's babies. Would that light in his eyes ever dim, could she be happy in his house, in his arms, cooking his dinner and raising his children.

"Susie will be worried about you Miss Hannah."

"And you as well, I think." Carl pulled his hat lower of his ears.

"I know Miss, plus Odette is waiting for you before starting lunch."

A bitter thought crossed her mind that she had driven Nicholas from his home. Hannah need time to think over the Doctors offer and she didn't want to do it where Nicholas couldn't shake her convictions.

Hannah spent the next few hours pacing the porch waiting for Nicholas to return. Carl had crossed from his lodgings, a small outbuilding, fondly referred to as Carl's Shack and dipped his head in greeting. On the fifth time Carl crossed the yard, Hannah figured it was time to end her sentry post.

Odette served large salted pork for dinner with potatoes and bread, but Hannah couldn't lift her fork. The sun had long dipped the horizon and dark shadows encroached upon the homesteads' porch, when Hannah finally heard Nicholas return. Embarrassed at the earlier confrontation, Hannah's brushed down her skirts and straightened her back. She entered the front sitting room ready for round two. Nicholas stood there, dark curls framing eyes that melted to cerulean, the grips from his service pistol hanging low on his hips.

"Well his alibi checks out."

"Really?" None of it made any sense, Hannah thought. Lance worked at the boarding house. Were the two bodies in the grave, ex Doves?

Nicholas pulled his coat off and Hannah took it from him and hung it on the rack. He unfastened his gun belt and stored it in a small lonesome table in the hall.

"Pippa recalled seeing him for most of the day at the Boarding house, when he was absent from there, he'd been over at the Tavern helping Joseph with all the cowboys and their drinks." Nicholas followed Hannah into the kitchen. A serving of dinner had been set aside by Odette and Hannah brought it to Nicholas at the table.

Hannah sat down on the nearest chair "And his jacket?"

"He reckons it was stolen the day of the auction. He'd left it at the Horses Gait when the heat had started and when he went back the following day. Gone. I spent the rest of the time chasing up anyone who might have seen that damn coat."

"I tried to think of why he might have been involved, and I wondered if any working girls had gone missing from the boarding house."

"None. I'd already thought of that," He managed to say around mouthfuls of pork and gravy dripping bread. "I did find three women who had birthed babies in that time frame, one is in Buck Town safe and well, the other two unaccounted for so far."

"Unaccounted for?" Hannah leaned back into her chair. "Do you think they could be the women in the graves?" she said, despite the topic, Hannah's shoulders relaxed.

"Possibly,"

Hannah stared at the table top. Years of Hoffman family dinners had marked the oak with notches and scratches. "I spoke with the Doctor today."

"So did I. I know about your time in Philadelphia. All of it."

Hannah dipped her head. What lecture on morality would she have to suffer now?

"Then you know why I make the decisions I do."

Nicholas placed his hand over Hannah's the simplest touch ignited a new rush of flames. She stared at it for a long time, wondering if the fire would ever burn out, and leave his touch cold to the skin. Would he blame you for the trappings of matrimony you shackled him with? No Beth or Suzanna for him, but a poor schoolmarm with medicine in her blood and whores in her past. "The Philly return comes in two days. I expect to be on it." Hannah entered the kitchen to avoid his ice blue stare. When she returned to collect his plate Nicholas was gone.

Nicholas walked out to the barn to retrieve his haphazard medicine chest for Hannah. Words had failed in the past, he thought before he returned inside. When he reached the sitting room Hannah had gone. He walked up the stairs to his bedroom, currently occupied by Hannah. The door was shut and no light emitted from the door sill. Nicholas raised a fist to knock and thought better of it. He placed the chest on the ground outside the door and retired to the downstairs chaise.

Chapter 15

Hannah had retired to bed early after Nicholas had stormed out. When Hannah woke, the night darkness still lingered and a chill hung in the air. As the birds began to stir, she opened the bedroom door to freshen up. In the grey darkness, Hannah's toe kicked a heavy solid object on the flooring. Holding in a curse, she bent down and collected the chest. She took it inside the bedroom and lit a candle.

The light revealed an old travelling truck that had been covered in leather, and when Hannah opened the lid, she gasped. All manner of bandages, glass jars filled with balms and liquids, a stethoscope, and needles lined the interior. Peering out the window she saw a glow in the barn and dressed as quick as she could. Hannah dashed out to the barn, and only when she lost her balance in a puddle of water did Hannah noticed it was raining. She took a moment to spy the ash light of pre-dawn washed with a little shower of rain. The cock crowed in the distance as if to spur her on.

As she approached, the grey darkness outside kept her hidden from sight and she looked upon Nicholas saddling Ranger. He wore a black shirt, covered in a black vest, the silver star of his office prominent on the left breast. Nicholas pulled a hand through his wet curls and caught her watching him.

"I wanted to thank you."

"You are getting good at these thank you's." Nicholas smirked, his smile widening into his square jaw.

Hannah smiled, "I appreciate the thought, even if you don't agree with my choices."

Nicholas stalked towards her, gun belt swinging with every step. Hannah held her palm out to forestall him. I have made my mind up, she thought.

Nicholas let her hand fall to his abdomen and Hannah withdrew as if scorched. Nicholas lips slanted across hers, gentle, with a hint of intensity held at bay. Hannah parted her lips and allowed Nicholas to overwhelm her defences. The sweet sting of desire raced through her blood and weakened her resolve as his tongue sought hers. She threaded her fingers through his wet curls, stroking the back of his neck. Nicholas's hands trapped her waist, before he placed one hand protectively across Hannah's lower abdomen, his fingers splayed and warm, "We need to talk about your predicament."

Nicholas' fresh scent mingled with the earthy aromas of leather and straw, the familiar blending with the homely. The frantic splattering of rain echoed Hannah's heartbeat. My predicament?

"I wanted to ask you something last night, but you disappeared." His hand cupped her chin and he turned her eyes to his. Hannah gently pushed his hands away. If Nicholas said those words she wouldn't be able to refuse him, and worse she wouldn't know his reasons for asking.

"Nick, I must go." She turned on her heel and took the next few steps with measured calm. By the time she reached outside she began to run, the rain drops joining the tears stinging her cheeks.

Hannah threw herself down on the coverlet, hearing hooves flying in the mud. She listened, heart aching as Nicholas galloped up the drive and out of her life.

Hannah woke to the sounds of Odette making breakfast, the late morning sun chasing away the memory only hours old of Nicholas' clenched jaw. Hannah rose with a familiar tightness in her abdomen. By the time she had freshened up her suspicions were confirmed and relief flooded her veins, spiked intermittently with disappointment.

Hannah walked down the stairs and ate with renewed hunger. The arrival of her cycle seemed poignant to the moment. She glanced at Susie serving Carl a hearty breakfast, Rosa pointing at letters by his side. Nicholas should feel relieved no social constraint would gnaw at his morality, forcing them to marry. Then why did she suddenly feel lost. Any obligation between them had ended, Hannah should feel elation, and yet her own freedom made her feel cast adrift in the ocean. She had nothing to hold onto, nothing tangible, to prevent being swept away. Maybe in time, she could have made Nicholas love her and the anchor she had tied him with. For now her decision had been made, despite what her heart yearned for.

At lunch time, Hannah sat on Nicholas's porch seeking direction and forgiveness in Ms Baker's Bible when Feronica and William Frey arrived carting donated goods from the community. Hannah placed the Bible down and greeted Feronica warmly. She nodded at William Frey.

"Where is dear Cousin Nick?"

"I haven't seen him since this morning, ah something about his investigation." Hannah's mouth snapped shut.

"Never mind, I'll find Carl to help me unload this." William got straight to work unloading the cart as Feronica started displaying and cataloguing the donated goods for Hannah to see.

"I don't think this is all necessary Feronica, although I am grateful for the thought."

"Don't be silly, Hannah. Why would this not be necessary? You have suffered, and the community, our Family has answered. We take care of our community Hannah."

"I appreciate the effort, I really do but I have decided to return to Philadelphia. I will leave tomorrow."

"Oh Hannah, that's such a shame." The fair haired woman clasped Hannah's hands in hers. "Well the clothing will help anyway. A woman can never have enough dresses."

The community had hated Ms Baker and yet here they were sharing concern for Hannah. It warmed her heart, temporarily.

"William Dear, only the clothing for now." Feronica chimed over her shoulder. Hannah awkwardly grabbed an armful and walked inside. Feronica began laying the clothes out on the bed and hanging them into the cupboard.

"We didn't interrupt your reading there did we?" Feronica asked,

"No, not at all, I am most grateful for the distraction."

"Seeking solace and guidance in the Lords words?"

"Yes, the only thing I could save from the fire at the Lodge. Ms Baker treasured that Bible."

"Yes, God rest her soul she did. This one was one of mine, I love the cut of it, but the colour doesn't suit, it would look lovely on you though." Feronica held up a finely tailored deep blue satin dress, cut low along the neckline. Instantly Hannah thought of Nicholas and turned her thoughts aside. "Perhaps just for special occasions then." Feronica said and hung it up with the others.

William brought up another crate of shoes and hats and placed it next to the others.

"If you change your mind, I'll come back with the rest. It's household goods, knick knacks and linen, I'll store it in our barn for now. William and I are arranging a lunch-box social day to raise money for a new house to be built,"

"Oh, I don't know what to say,"

"I suppose a new teacher will need a house to live in. That is if we don't manage to change your mind. It would be a shame to lose you." Feronica squeezed Hannah warmly. She is losing the closest thing to a friend she's ever had, Hannah thought dryly.

William Frey glanced around Nicholas's bedroom, the neatly made bed, Hannah's box of jewellery and makeup from the boarding house, a hair brush on the dresser, "Yes, a shame to lose you."

The Frey's left Hannah even more confused. Between the community support and Nicholas heavy handed proposal Hannah's heart rested heavy in her chest. Hannah started packing the donated clothes when Susie joined her.

Susie isolated the dark satin dress Feronica had donated. Her slim brown fingers traced the neckline and smiled at Hannah, "More mesh?"

"I don't think so Susie."

"Why not Ms Hannah, has the cow been bought?" Susie winked at Hannah.

"Not if the cow doesn't want to be tied up in the barn. Hand fed and regularly bred."

"Would that be so bad Ms Hannah?" Susie's wistful tone made Hannah stare. Susie slowly moved about the room, glancing down at Carl's shack every few paces and Hannah smiled. At least Susie would be happy.

Together the girls continued packing allowing Hannah to muse of Susie's comments. Would it be so bad, if it was Nicholas?

Hannah looked at the leather covered medicine chest and thought about Nicholas's last words. "Does he love you?" Hannah asked out loud, surprised when Susie answered.

"He said so Miss Hannah."

Nicholas struck out early this morning, with no real place or purpose in mind. He'd hoped after Hannah had found the chest, she'd come around. What the hell was he supposed to do with a woman who could be carrying his child, yet refused to marry him? Could he let her go and raise his bastard on her own? His answer thundered in his chest. He had a single day to make her reconsider.

At lunch time Nicholas, ate Odette's leftover, pork surprise, and poured over his and Christians notes until the scratchy words on parchment fused together. By the end of the day, Nicholas had gotten no closer to an answer. He watched the comings and goings of the townsfolk, Lance, Dammier and the Krouse brothers choking his thoughts.

He rode Ranger to the end of town, letting the big stallion set the pace. As he approached the gates to the school, he led the horse up the drive and to the back field. From this view he could see what Ms Baker would have seen, the trees now cut down, letting the dirt bake in the afternoon sun. The Krouse brothers won the contract for the construction of the new bridge. The Mayor had approved the construction. Then wouldn't the brothers set the foundations elsewhere, the Mayor surely would have had a say in the planning. Dammier wouldn't have let them dig up a dirty little secret. Had the brothers sent Lance to finish the job, tie up loose ends or bury any shred of evidence Ms Baker still had? Instead Hannah had been caught in the crosshairs.

Naturally his thoughts lost direction again. Nicholas had thought of Suzanna too, making her choice of husband, just like Beth had. Except Hannah didn't want a husband? Arguing and issuing demands to Hannah did no good, either.

Nicholas watched as a chicken hawk swooped down to the adjacent field striking dead an unseen target.

Harriet Swan. Alive or Dead? He'd have his answer soon enough, he'd sent Leonard on to Spring Creek, and Christian relished the opportunity to ride to Sunbury in Northumberland.

The chicken hawk took flight and returned to a nest in a nearby tree, where Nicholas could hear the squawking demands of the hatchlings. An idea dawned on Nicholas, suddenly he stood up. He'd been looking for the wrong person. Nicholas rode into Franklins Shallows as if chased by the devil himself and headed straight for the courthouse. There he managed to catch Stephens leaving for the afternoon.

"Stephens,"

"Oh Sherriff, don't you look worse for wear, any luck with your search?" He shuffled his keys and papers and almost lost the lot until Nicholas caught the precious silver ring.

"No luck so far, but that's about to change. What do you need to registrar a birth?"

"A baby for one," Stephen's pushed his wired glasses up his nose with a nobbled finger and shuffled his load, "a witness normally the widow Charles, has to attest to the birth."

Hairs rose on the back of Nicholas's neck, "Normally" he said.

"Yes, normally, she will attest by…."

"When is it not the Widow Charles?"

"Well, Doctor Fitzgibbon is another, or whoever assisted with the birth. They have to attest to the birth of the child by that mother." He said this so matter-of-factly as if Nicholas should know this already. "Why I was just telling Sue-Lyn that although I know she had little Addison with her, I needed Dr Fitzgibbon to witness the forms."

"I need your keys."

"I beg your pardon Sherriff." The small man clutched the silver chain to his chest.

"I need to search your records by birth."

"Searching by birth is going to take considerable time."

"Your dinner will be ice by the time I'm done." Nicholas said, hand out, palm up.

The bony forearm of Stephens gingerly extended, "Fine Sherriff, but -"

"Don't worry I'll put it all back, the way I found it, I promise."

"I'll collect my keys tomorrow first thing in the morning." He handed over his treasure detailing which key would unlock what door or cabinet. When Stephens finally walked off, Nicholas entered the Registrar's office and lit a lamp. He'd raced off trying to pinpoint the potential mothers before realising his mistake. As each page flicked past Nicholas' nose it reaffirmed his hunch. He'd been looking for the mother who had given birth. That part was known, if not fully known. The mothers lay in the grave. He should be searching for the children.

Hannah rested in the front sitting room. Susie and Rosa sat with her, slowly reading to each other with a lamp to light the way. The Philly Return departed tomorrow. She had packed her second hand clothes and her medicine chest yet weariness crept into her bones. Hannah imagined Nicholas's face when he returned to discovery his house empty. She ran her hands over the cover of Ms Baker's Bible again. Was returning to medicine in the Lords plan? Was Nicholas Hoffman not included in His plan? Hannah opened the cover and stared at the Frey Family tree. Ms Baker had spent hours detailing each branch and off-shoot. Each of the Four Families had its separate page, the names repeated on each branch when a marriage occurred. Hannah had flicked past it so casually every time she opened the book and now she actually read it. Her fingers idly traced the names down each branch. The names of the children caught Hannah's eye. Such an incestuous family line, the same names had been passed down after each generation. No wonder Ms Baker decided to make notations of their birth dates and death dates. So many children died so young, one year old, two years old. The women fared no better, dying in child birth, only one or sometimes two children to their name, the Treschells family line especially. Hannah considered Nicholas's family. His sister. What would have happened to Beth or Suzanna? Hannah turned the page to read the Hoffman's family line and a light in the barn caught her eye.

Nicholas? Hannah placed the Bible down and made for the door.

"Hannah?" Susie cautioned.

"There's a light in the barn. I thought Nick had come back, I mean home –" The words sounded awkward to her ears. Susie grabbed Hannah by the shoulders.

"Miss Hannah if it is the Sherriff, he will come in." Together they stood on the threshold waiting, not one shadow of movement crossed the flames light. "I didn't hear Ranger Miss Hannah. That horse has heavy hooves."

A chill crept into Hannah's spine, "Where is Carl?"

"In the shack Miss Hannah. I'll get him."

"No, you can't" Hannah tried to grab Susie but she stepped back.

"You take Rosa upstairs Miss Hannah. I'll be quick." Susie whispered and dashed out the back of the house.

Hannah rushed Rosa upstairs, the cogs in her brain spinning as wild as her heels. Nick had firearms, why didn't I ask him where they were! She then remembered she'd donated his pepper gun to Franklins Shallows thanks to the Elk. Hannah heard light footsteps dashing up the stairs. Susie? Hannah opened the door a crack before it flew into her face, kicked with such force it struck her cheek and sent Hannah backwards, Rosa's desperate scream silenced by blackness.

Nicholas had given up looking for all but one name. Ms Elizabeth Baker. It took him through three volumes before he struck the answer. He slammed a clenched fist onto the pages. His suspicious confirmed in Stephen's own handwriting, the two names appeared on the one entry. Ms Baker's secret. My Family's secret. Nicholas searched the volume two years later and again the same names, the same entry.

Nicholas snapped the books closed. He locked up as Stephens would have liked, the Horse's Gait nightlife, the only light splashing onto Main Street. As Nicholas entered the worn bridge, he heard hooves of a second horse dogging his path. Nicholas steered Ranger to the shoulder. He waited until the horse and rider had crossed before drawing his pistol. At the crisp metal sound of the hammer cocking, the rider slowed.

"Oh Nick there you are?" Christian reigned in his pale mount and trotted over to Nicholas. "I thought I was seeing things, when you rode back into town. It's a long ride to Sunbury." His dishevelled appearance confirmed the Christian had driven himself and his horse to their limits on his thirst for adventure.

Nicholas holstered his weapon, "I'm glad you're back safely." He moved to flick the reins.

"Don't you want to hear about how I went?"

"No, something's come up."

"Okay, what can I do to help?"

"It involves - "

"The Family? When does it not involve the Family?"

Nicholas wished he could share in Christians' mockery, but instead tightened his grip on the reigns. Nicholas didn't want to believe where the evidence pointed, but he had to confront him. "Whatever happens, whatever is said, we are the Law."

Christian nodded.

Both men turned their mounts to the North. Nicholas held those words tight to his chest as they passed the large stone archway, that marked to entrance to the ranch of William Frey.

Chapter 16

A soft stifling of tears roused Hannah. The smell of horses and hay indicated she was in the barn, desperately trying to focus on shifting shadows through swollen eyes. Hannah moved her shoulders and found her hands bound to a pole at her back. Hannah flexed her hands pumping blood painfully to her fingers. Susie slumped to the right and Rosa on the left, her little eyes closed tight, tears racing down her cheeks.

A thin river of red trickled down Susie's right cheek and snaked around her chin to fall in the dirt.

Movement at the entrance to the barn drew Hannah's eyes as a dark clothed figure entered, carrying a lantern.

"Feronica?"

"Urgh, you're awake."

Hannah blinked rapidly, causing her left eye to swell further. Fernoica? Hannah's heart sank when she saw the limp frame of Carl dragged by his ankles into the barn, the assailant concealed in a brown leather jacket.

Nicholas knocked loudly on the double doors, the noise reverberating through the vast interior, eventually a servant answer the door.

"Where's William?" Nicholas demanded not waiting for an invitation before entering.

"In the library Sherriff."

Christian arched a questioning eyebrow. "Keep quiet, but be ready."

"Dear cousin Nicholas and cousin Christian, what can I do for you lawmen at this late hour?" William Frey reclined in a large wingback chair, pipe in one hand and whiskey in the other.

"We need to talk."

"Family Business or Sherriff's business?" William crossed one leg over the other.

"Both."

"Both? Nick, you sound serious. Sit down, what's the matter?"

Nicholas refused the chair and took a deep breath, "I know Will."

William Frey leaned forward slowly to strike a match against his side table.

"Know what Nick?"

"About Baker and the two murdered girls."

William froze, the match burning in his slender fingers, inches away from the tobacco pipe, "What?"

"The bones in the graves. The missing girls."

"I don't understand."

"Will, I'll ask you to phrase your next answers carefully." Nicholas watched William's face intently for any acknowledgment of guilt, any admission that his children's mothers had been identified. The patriarchs' hazel eyes focused and unfocused. Words formed beneath his manicured moustache yet failed to surface. William's normally pale complexion drained of all colour. He didn't know. Feronica!

"Where is Feronica?"

"Upstairs, in her drawing room, but I don't understand - "

Nicholas interrupted, "Fetch her."

Christian dashed up the wide spiral staircase.

"Now wait just a minute here - "William rose from the chair. Nicholas drew his pistol, resting the weapon on his hip. "God damn you Nick! Explain yourself, you come barging into my house guns drawn and *fetch* my wife."

"Ms Baker was blackmailing you and your wife for murdering those girls."

William sank back in his chair, "Nick you're mad!"

"The doors locked!" Christian called from the level above.

Nicholas sprinted up the stairs, William in a daze behind.

"The key!" Nicholas shouted at a servant who loitered nearby.

"The mistress never gave me a key." She whispered, and dashed down the ornate hallway.

Christian kicked at the door causing the lock to snap, the door slamming open to reveal the personal quarters of Feronica Frey. Rich dark furniture crowded the room as pale pink curtains covered the full length window. The walls splashed with frame after frame of preserved butterflies.

"Nick, enough! Tell me what's the devil is going on."

Nicholas scanned the room, unable to meet Williams questioning glare, "Tell me about the birth of your children Will?"

"Little Will and Violet?"

"Yes. Now."

"Well, what can I tell you? I don't really know." William rung his hands together, the pipe and whiskey discarded somewhere downstairs.

"You can't or you wont?"

"I can't Nick! I wasn't here."

"Explain yourself." Nicholas prodded, re-holstering his pistol.

"I don't see how this matters but fine, I had a stock run when Little Will was born, I camped in the northern fields. When I came back, I saw my son for the first time. He was a week old by then. I thought I'd make it back in time."

"And Violet?" Nicholas paced around the room, picking up items, turning them over and opening drawers.

"I remember that quite clearly! Damn New York City buyer had me all in a rush for no God Damn reason! I had taken a dozen of my best horses into Philadelphia. Kept sending me damn telegrams that he was on his way, but never showed! I had to sell them at a pittance. I was gone a full fortnight, when I got back Violet was my little ray of sunshine." A broad grin ruffled his moustache.

"And what of Feronica?"

"What of her?"

"How long - " Nicholas couldn't find the words, "Had you ever - ".

William's sandy eyebrows twitched in the candlelight.

"Did you and Feronica ever - I mean surely you saw her while she was - ?" Nicholas paused again. He couldn't think of any reason or circumstances that would keep his hands off

Hannah, if he had the chance. Clearly passion had never featured in Will and Feronica's marriage.

"When she was what Cousin, spit it out."

"Did you ever see Feronica pregnant? See her in the flesh?"

"Of course not! Once the roosters in the hen's house, it's time to look for another hen!" He chuckled to himself. William tapped his pockets searching for his pipe. Nicholas picked up a jar of Feronica's latest butterfly sample. The creature slowly fluttered its delicate wings in silent protest at its captivity.

"And did you?"

"Did I what? Find another hen, Nick?"

Nicholas sighed, "Do you remember if anyone else, in your household was with child at that same time?"

William wrung his hands together and Christian who had stayed silent for the longest time spoke up, "We need to know, William."

"Well…" William Frey turned to the Deputy, "Cece, I mean Cecille."

"Where is she now?"

"Feronica decided to end her employment about that time."

I bet, Nicholas thought. "Where did she go, what happened to her?"

"I don't know, Feronica is in charge of the running of the house, she moved the girl on."

"How long were you and Cece intimate?"

"For God's sake Nicholas, am I on trial for something?" William stood up and stormed around the back of his chair. His hands clasped onto the back of the brown leather and squeezed tight.

"Maybe."

"Yes oh righteous cousin, Nicholas" he sneered. "Feronica ceased Cece's employment when she discovered my involvement with her."

"When was the last time you saw her?"

"I told you the time I rode off to muster! Feronica told me that Cecille would be gone by the time I came back. I argued and bickered with Feronica that she couldn't be that unkind to send a pregnant woman off into the world with no means to support herself. Fenorica agreed to take care of Cece and make sure she would have an income, somewhere – " He turned away from the rising scorn on Nicholas' face.

"Were you the father? Was she an innocent?"

"To be honest, I don't know, she was a real looker that Cece, could have been any ones I guess."

Nicholas let the comment slide by, "What about when Violet was born, any other women with child at the time."

"I don't remember."

"Don't waste your breath lying now William. You've fathered two children and neither of them with your wife."

"How dare you!"

"How dare you, those girls are dead!" Nicholas reserve snapped. The man who thought he was above every law, couldn't deny the retribution he had caused those girls.

"No, not Margaret - "

"Yes I bet Feronica promised to set her up nice and safe. Out of your reach, but in harm's way!"

"She never knew, at least I didn't think – Nick you're saying that Feronica -"

"For Christ's sake Will, Feronica murdered them. She stole their children and murdered those girls. I'm going to assume that Margaret had a mop of silver curls like Violet and Cece was dark eyed and dark haired. Your children's mothers are dead! And it's because of you!" Nicholas heard his own words and turned away, William wept into his hands.

Nicholas paced around the room again, clenching his fists. Nicholas recalled William returning furious from Philly and cursing like a demon. Obviously Feronica had rushed William out of the way and kept him there with fraudulent telegrams. Nicholas didn't doubt William's statement about arguing with Feronica for Cece's wellbeing. William Frey would have maintained their income for the sake of his children. That would have rankled Feronica even further. William was a dirty rotten philander but not cruel. Feronica could have quite secretly bought those children, she could have sent the mothers off with money and the prospect of a new life. Feronica chose to end them, she chose to keep the secret quiet and close to home. Same as Ms Baker, Feronica could have let the old woman retire in peace, but she chose to end her. Nicholas let William prattle on about the women. Cece was a bastard born in Buck Town and had been raised as an orphan. The orphanage would not be looking for her. Margaret had come from Philly as a serving girl in a minor house. William knew nothing else of her background. It seemed clear that she also had no parents or someone to search for her since her death had remained undiscovered since now. Ms Baker, as unlikeable as she was, had held his family secret for over 7 years.

Nicholas picked up the newest butterfly specimen ready for preservation. "Do you know how Ms Baker died Will?"

"The Doc mentioned poisoning. I didn't kill her Nicholas, I swear." William kneeled in front of Nicholas clutching at his chest. Christian stared at his own boots. "You have to believe me, Nick I didn't kill anyone!"

"Did you know how to preserve butterflies, Cousin?"

"I don't know – " William stopped and snatched the bottle Nicholas tossed into the air. He read the label out loud, "Cyanide."

"We need to find her, where is she?"

"I honestly don't know, she talked about finishing some charity thing or another, I didn't listen – "

Nicholas's thoughts raced through his head like stampeding cattle, William ran his trembling fingers through sandy hair, trailing to rasp at his unshaven jaw.

"Is there any other hens of yours in Franklins Shallows I should know about?" Nicholas said off the cuff not expecting a response. Maybe Feronica would try to destroy birth records or the like. Nicholas's mind tripped over thoughts, one after another in his head. Thoughts of the fire, Ms Baker, the bones in the graves, all crashed into one name he knew was now in danger. He said her name out loud just as William said another.

"Susie."

"Hannah."

Chapter 17

Hannah shuffled herself upright as well as she could, one leg trapped beneath the other and her hands tied behind her back.

"You remember Richard, Hannah?" Feronica reintroduced the dark shadow of the man who stood behind, in the manner she had introduced guests at the welcoming feast. The man threw back the hood and Hannah recognised the round youthful face of Richard Treschells.

"He's not here." Richard snapped, his feminine voice sounding distant and hushed.

"Well then we wait. We can't let one slip through again."

Richard nodded and closed the stable doors behind him.

Nicholas! They will kill him too. Something must have happened, he'd come too close to unearthing their secret. The pages of the Frey's family tree flickered through her head. As if Feronica had heard Hannah's thoughts the woman spoke, "Stupid Ms Baker. It didn't help that she wrote it down so accurately."

Hannah's eyes blinked independently of each other, the swelling to her left eye preventing any clear vision of her attackers. Carl lay prone on the ground, a stream of blood trickled from his scalp but stopped. Not so serious, yet, if only Hannah could help them.

"Wrote down what so accurately?"

"Don't play coy with me. I know you worked it out, where's the book?"

"The Bible?"

Feronica's thin lips contorted into a grimace and she nodded. The pieces had fallen into place. The fire had been set to destroy the Bible. Such a detailed reminder of how the Treschells women could not survive birth. Hannah heard her own words repeated back to her from the horse auction. She had commented to

Fernoica that she intended on treating all the children, the same. Feronica thought she meant Will and Violent, not all the Frey children. Feronica Treschells had never given birth.

"You don't have to do this. I'll keep your secret safe. Just let Rosa and Susie go, they have nothing to do with this!"

Feronica's olive eyes narrowed into dark slits and her mouth became a nest of vipers. She laughed. A noise so thick and vile it rent the air around them. Hannah turned to Susie, still unconscious. Tears streamed down Rosa's tiny face as she her bright brown eyes stared at Feronica and then back to Hannah, pleading. "The only one of my husband's bastards I couldn't claim." Hannah stared at Rosa. No! In the little girl's wide-eyed panicked stare, Hannah caught a fleck of hazel "No I don't think so."

"Try as I might, I could never catch a break, either the whore's kids or this bastard was around." Richard smirked, a slick wild thing that twisted his features and made Hannah shiver.

"Look inside for that book, brother."

Richard reached a tan coloured mare and retrieved a shot gun. He handed it to Feronica before disappearing, making sure the barn doors closed silently in his wake. Hannah couldn't hear his footsteps on the porch, yet heard the familiar squeak of the front door hinges. Richard would have no trouble finding the Bible, Hannah had left it on the seat by the front window. Ms Bakers voice returned to haunt her, *Birthed some myself.* Ms Baker had been Will and Violet's midwife, she'd been so accurate she had written their dirty little secret into her Bible without a second thought. Think quick Hannah! She tried to clear the fog in her mind.

The hem of Feronica's red riding skirt kicked dirt and hay as she stalked towards them, Hannah's voice quavering at each approaching step. "That's why you fought so hard to save Old Thom. You knew those girls would be found."

"Yes the construction had been discussed many times during the Family meetings, Richard only had to ask once about the supply of timber and he had the whole surveys revealed. The Mayor was more stubborn than I thought, even after I offered to vote for Suzzana and his son." Feronica pushed a hand through the fair strands that swept loose across her brow, "And before that bitch was finally out of the picture, she puts you in the middle of it. Honestly Hannah you should really blame Elizabeth for all this."

"Elizabeth? Ms Baker? She never betrayed you."

Feronica's eyes glassed over in the lamp light for a moment before hatred returned in full force.

"I promise I'll keep your secret, just let us go, whatever happened it's not-" Hannah didn't dare risk drawing attention to Susie laying helpless on the ground. How did Susie keep her secret for seven no eight years? Elizabeth had mentioned Susie's wages were already settled and paid for. Of course, Feronica had given over Susie and Rosa for Ms Baker to watch and control. Now Ms Baker was out of the way, Susie was a risk. That and the fact that no-one would believe the dark skinned girl, had birthed a Frey child. Feronica said it herself, she couldn't claim Rosa, but she could claim the others. "It's not their fault, it's Williams."

"Yes, see I knew you'd see it my way, Hannah." Depsite the shotgun in Feronica's arms, she spoke as if they stood at a lunch box social. "He couldn't go on forever, fertilising all the soil in this county without results. I thought I'd have to wait forever."

"You waited?" Hannah gagged on the dust rising in the air.

"How else could I be sure? I had to be certain Hannah. Don't you understand, I had to push him away." Feronica said, her throat tightening, "I had to deny him every night that I could. I had to destroy the ones that formed in my belly. I had to survive. And when I'm done," Her shoulders squared and the muzzle of the gun rose to Hannah's chest. "I will be the only one that survives." Feronica took a deep breath.

"You did this? How long did you plan this?" So long as the woman was talking, she wasn't shooting. Tiny fingers worked around Hannah's wrists. She could feel the desperate, pulling and plucking, at the ropes.

"No, no don't you start - he did this. You remember that Hannah, William did this!" Feronica stared down Hannah as if to make the words gospel.

"Feronica you still have a choice. You can let us go. I will keep your secret. I promise, Rosa's just a child. Just like Will and Violet" Hannah tried the tears spilling forth rapidly from her one good eye. Hannah let the sobs cover the movements of her wriggling.

"Don't you compare this half-breed to my children!" Feronica screamed.

"What about Will and Violet, then, what will happen to them?"

"They are *my* children!" Feronica sniffed the air with her nose and turned side on. Hannah bit her tongue and changed tactics, lest the woman decided to inspect her other prisoners.

"You did this for them, then?"

"Them? No Hannah, for me. The first born Treschells daughter must marry a Frey remember. Will must inherit his fathers' fortune. " Feronica giggled an unnatural girlish sound, her eyes wide and for a moment, her arms lagged, the shotgun weight eroding Feronica's strength.

"So you couldn't have his children, even if you wanted to?" Hannah asked. Rosa's tiny fingers kept working at her bonds and finally they slackened. Hannah spied the wooden handle of a shovel laying blade down in the hay.

"Not with a Frey, not if I wanted to live."

Hannah knew it all now. Feronica couldn't inherit any of the Frey's wealth without her children. But if Feronica had dare birthed a Frey child, their inbred bloodlines would have killed her. Her child, if it lived, would inherit William's money while she lay in her grave. Who knew how long Feronica would keep her husband around after this, and what of little Will when he inherited that wealth?

"And what of your husband, what ills would he suffer, a horse riding accident, perhaps. What of your children?" Rage boiled so hot and suddenly in Hannah she didn't care what poisoned words flew from her lips.

"Oh honey, who knows? I think I might actually like Violet."

All moisture evaporated from Hannah's mouth and she choked back bile, there was no limit to the evilness of this woman. Feronica turned to the sound of footsteps splashing in the rain. Hannah had hoped for a rescue of some sort from anyone, but instead Richard entered the barn, Bible in hand.

"No sign of Cousin Nick yet,"

"Well we don't need these anymore," Feronica tilted her chin at the captives.

Hannah's heart erupted in her chest, time had run out. More and more slack entered the ropes at her wrists. Hannah wriggled as gently as she could, keep her shoulders still and elbows tight into her waist. "You won't get away with it,"

"Of course we will." Richard Treschells stood next to his sister, fair hair and hazel eyes in chubby cheeks, staring down at Hannah. He had been the man to drag her into the Lodge, he had struck her and left her to burn. Hannah licked her lips, her parched words coming out in a rush, hands almost free.

"What about Nicholas then? What if he doesn't come back tonight, what then?"

"He's not very good at hunting Elk is he? Who knows he might be unlucky, knifed in the back from a Tavern fight. I do like you're idea of a horse accident."

"Feronica – " Richard barked.

"Who care's now Rich, she's all but dead, and besides I've always hated Nicholas!" She said it with such toxicity. "All the Hoffman's, think they are too good for their own family. Traitors, the lot of them, right from the start! Why do I have to suffer when he doesn't? Always trying to keep the bloodlines pure and at the expense of our hearts, our bodies and our lives? Why should he get a choice?"

Richard offered a gaze with soft hazel eyes to Feronica as if to offer her small comfort and justification for their despicable actions. Then the moment passed and Richard knelt down as far as his bulk would allow in front of Hannah and grabbed a wad of cloth from his jacket pocket.

"Who were they?"

"Servants, Dear. I told you good help is hard to find." Feronica smiled. Richards soft pudgy fingers, anything but gentle as he shoved the wad into Hannah's mouth, sealing her lips with a handkerchief, the stiff fabric biting into the sides of her mouth.

Heavy hooves flew up the gravel drive and Hannah heard Nicholas voice crisp and agitated, "You go around the back." Waves of relief and fear crashed over Hannah.

Richard dimmed the lamp and returned to the barn door peering outside through tiny cracks.

Hannah knew if she made a sound, Nicholas would rush to the barn and then to his death. She wriggled her hands again, shoulders inching upwards until the last of the rope fell loose. Who did he have with him?

Richard pulled a Colt pistol from within the folds of his jacket, he handed Feronica the hefty Bible and pealed open the heavy oak doors. "You watch them, I'll thin the herd."

Nicholas would be shot from behind, Hannah just knew it. With the heavy book with one arm and the nose of Feronica's shotgun lowered, a reckless wonder stolen over Hannah. Richard was paused at the door, peering into the darkness, waiting to seize his moment.

Hannah stole a deep breath, as deep as she could through her nose and then launched. She landed belly first into the hay, and emerged with the shovel in her hands, the dirt grinding into her knees.

"Richard!" Feronica screamed dropping the Bible to pull the shotgun up to height. A shot rang out as Hannah brought the shovel down on Feronica's arms, a sickening *crack* sounded before the firearm clattered to the ground.

Nicholas was in the upstairs bedroom, his hand caressed the shattered door frame, a splash of blood on one edge, a smear of red on the floor. Suddenly a shot cut through the chilled night air. "The Barn!" he shouted to Christian. He covered the stairs two at a time, a lead weight in his chest. He tore through the front door, Christian hot on his heels.

Feronica sank screaming into the hay her right hand dangling helplessly.

"You bitch!" Richard stormed towards them, snatching Feronica and pulling her backwards from the waist. Hannah swung the shovel again, and Richard released his sister to block the blow. He clawed at Hannah's dress, tearing the shoulder while, his other hand clenched in a tight fist, aimed at Hannah's head. "You're dead!"

Hannah would have screamed if not for the gag. The shovel connected weakly to his soft belly and Richard twisted aside. Hannah's only weapon tangled in Richard's boots and he kicked it away as his thick pudgy fingers closed on Hannah's throat. Richard's girth knocked over the lantern as he dragged Hannah to the ground. Breath rushed out of her lungs as his weight compressed her into the soil, his fingers squeezing the life from her throat as the gag stole all hope of a reprieve. Fear shredded her nerves and long black shadows threatened the little sight she had.

Hannah frantically plucked and scratched at his hands, her nails dragged across his skin to no avail. They tightened around her windpipe. A sickening slow rhythm pulsed through her ears, the sound of her own death marching closer leaving Hannah deaf to the world around her. She threw her arms wide as her teeth ground into the cloth gag, fingernails snagging through dirt and hay. Suddenly her grip tightened on the timber butt of a long arm. Ferociously it was yanked from her grip, the tiniest amount of air returned to her lungs and she sucked as deep as the cloth would allow. The shotguns' muzzle pressed hard under her breasts, Richard knelt on the other end, his hands moving to the trigger.

"Kill her Richard!" Feronica howled in despair.

The trigger answered to Nicholas's gentle tug and Richard's eyes flew wide, blood pooling on the front of his cream coloured shirt. He collapsed forward onto Hannah.

A warm wetness oozed onto Hannah's belly and thighs as the sound of spits and crackles surrounded her. A deadly heat licked at her cheek and Hannah realized the barn was alight. Hannah tore at her gag, sliding the handkerchief down passed her chin, and drew deeply of the air, slowly filling with smoke. She wriggled her torso free just as Nicholas reached her, his powerful hands dragging her clear.

"Get Rosa and Susie," Hannah gestured, coughing into her fist.

Nicholas pushed Hannah forward and dove into the barn. Through one eye, Hannah thought she saw William Frey of all people dragging Carl clear of the inferno. He dashed inside again and returned with Rosa in his arms.

As the rain splashed down on Hannah's face, she sucked in long hard breaths, hands gripping knees, waiting to see Nicholas emerge. She sat down with Rosa and checked her over, as William re-entered the flames.

Hannah's shaky breath barely held back the tears. Examining Rosa stilled her desperate prayers. "Are you alright?" She asked. The sweet little girl nodded, tears streaming down her face, but a smile on her lips.

The flames licked the highest beams as the structure suddenly became engulfed. The barn doors swung open in a flurry and Nicholas appeared carrying Susie. Hannah's heart snapped and she scrubbed tears of relief away from her cheeks with the back of her hand. The motion brought sharp pain to her wounded cheek but it disappeared the moment she saw Nicholas. His face was awash with relief as he reached out to Hannah, and then withdrew his hand. She checked Susie, gently tapping her cheeks and calling her name. Susie's dark lashes opened and her eyes focused. William Frey saw to Carl, splashing water on his face to stir him.

"Rosa?" Susie croaked.

"I'm fine mamma." The little girl squeaked and ran into her arms.

"Where's Feronica?" Nicholas asked, the smoke charred his voice to a harsh timbre.

Hannah faced the flames as a dark shadow crawled from within the barn.

"This is on your head William Frey!" Feronica howled as she stagged out of the smoke. The shot gun leaned across her right arm, the wrist dangling at odd angles. Her dress blackened by smoke, fair hair and fair eyes wild with hatred. "You and your – "

A shot rang out from behind them and Hannah spun around, to see the long slender barrel of Christian's rifle, steaming in the rain.

William ran to Feronica and held her limp frame in his arms, smoothing the hair away from her face. Unknowingly for William he would have been the next to meet his maker, and then perhaps little Will. The acrid odour from the burning barn clogged Hannah's senses and her reserves gave way. Hannah collapsed forward, her hands sinking into the mud. Nicholas scooped her up into his arms, and removed the handkerchief from around her neck with one hand. He ran his thumb over her swelling cheek, a dark scowl raced across his brows.

"Thank you." Hannah said sobbing and laughing at the same time. She buried her head against his shoulder. The tension in Nicholas eased. Gently he rubbed his chin along her hair, not trusting his voice with the words he wanted to say.

Hannah saved him the trouble and pressed her lips to his. All his pent up fear and anger washed away and defeated as he savoured the salty tear stained kisses. He set Hannah down as farm hands awoke at the sight of the flames. Soon a chain gang formed. As pitch black parted to grey pre-dawn, the exhausted men called a halt, half the barn had been salvaged. Christian returned with Doctor Fitzgibbon who checked over his patients one by one.

Exhausted and delirious Hannah watched William sitting silently on Nicholas's porch. Nicholas stood in front, his hands tucked into his belt, one knee resting nearest to his cousin. William hadn't spoken since the undertaker had taken Feronica and the remnants of Richard. Hannah joined them, touching William gently on the shoulder.

"It's all my fault. They are all dead because of me and my sins."

Hannah sighed, "No, William." She put an arm around his shoulders, "You have sinned William, a lot. But, Feronica told me things, before she - " Hannah bit her bottom lip. Is William ready to hear this? "She told me about children she might have borne from you and how she voided them so she could survive."

Nicholas shifted his weight to the other leg, and Hannah eyed him cautiously. He was the Sherriff, he would ask her these questions anyway. Best to only have to tell it once.

William's red eyes, tight and hard lined raked over Hannah's face, his moustache dishevelled over pale lips, "No"

Hannah shuddered, "She talked about how the Treschell's women were cursed in child birth. She was never going to have your children and risk that fate, or risk your…"

"Your fortune," Nicholas added.

"Yes" Hannah didn't want to go on. "She pushed you away so you would *provide* her with children. Other people's children, she did it for herself, for your wealth. The way she talked…"

"This was all about money?"

"I believe she had no intentions of ever being a wife or mother, no more than she had to. She wanted to be a widow. A rich widow."

"She said that?" Nicholas leaned down on his knee, his face closer to Hannah's.

Hannah answered Nicholas but faced William instead. "In less words, but yes, I believe you and little Will would have been next."

William Frey stood up and stalked into the pre-dawn without saying another word.

Hannah sat on the porch for a few minutes more watching the sun rise over Nicholas's fields. She could see the last morning stars twinkling out of existence as the sun raced across the sky. Nicholas hadn't said one more word since their kiss in the mud.

Hannah stared up at him, clad in black, the exhaustion of the night straining his features. His lips thinned in anticipation of some thought he might voice when Doctor Fitzgibbon interrupted to examine Hannah.

Nicholas scanned Hannah's dishevelled state, "Doc you better check – "

"No Nick." Hannah cut him off. With all that had happened, she'd forgotten to let him off the hook about his parental duties. "There is no need. There is no predicament to speak off."

Nicholas eyes narrowed and his jaw tensed. So she wasn't pregnant. Why did he feel so bitter? He walked away. A little disappointment leaked into his chest, followed quickly by shame. Hannah's injuries were Nicholas's fault. Mine and my families, he thought. He clenched his fist by his side. Just like that she shut him out. She knew what he had intended, he had made himself clear and yet Hannah managed to do everything but answer him. He dared not comfort Hannah now, while the anger and hurt inside would force his hands to be anything but gentle. He wanted her answer either from her lips or he would drive it from her body with his own.

Greed, control and domination. His family had fought and killed each other and innocents for all that. He dared not ask again while Hannah sat there poked and prodded by the Doctor. Even as her lung had burned with smoke and her eye swelled from some other force, Hannah had managed to check the others first. She had put their needs above her own time and time again. And what of your needs Nick! He saddled Ranger.

Hannah let the Doctor check and double checked her swollen eye.

"Did you tell him about all the AMA's requirements?"

Hannah sighed, "No."

"What happens in a month's time, Ms Evans when you return to Franklins Shallows as my apprentice? What then?"

Hannah mulled over his words. If Nick had truly loved her, he would have said so. His proposal, no his demands had come from obligation, morality and shame. Not respect or love.

Hannah tiptoed up the stair case and cracked open the second bedroom door. Susie stretched out in the middle of the bed, watched by a sleepy-eyed Carl. He raised his head to nod at Hannah without making any more movements then necessary. He gently patted Rosa's sweet head when she stirred briefly in his lap. Rosa *Frey*. What would Nicholas write in his report about her? About Little Will and Violet?

She entered Nicholas bedroom that had been hers and thought better of it. Nicholas could come and go without her knowing if she slept up here. She resigned herself to the chase in the sitting room, praying she would hear him enter and rouse her exhausted self to confront him. She had to tell him.

Hannah's eyes opened to the late afternoon sun-streaking across the peach coloured sky before she realised how late she'd slept. Vaguely Hannah realised, she'd missed the Philly return and would have to stay in Franklins Shallows another fortnight. How could she go on living here each day facing Nicholas? Her heart ached when he rode out on Ranger this morning and he still hadn't returned. Hannah gathered her things.

Chapter 18

Hannah kept herself busy for the next week, the school year finally started and she eagerly awaited the arrival of her replacement. The Doctor had offered her a room at his house, as cluttered as it was with the belongings of his long deceased wife, it was a pleasant option compared to Jasmines offer at the boarding house. Hannah had politely refused and instead taken the small room above the surgery. Compact and functionally, a single bed took up one side, the roof sloped down on the other and the jovial sounds of the Tavern kept her awake most nights. That and thoughts of ice blue eyes and dark curls.

Hannah had successfully avoided talking to Nicholas, but didn't manage to avoid the long possessive stares as his eyes watched her walk the streets of his town. Each time she entered Main, he appeared lounging in black, arms crossed and knee raised, back flat against the door frame to the Sherriff's Office. At night when she locked the surgery she could see a single lamp burning low in the Sherriff's window. She was now safe, so why did he continue keeping a night time vigil.

Hannah's eye had finally turned a dark purple and receded to a fine sheen of grey by the time she actually had to deal with Nicholas.

In the race for silver, a few miners and prospectors had arrived in Franklins Shallows and the boarding house flourished with life. One such miner took a rough hand to one Dove and therefore landed in the street from the second storey windows.

Just passed supper time, Hannah awoke to frantic banging on the surgery's door. Hannah opened the tiny window and peered down to the street below.

"Christian?"

"We got ourselves an injured prisoner Ma'am,"

"I told you not to call me – " Hannah sighed, was Christian grinning?

"I'll go get the Doctor,"

"Um no time for that Hannah, come on." Christian stepped backwards and looked up at her. She realised he was most definitely grinning and Hannah breathed in sharply when her hair fell past her shoulder. "He's cut up pretty bad."

"Who is?"

"I don't know his name, he's not talking."

"Okay fine, but give me a minute."

Hannah dressed as fast as she could, pulling on boots and fastening her hair roughly at the nape of her neck. She lit the surgery's lamps and opened the door. Suddenly Nicholas and Leonard entered carrying the unconscious miner. They rolled him flat onto a trolley in the back room.

Hannah looked past the three bulky Hoffman's, Nicholas splendid in all black, to the stranger. Five days growth sprouted across a wide jaw, dirty brown hair flat where a hat had plastered it to his scalp and eyes closed into sunken pits. Hannah bet his belly was as empty as his pockets. His lips bled from a tooth poking through the flesh, and multiple cuts, either by a knife or glass covered his torso. He wore a dirty brown shirt torn at the shoulders, which was rapidly turning pink.

"What happened to him?" Hannah asked, ice blue eyes pinning her to where she stood. She withheld a sigh and mentally cursed herself for being so weak.

"He gave Jasmine a touch up."

Hannah heard the thinly veiled anger in Nicholas' voice and it coated her insides, causing her heart to leap into her chest. Nicholas's wounds were still too close to the surface.

"Oh?" Hannah managed, "Is Jasmine alright?"

Nicholas smirked at Leonard, "Yeah she's fine."

Somehow, his grin made Hannah look twice at this man's injuries. Had Nicholas been visiting the boarding house? No. Hannah glanced at Leonards knuckles and saw minor signs of damage. Pity for the man on the table disappeared.

Christian helped rid the stranger of his shirt and Hannah examined each laceration that demanded urgency. At the first splash of alcohol, the man came to. He squirmed in pain and curses flew from his lips.

Leonard charged from the darkness to restrain him but Nicholas barred his way.

Hannah rolled her eyes, "Sit tight and I'll have these fixed. Move and you'll end up looking like yesterdays –" Hannah stopped when she considered where the man had come from.

The man's eyes focused on Hannah and she turned away from the whiskey and tobacco stench of his breath. "Well thanks boy's for bringing me here, I thought my night was done but not with this pretty little thing."

Nicholas jaw clenched, "Go on." He spoke so softly that the stranger swivelled his head to answer the threat. Hannah shuddered under that unmoving icy stare and the drifter rolled his head to stare upright at Hannah.

"Never mind, Miss I appreciate the help."

"Good, now stay still."

As the night wore on, Hannah had lost count of how many stiches she lay in his multiple wounds. The patient had long fallen into a shallow dream state, either by blood loss or alcohol. Leonard and Christian carried him across the street to the lock up and Hannah cleaned the room.

Aware that a presence still lingered behind her, Hannah took extra care in washing away the strangers scent. Without saying a word she turned down each lamp, leaving one to walk out to the foyer. Nicholas followed. She set the lamp down on the window sill and opened the glass paned front door.

"I thought you'd come and check up on your patients." Nicholas made no move towards the door.

Hannah had seen Rosa every day this week at the school and Susie twice. She'd already found out about Susie's decision to stay on at Nick's homestead, although Carl weighed heavily in that decision too.

"I think Susie made the right choice for Rosa and herself."

Nicholas rested against Doctor Fitzgibbons desk, hands beside his thighs, rolled shirt sleeves showing the delicious ropey muscles of his forearms. Would he ask her to look at his injuries? After all she had stitched him up.

"I've also finished the reports."

Hannah clicked her tongue. The torment of his presence eroded her self-control. Work? He wanted to talk about his work? She buried her hands in her skirts.

"Yes,"

"I thought you should know. I did it for Little Will and Violet, and Rosa. Not for the Family."

"Did what?"

"I won't ask you to lie, so I won't be asking for a statement or affidavit on your behalf. I closed the file that Richard had murdered those girls, with the help of Feronica. The Bible was destroyed in the fire. I need you to understand, if the truth had come out, Rosa, Will and Violet would be ruined in this town. I did it for them."

"I see."

Even though Nicholas had done the right thing, his actions covered up more Frey lies. What other options does he have, Hannah asked herself. Expose it all, Feronica's abortions, the true paternity of Will's children to murdered serving girls. Hannah shook her head.

"What about Will and Violet, who will tell them about their mothers?"

"I'll leave that to William, he has some atonement to make for all this."

"I think all the Frey's have."

Nicholas nodded. The irony was not lost on Hannah that Nicholas had been ridiculed for being a Hoffman.

"What's going to happen with Leonard and Jasmine?" Hannah asked.

"He's about to make her an offer. Move west with him, taking Jimmy and start out new." Inwardly Hannah smiled, "Doctor Fitzgibbon dropped the death certificates to my office yesterday," Nicholas started and dread sunk into Hannah's bones. He knew. Of course the good Doctor Fitzgibbon would have told him.

A feather light touch dragged a tendril of her hair back from her neck. Shivers stole down her spine to behind her knees, fleeting warmth spread through her abdomen.

"A man can wait a month,"

His wet pine and leather scent washed over Hannah and every muscle wanted to turn and face the man that she loved. What did he say?

"You won't marry for wealth, for security or for morality, but what about love Hannah? Would you marry for love?"

Hannah melted inside, as his touch trailed down her spine, stroking the fire that threatened to overwhelm her. She didn't answer, her voice trembling as much as her body.

"You can't or you won't love me?" He pressed his lips to her ear and Hannah's instinctively reacted pressing backwards against his strength, letting his kisses fall on her neck.

"I do love you." Hannah moaned.

Strong hands grabbed her waist and spun her, and Nicholas seized her lips, his hot tongue seeking hers. She relented, letting Nicholas devour her heartache. Hannah threw her arms around his neck and pulled him tighter against her. He responded pressing backwards, trapping her beneath his pulsing body and the door frame. Her body answered, calling forth the slick heat that Nicholas enticed. His hands roamed over the fabric of her dress, feeling the lack of corset and the firm swell of her breast. His groan's silenced by Hannah's fevered kisses. One hand snared the back of Hannah's neck as the other found any opening it could to reach her flesh.

"I need all of you Hannah. I need to cherish you, to love you and to have you give all of yourself to me." Nicholas fumbled over the words, "I could spend the rest of my life, searching for my perfect fit, a woman made just for me," His lips found her nipple, already hard and waiting. Hannah gasped in pleasure as thoughts of refusal vanished on the wind.

"Am I that woman?" She pulled him tighter into her breast, arching her back and letting his desire press against her thighs.

Nicholas licked and suckled the hollow in her neck, trailing kisses along her throat and finally demanding more from her mouth, he released her and Hannah gazed into the azure depths of his soul, "You are and more so, let me have you, now and forever."

"Yes Nick, now and forever." The fire raged inside Hannah and she succumbed to the torrent, rocking her hips forward to reach him, to feel more of his arousal kindling her own.

Nicholas self-control snapped. He slammed the surgery door and pulled Hannah into his arms. He climbed the stairs two at a time and pressed Hannah into the soft mattress, her legs trapping his hips. His flesh strained to be free, fought to be sheathed inside the honey silkiness of Hannah and he peeled away his shirt. Her fingers trailed over his skin, soft yet direct. Her fingertips grazed the scar on his rib cage, the muscles trembling at her gentle touch.

"I didn't know it then, but I do know. That day, you became part of me."

He kissed her fingertips and she cupped his face in her palm, "At the party at the Frey's, I couldn't help feeling overwhelmed, and yet amongst it all, I kept searching for you, for your presence. Deep down, I knew then that I would keep needing your strength, your support and your comfort. You were the centre of my world that night. I just kept trying to deny it. But no more,"

Hannah reached up and pressed her lips to his, a lingering soulful kiss, that drew Nicholas forward to answer her passion. Hannah clawed at his skin, the muscles rippling, as his hands climbed with purpose and found her upper thighs, powerful fingers kneading and teasing her flesh.

"All of me, Nick. All of me for you."

The gentle words of her promise tugged at his heart. He kissed her with all the essence of himself, letting her feel, how much he treasured her, how much he loved her. Nicholas devoured each kiss, his lips scorching her throat, the rounded curve of her breast and finally the cherry centre.

Her clothing landed on the floor, and she couldn't recall if she had removed it or Nicholas, as his teeth nipped at her skin. She released his gun belt, hands confident, demanding and direct. Hannah unbuttoned his pants to stroke Nicholas, his cries of pleasure spurring her on.

"All of me for you," Nicholas said as his hand found her slickness and stroked the internal flames that burned within Hannah. She rocked forward letting his maleness dominate her every sense, letting Nicholas capture her, penetrate and lavish her.

Between ragged breaths, Nicholas shucked his pants, laying a trail of hot kisses down her belly as he did so. Hannah smiled.

How could she manage to ever let him go? Nicholas surged forward and she cried out when the first wave stormed throughout her body.

The tremors rocketed through Hannah and she bit down on his bottom lip. Nicholas couldn't curb his need any longer and he entered the silky heat that beckoned. The tightness stretched around him and a moan escaped his lips. Hannah's legs wrapped around his hips and he surged forward again.

Total completeness overwhelmed Hannah, her lover had come to claim her and she parted beneath him. At each movement Nicholas called forth a tidal wave of emotions that overflowed into the well of pleasure he had created. She had called his name into her heart that first night and now, she burned it onto her soul. He was hers and hers alone. Hannah trembled beneath him, her shuddering giving him miniscule warning to withdraw. Hannah broke from his kiss as his hot seed spilt on her upper thigh.

Through lids heavy with satisfaction, Hannah watched him, "I love you. I thought I was your woman, Nick?"

"You are and I love you more than you'll ever know Hannah, but I can't marry you yet." He pulled down the blanket covering them both and folded Hannah into his arms, the rhythm of his heart matching the dance of her own. "I said I wanted all of you, not half. In a month you'll be back and we'll marry then." Nicholas stole any argument from her lips, savouring each bead of moisture she offered, a smirk edged up the corner of his lip, "I am a Hoffman after all, and I will only marry a Doctor."

The End

Epilogue

Doctor Hannah Evans watched the tall pines pass as she urged the coach faster on its return journey to Franklins Shallows. Hannah had answered each of Susie's rough letters begging that no word of her surprise should reach the ears of her soon to be husband. Hannah had marvelled at Susie's weekly improvement in each letter and the news of progress within the town.

James Dammier had indeed found silver on his land and the Frey's had approved of his marriage to Suzanna Treschells. William Frey had bought the Timber Mill and the Grist Mill and Feed Exchange but was rarely seen about the town. The railway had finally agreed on line placement and Jasmine had accepted Leonards offer. They had set off last week to claim their land. Hannah drew her hands up to her heart.

As the horses slowed, Hannah peered out the tiny window both excited and relieved for her homecoming. She glanced at the Sherriff's Office, Ranger tied up the front and Hannah crept to the edge of her seat. When the door finally swung open, Hannah stepped down and turned.

Nicholas stood there, hands on his gun belt, ice blue eyes raking over the creamy white skin of his bride to be.

"Susie?" Hannah smiled exasperated.

"Carl."

"I should have guessed."

Nicholas dragged her into his grasp. Her intoxicating vanilla scent rested gently against his senses as he kissed her, and Hannah answered with her melting softness.

"I hope the new Doctor is not too tired." He whispered against her ear and she laughed, her sweet throat vibrating against his lips.

"Apprentice Doctor. Is the handsome Sherriff about to give me a tour of his fine town?"

Nicholas laughed, "Only a short one my love."

Nicholas slipped his hand into Hannah's and crossed Main Street. Hannah grinned as Nicholas pointed out the site for a new Inn, suspiciously close to the freshly painted boarding house.

Nicholas paused at the hitching post outside the Sherriff's office. A dark grey mare snuffled Ranger's bridle, a delicate saddle on her back.

"She's beautiful" Hannah let the mare sniff her gloved hand before she gently stroked her long nose.

"She's yours, her name is Mist." Hannah watched Ranger sniff at the mare's forelegs letting the smaller horse nip and rub all she pleased along his shoulder. Mist seemed just perfect.

Nicholas boosted Hannah a top her new horse and then mounted Ranger, "Ready to go home?"

Hannah grinned from ear to ear, "Definitely."

Up ahead she spied a familiar face. Deputy Christian Hoffman strolled beside a blonde haired girl, her waist slim and eyes bright.

"Is that Lucy? Lucy Ramsey?"

"Oh you mean your replacement, Lucy Taylor."

Hannah tilted her head, "Taylor? I thought it was Lucy Ramsey?"

"Apparently there was already one Mrs Ramsey or so Lucy found out."

"Oh no," Hannah brought a hand to her mouth.

"She decided to come home and take up your teaching contract."

Hannah watched Lucy's enthralled gaze lock onto Christian as they entered the Café. Even spinsters need company, Nicholas had said to her once. "Maybe," Hannah grinned, "Maybe she came to marry a Hoffman."

About the Author

Louise Crouch loves all genres of fiction mixed with a healthy splash of romance. This is her first foray into the world of Historical Western Romance. When she is not writing, Louise spends her time frustrating her wonderful husband and raising their two marvellous children.

Her second novel is Hammer & Lock; A Texas Romance which is set in Texas in the 1870's.

After news of her fathers' death, Evelyn Lockwood returns to her small hometown Dew Springs, Texas to claim her inheritance, the Double E Ranch. Evie's plans of selling the Double E to resume her high society life in New Orleans and snag a rich husband is derailed when she discovers her fathers' strange bequeath to the rugged and boorish cowboy Cade Hamerton.

Cade Hamerton has had to shoulder his fathers' dishonest and violent reputation in Dew Springs his whole life. When Evie's father leaves him half of the Double E Ranch, he has a chance at redemption and to secure the closest semblance of a family he has ever had.

When Evie's railroad shares bankrupt, she must defend her only source of income and learn the true value of a man.

With Evie staying on at the Double E, Cade is forced to defend not only his entitlement, but his heart, from invasion. Find it here:

http://loucrouch.wordpress.com

www.ingramcontent.com/pod-product-compliance
Lightning Source LLC
Chambersburg PA
CBHW021140130626
46554CB00005B/1603
* 9 7 8 0 6 4 8 4 8 7 8 0 7 *